LIGHT IN DARKNESS

ALI WINTERS

LIGHT IN DARKNESS

ALI WINTERS

RISING FLAME PRESS

Published by Rising Flame Press
Edited by Schwartz Fiction Edits
Cover design & Formatting by Red Umbrella Graphic Designs

ISBN-13: 978-1-945238-09-3

www.aliwinters.com

MORE BY ALI WINTERS

The Hunted series
The Reapers
The Exodus
The Moirai
The Fallen
Flirting with Death

In The End duology
Sound of Silence
Light in Darkness

Shadow World
The Vampire Debt
The Vampire Curse
The Vampire Court
The Vampire Oath
The Vampire Crown
The Vampire Betrayal

Stand Alone
Cast In Moonlight
Favor of the Gods
A Sky of Shattered Stars
Army of the Winter Court

For Trish

Chapter One

The Quiet

Dark shadows move under the dim, flickering lights as I look around. I'm standing in the center of the light rail car and all the seats are empty. The doors slide closed. I stare at the face reflecting in the glass, but I don't recognize the person looking back. She moves when I move and, somehow, I know it's me. But I don't look like myself. My brown irises have changed to a clouded light blue, chunks of flesh are missing from my cheeks and jaw. I lift a hand and place it against my face, expecting it to be horrible and painful.

But I feel nothing.

The train car rocks slightly as something collides with it with a dull thump. Then again and again. I squint out the window into the darkened underground station and see a man a few yards away. He sprints toward me at an unnatural speed, hitting the car.

I jump back just as the metal box shakes again. He claws at the doors, his mouth open wide, saliva dripping between teeth and down his chin as he moans and growls at me like a rabid animal. His fingers claw and dig at the rubber sealing the doors.

He alternates between attempting to pry it open and pounding against the glass, his bloodied hands leave streaks of red across the smooth surface.

All I can do is stand and stare. I want to scream at myself to run, to find somewhere to hide, but there's nowhere for me to go. Goosebumps prickle along my arms and my body shivers and begins to shake.

The doors twitch and open the barest amount before snapping shut again. Wider the next time and the next, until the man sticks one arm through. He wriggles, slowly squeezing his body inside, inch by inch until his efforts snap the doors open. I can only catch the glint of the flickering light off his bared teeth before he charges.

In a blink, the train car is flooded with bodies just like his. I don't know where they've come from, but the smell of decay is overpowering. I'm slammed against the ground, my head smashing against the metal floor as stars explode across my vision. My mind is screaming for me to move and fight him off, but I'm frozen in place.

When the spots clear, he's straddling me until he's the only thing I can see. His face swoops down toward my neck, ready to rip me apart. His hand covers my mouth and I can smell his rotting flesh. Terror coils in my gut and swarms up my chest to settle in my throat. When I manage to twist my head to the side, a scream rips its way out of my mouth.

But no sound escapes, just a whoosh of air. I flail and squirm, waiting for the pain of being shredded to pieces. He's too strong, I can't break his hold.

Then he looks me in the eye and snarls, "Raylinn."

I squeeze my eyes tight, not wanting to give into death yet. I scream again but it's muffled by the hand over my mouth.

"Raylinn, be still." This time the words have warped, no longer sounding like a half growl, but more human, almost friendly. "Open your eyes, Raylinn."

I do. It takes me a moment to realize where I am and what happened. Uneven ground digs into my back and… Jace is straddling me, his legs pinning my arms to my sides, and it's *his* hand clamped over my mouth to stifle my screams. His amber eyes are nearly glowing, even through the dark, as he frowns down at me with concern.

I continue to squirm—afraid my nightmare has warped or that the unthinkable has happened and Jace is infected with the virus and I'm too blind to see it. Then, like a slap, it hits me—if Jace is infected then I would be completely alone in this world. Maybe it would be best to give in to it, then I could at least be with everyone I care about.

But my body continues to struggle, some instinct buried deep inside. I don't want to be infected. I don't want to die—

"Raylinn, please…" Jace whispers. His eyes dart around, looking left and right, as he murmurs, "You are safe. You are safe. Nothing is going to harm you."

It's with those words that I understand. My breathing is ragged but I stop struggling. I'm not in danger. *I'm safe. I'm safe with Jace.*

After a moment, he slowly removes his hand from my mouth and eases off me to crouch at my side.

I brace my hands on the ground and sit up.

"You had a nightmare," he says quietly.

It had seemed so real. It wasn't like the nightmares I used to have where I would feel the fear from start to end. They had slowly changed over time, as though my mind was now resigned to my fate. I was losing my fear. But now that I'm awake, that might be the most terrifying thing of all—*resignation*, I shutter at the thought.

Did I scream? I mouth silently.

He shakes his head. "I stopped you in time."

I let out a low breath then scoot so the tree presses against my back. Our fire, if it could even be called that anymore as it is nothing more than a small bed of coal, still flickers. On most days, we don't dare even that. The smell of burning tinder might attract the runners to our location, but with last night's chill, we decided to take a chance and build a small one.

The winters are the hardest. The cold weather makes moving from place to place difficult and it forces us into buildings to take shelter. Staying in one place for more than a day is dangerous, and I hate the feeling of being surrounded by walls with only one or two options for an exit strategy. At least in the open we can go in any direction, usually for miles. It also means we can see danger coming from a distance and be long gone by the time it arrives.

Jace wraps one of our threadbare blankets around my shoulders and crouches in front of me. It's partially out of concern for my emotional state, and partially so he could see what I cannot. Everything we do anymore is connected to watching each other's backs.

Sleep, he mouths. A single word that might seem like a command but is really much more than that. He's telling me that I am exhausted and need more rest, that it is not time for me to take over the watch.

I look through the sparse branches of the trees. The moon has arced through the sky since I'd lain down and is nearing the horizon. He should have woken me sooner. It's then I notice the dark circles under his eyes.

I shake my head, and jerk my chin toward him, then point at the moon—my meaning is clear. *It's* my *turn to watch.*

He gives me a one shoulder shrug as if to say, *I tried,* then settles into his blankets. Jace lays on his side facing me.

As he sleeps, Jace tries to listen for anything that could come at me from behind even knowing I'll be watching his back until we pack up what little we have and move on for the day.

It's not that he doesn't trust me to keep watch—it's the need he has to try to protect me at all times.

In minutes, his breathing slows to a deep rhythmic pace, leaving me with the sounds of crickets chirping as the only thing for company. Their song is constant and friendly. Absentmindedly, I reach up and tug gently on my left earlobe.

The night has an eerie feel to it, and I can't tell if that's because I was born and raised in the city, or if it's because I know exactly what's out there.

The moon continues to dip toward the horizon as the sky gradually begins to lighten from a dark muddy gray to hues of purple and orange. All the while, my nightmare still echoes through my mind.

I am thankful the rest of the night is uneventful, though most nights are. We'd only suffered bad nights in the first several weeks after we initially left the city, before we knew what signs to look out for and how far away from the nearest populated area we needed to be to remain relatively safe. We quickly learned what to watch out for, but we know there is no distance that can guarantee our safety.

My eyes burn as tears prickle their way forward. I squeeze them shut, pushing the rush of emotions back down. He's the reason I'm alive today, and I am the reason he's alive as well.

That irresistible pull that had been there since the day our eyes met is still there and as strong as ever. I still feel safe with him, at peace with his proximity, despite everything that we've been through, and I still crave him every bit as much. Even now, I long to reach out and stroke his hair off his forehead. But I keep my fingers tightly clasped together in my lap. We don't have time or room for small comforts, those distractions could cost us everything.

It's still hard to wrap my head around the fact that I could feel so strongly about someone I had barely known. Weeks after we'd been on the road, I finally asked Jace about it. He said that the initial attraction had been our pheromones reacting, and something to do with an evolutionary safeguard to make sure they weren't rejected on a potential new planet. Which I suppose makes sense, however unromantic it is. It was more lust than love in the beginning. But now, what I feel for him is infinitely deeper than I ever thought possible. We've been through so much together.

But in those first days…

I let my eyes slide closed for just a moment, remembering the banquet, the dance, the stolen moment hidden between the trees. I breathe a sigh and open my eyes, scanning our surroundings looking for any sign of movement.

I had been blind to the world around me until it was too late, too wrapped up in what I felt for him to see the signs of what had come to pass.

Was I foolish for letting myself get so wrapped up in a romance that burned like wildfire through my veins? Looking back, if I'd known how it would end — I would say undoubtedly.

But what eighteen-year-old girl would expect something as horrible and deadly as a virus, or runners, to decimate the world?

It had been my senior year and I wanted it to be a blast before I had to submit myself to society's demands of a nine-to-five job I hated. I wanted a carefree, all consuming love affair that would put the romantic movies and books I loved to shame.

But what I got, instead, was a nightmare.

As it nears the time when I need to wake Jace, I gaze down at his sleeping form. He looks so peaceful so I decide to let him sleep a while longer. He needs the rest and, besides, if we aren't sleeping, then we would be walking to the next city or town, somewhere fresh to scavenge so we could survive one more day.

We are always focusing on survival.

Truth be told, I wouldn't mind a little more time to myself. Just a few more moments where I don't have to pretend to be strong for him. Not that he wouldn't understand, I just hate burdening him with it, knowing he feels the same. Dwelling won't help either of us.

I wish my mom was here. I miss those times she'd put her arm around me when I was upset and hold me as she stroked my hair. I miss my dad's jokes and Toby's sarcasm. It's hard not to feel alone. After Jace and I got sick, I thought we would die, and I think part of me was looking forward to it.

Then we got better, and I was too stunned to think of the implications or to realize how much it would hurt when it finally hit home.

I pull my knees to my chest and wrap my arms around my legs.

Two days on the road. That's what it had taken before the reality of what happened set in. It was mid-day and we were on the edge of a town. It had been all Jace could do to keep me quiet enough not to attract runners to our location while he tried to find an abandoned ship for us to sequester ourselves in until I could calm myself.

We had stayed there a week. It was all we had dared. I curled up in a dark closet at the heart of the ship, alternating between crying and sleeping. It was only in a moment of clarity where I had to force myself to act logically despite wanting to stay there and never leave.

It was move or die and it had been that way every day since. Never staying in one place too long.

There are times when I wish I'd suffered the same fate as my family. Wish I could be with them… wish I had stayed, and that I could just give up and find the nearest runner.

But I would never tell him any of this. He lost his family too, his friends… and without me, he's alone too. We have each other, which is no small thing. But love, a deep soul connection like this, could never replace the love of our families. We both know that.

His form wavers before my eyes and I lift my face to the sky, blinking away tears that form against my will.

Now is not the time, I scold myself. I need to keep my eyes clear and my mind focused.

I wince and look down at my hands. My nails dig into my palms, leaving deep marks but luckily not breaking the skin. It still stings like a bitch though.

I blink out of my haze and jolt to awareness, scanning the area. Something is off. I jolt to my feet and strain to listen. Nothing. It's completely silent.

The crickets have quieted.

Chapter Two

A Foolish Thing To Do

My heart hammers in my chest and I struggle to keep calm as I crouch down to place a hand on Jace's shoulder to shake him awake. All the while my gaze darts around, looking for any sign of movement, any snapping twig.

Jace is up and on his feet the second he sees my expression. He tilts his head to listen, zeroing in on something I can't hear yet. My hand goes up to my left ear again and I tug on my earlobe, a little harder this time. It's like having water stuck in there—sounds are muffled, only with this, it will never go away.

We stand a few yards apart, each looking into the dark shade of the forest, straining to see and hear. My gaze flicks to Jace for a second as he takes one step forward. He hears something.

A twig snaps and I see the rustle of the tree fronds as they brush up against each other. I turn to say something to Jace but looking away is my first mistake. As soon as I open my mouth, I'm slammed to the ground. My head bounces off the dirt and galaxies explode across my vision, soon replaced with dancing dark spots. Something that has been ingrained in me over the last two years keeps me from screaming, even as a heavy weight sitting on top of my middle makes it difficult to breathe.

There's a painful crack to my jaw right before the weight is dragged off.

I sit up and a sharp pain shoots across the back of my skull. I hiss through my teeth as I look up at who, or what, hit me.

Jace's arm shoots out, then there's a quick flash and the offender stumbles back into a tree where it slumps to the ground. My jaw drops and Jace advances until he stands over him, glaring down.

"Stay," he orders in a low voice, almost a growl. Then Jace is at my side, one hand on my forearm, the other on my upper arm, helping me to my feet. He looks me over and mouths, *Are you okay?*

I nod.

We've defaulted to saying as little as possible most of the time. Habit. At least it is when we aren't sure about our surroundings, which seems to be most of the time.

There's a groan and we spin to face the man who attacked me. He rubs his chest as he sits up against the tree with a dazed expression on his face, but one look in our direction has him freezing. My head spins and I can't focus on him enough to see if he's a survivor, or if he's in the process of turning into a runner.

Jace openly glares at him, watching for him to make a move, ready to defend us. Then the watery light of dawn washes through the trees and I can see the man isn't a runner, but a survivor like us. His mouth hangs open as he stares between the two of us with an expression I can only describe as dumb shock, like he reached the same conclusion about us.

I rub my jaw. It's tender and already feels swollen. My hands tighten into fists at my side but as much as I want to return the favor, I restrain myself.

His face is covered in a layer of uneven stubble, his clothes dusty, though no worse off than ours, and he's wearing a leather jacket with a bag flung over his shoulder.

"You're not runners," he says, as if there had been a question about it.

I wince at his words, he's louder then we ever let ourselves be. Habit has me scanning the area, straining to see if he's attracted any runners by all the noise he's making.

"No, we are not," Jace says pointedly positioned between us, but not enough to block my view of the guy. He crouches before the man and says, "Keep your voice down."

"I thought—" he starts but cuts himself off before lowering his voice. I can't make out what he says next, but Jace can. Whatever it is, Jace is pissed.

He points to me without looking. "The only thing wrong with her, is the giant bruise you gave her."

I clench my fists. *He* pummels me and has the nerve to ask what's wrong with *me*? I stifle down my ire. There's nothing good that can come of snapping at him… or punching him back—no matter how much he might deserve it.

After a long moment, Jace takes a step back and motions for him to stand. The two of them talk a little longer while I keep an eye out for any runners or other survivors following in his wake.

Normally we try to avoid others at all costs, for several reasons. The two big ones being: One, we don't want to be killed for our supplies and two, we still aren't sure if the rest of the world knows about the connection of the virus and a select group of the Vor'onins who decided to pull a very humanistic move—or, if everyone is blaming the government… Then again, everyone could be so focused on survival they haven't spared it a second thought.

I nearly jump out of my skin when a meaty hand touches my arm. I snap my head up to see our "guest" standing next to me. I jerk my arm away and he lets go without resistance.

"I apologize for punching you," he says somewhat sheepishly, then extends his hand and says, "I'm Brian."

I nod, accepting the apology and his hand, letting go of my irritation. I only manage a half smile as my face still aches. It's going to leave quite the bruise. But I've had worse, and if I'm being honest, I can't blame him. His caution can hardly be helped. At least he didn't come at me with something bladed, trying to remove my head.

"I'm Raylinn, and this is Jace," I offer.

Before I can say anything more, we all turn toward the pitiful moan coming from the same direction our new friend had.

Jace reaches out in a movement faster than my eyes can catch and grabs the guy by the front of his shirt. "Why didn't you tell us a runner was on your heels?"

"I-I didn't realize," he stutters.

I quickly snatch up my bag and fling it over my shoulder as Jace slips a machete from the sheath attached to his pack. I glance at it, wishing I hadn't lost mine.

I break into a run with Jace at my side and our new friend close behind. We don't move as fast as we can, opting for as much stealth as we can manage. It's still dark enough that we can use the shadows to hide.

Though the constant snapping of dry twigs coming from behind me makes me wonder how Brian has managed to survive as long as he has. He couldn't sneak up on a bush.

Jace halts abruptly, holding out an arm to stop us. He cocks his head to the side and listens. I strain to hear what he does, but I can't make out anything. Again, I reach up and tug on my left ear.

Then I hear it. A snap of a branch in the dry brush and a moan as a runner makes its way closer. Another snap and I whirl to face it.

"We're surrounded," Jace says through gritted teeth. "There's at least three... maybe more—it's hard to tell."

Jace takes my hand and we run back toward the clearing as fast as we can. I have to work to pick up my feet to avoid tripping on tangles of roots.

In no time, we burst back into the small clearing where we'd been camping. The groaning noises are almost on us. The three of us stand with our backs together and wait.

"Hell," Brian says. "They're coming from all sides."

"Not this one," I say, pointing away from the direction of the road.

Jace turns to me and grabs my shoulders, spinning me to face him. "Go, we will slow them down."

"Are you insane? I'm not leaving you to fight alone."

"We'll be fine," Brian cuts in. "There can't be more than two."

Well, that's a damn lie if I've ever heard one. But now isn't the time to argue. Even though I hate the idea of running to save my own hide, I don't have a weapon and I trust Jace. He wouldn't put himself in so much danger that I'd risk losing him. So I run, looking back over my shoulder only once.

Jace widens his stance and prepares himself, Brian picks up a thick fallen branch and does the same. Then I look ahead and move a little faster, telling myself they will be right behind me.

The farther I go, the more I reduce my speed, until my breathing evens out and I'm moving at a slow walk... hoping they'll catch up soon.

I don't know how far I've gone when I finally stop, my

back to a tree and strain to listen for them or something worse. The gait of a runner is clumsy, and that of a survivor is more deliberate and careful.

Grunts and obvious sounds of a fight reach me. Even cupping my hand to my good ear, I can't tell how many there are. All I know is that they shouldn't be taking this long.

I have to do something!

There's not much in the way of anything I can use lying around. The frustration of feeling so useless is too much. I'm going to make it a priority to find a weapon of any kind, because we can't go on like this with only one between us.

My eyes catch on a bright spot through the brush. I glance behind me to make sure the coast is clear. I move forward. Just on the other side of some dried brush, is a small barren patch of dirt that extends for a few yards before dropping off in a steep slope any normal person would need a rope to traverse.

A half smile forms on my mouth and I know what I can do.

Turning on my heel I bolt back toward where I left Jace, stopping dead in my tracks at the edge of the clearing.

Two runners lay unmoving on the ground. Jace and Brian are each fighting one off. They both look exhausted, but the runners look like they have a never-ending supply of energy.

Jace's machete is lodged in the neck of the runner near his feet. Brian's branch lays cracked in half on the ground and they are barely managing to hold them off.

This is bad. Very, very, *very* bad. Guilt and anger at myself for having run off in the first place sets my teeth on edge.

"Hey!" I call out, and everyone's attention falls on me.

"Raylinn? What are you—?" Jace asks as he continues to fend off the runner straining to bite him. Saliva drips down its chin as it continues to gnash and chomp its teeth in his direction, even with its eyes now focused on me.

The two runners disengage with the guys, pushing them away, and make their way toward me. If I didn't know better, I'd say they assume I am the easier prey and are trying to flank me.

But I don't have time to debate or worry about their seemingly advanced hunting skills. I turn back toward the drop off and run.

They crash through the brush behind me. I can hear the loud clack of their teeth as they snap their jaws in anticipation of catching me.

My breath comes in fast bursts and a stitch forms in my side, but I can't slow down. My muscles strain and burn and I'm either getting slower or these things are getting faster.

Jace calls my name from behind. I keep running, refusing to slow. I call out to the runners making sure they keep their attention on me.

Finally, the light through the brush appears. *I'm so close.*

I break through to the open space looking out across the valley, sliding to a stop a little closer to the edge than intended. The first runner bursts through the brush barreling forward. I dig my toes into the dirt ready for it.

The runner lunges and I throw myself to the side.

I'm falling face first toward the hardened dirt and ready myself for the impact even as the second runner continues to advance. My body jerks sideways, taking the breath out of my lungs as I stumble.

The first runner has somehow latched onto my pack, keeping me from falling. Its body slides, pulling me along with it. I claw at the air for a branch, bush… looking for something, anything, to hold onto, but there's nothing.

I feel it go over the edge, and I'll be dragged along soon if I don't do something. I twist my body in an attempt to shrug off the bag. The second runner sees me flailing, but I manage to sidestep, and it continues headfirst over the edge.

Bending forward at the waist, I let the bag slide off my arms and over my head.

The runner clings to the bag as it growls and snarls and it is one hundred percent focused on me, wanting nothing more than to rip me to shreds and devour my insides. My eyes lock with its milky, cloud covered ones, then I feel the world tilt as the abyss of open air threatens to swallow me up.

I circle my arms, trying to regain my balance as I watch it fall, tumbling down the slope, still clinging to my bag. The sick crack of breaking bones echoes upward.

Time seems to slow down. I'm half on the ground and falling forward. I wait for my life to flash before my eyes, but it never does. An arm snakes around my waist and pulls me away from the drop mid-fall.

Jace pulls me back to safety and crushes me to his chest. His familiar and comforting scent envelops me. I cling to him as I let my breathing and pounding heart slow.

"Are you okay? Did either of them bite or scratch you?" he asks.

I pull back to look him in the eye so he can see the truth. "No, I'm fine. Thank you for catching me."

"That was really foolish, Ray. You could have ended up down there with those things." He jerks his chin down the drop.

"I know, but it worked. Besides, you know one of you would have been bitten if I hadn't done something. You were barely holding them off as it was and neither of you were armed."

"You should have kept running."

I close my eyes and take a breath before looking at him again. Brian hovers in the corner of my vision and takes a step back, looking uncomfortable. I rub my forehead. "Jace, no one can survive out here on their own. You can't always keep me safe. We have to work together."

Jace frowns and I can see the logic of what I said and his instincts warring in his mind. After a long pause, he says, "I just hate seeing you in danger."

He might try to pull this protector crap on me, and even though I know it comes from a place of worry and love more than anything else, that doesn't make it any less frustrating... and it still pisses me the hell off. We've been barely hanging on for the last two years out here working together. Allowing him to take on the burden of everything would only get one, or both of us, killed.

"At least it was only my pack that was sacrificed this time," I offer with a shrug, trying to lighten the mood.

He clenches his jaw, clearly not having any of it. "We'll have to go into town soon and get you another. But, Raylinn, this isn't a joking matter. I don't want you to do anything dangerous like that again, okay?"

"Forget it," I snap, cutting my hand through the air. "I'll do what's necessary. End of discussion." Then I turn and walk away.

I feel bad being angry with him because he was worried, but I'm not helpless, even if I have a slight disadvantage. Brian has his back to me, pretending to examine the leaves on a branch as if he didn't have to witness our little tiff.

Jace means well, I tell myself. But that doesn't stifle my irritation at being treated as a delicate flower.

There's no room for flowers in this new world—only steel and sharp edges. And the sooner he realizes that, the better off we'll be.

Chapter Three

A Risk Worth Taking

Jace catches up with me and we walk side by side in silence, with him taking the lead, me in the middle, and Brian trailing behind as we keep to the cover of trees, moving quietly. The two guys seem to have come to some agreement that they need to flank me. While it's nice to be protected and all, it's far from practical and I roll my eyes at the notion.

We walk for a long time before Jace says quietly, "I'm sorry."

I open my mouth to say it's fine, just as I always do. But it's not, it's far from fine and I need to make it clear now. I need to stop giving this behavior a pass. We have to fix it now before something bad happens and it's too late.

"I know," I say, reaching out to put my hand on his arm. Jace looks at me with a storm brewing behind those golden amber eyes of his. "I know it's in your nature to be protective, but it's dangerous for both of us if you treat me like I'm helpless. You have to trust me and let me pull my own weight." As if on queue, both our gazes flick to our guest. "We'll talk about this more later," I say.

He nods, giving me a tight lipped smile that I'm pretty sure is more for Brian's sake than for mine. "You're right, we need to get moving if we're going to find a town and get you a new pack."

Jace turns to Brian and motions for him to come join us. He'd been keeping his distance, but it's awkward enough fighting with Jace when a practical stranger is standing a few feet away.

"If you will be traveling with us for a while, then you need to learn how we do things. Our way has served us well over the last two years. If you don't think you can adhere to that, then it's best we separate now," Jace says sternly.

The three of us form a tight huddle and we give him a quick rundown of our rules. Most of which comprise of doing everything as quietly as possible to avoid calling the runners to our location. Keeping downwind of runners and staying out of sight of them when possible. After all, we aren't sure exactly how they find us—sight, sound, or scent. Though their eyes turn milky white, there have been enough times when I could have sworn one looked right at me.

Brian nods, silently absorbing our rules.

I pull out our worn map and crouch down, spreading it over a relatively flat spot of ground. I search the map until I find our approximate location while I let Jace fill him in the rest of the way.

I frown. We are somewhere near the southern middle area of the Zion national forest the last time I checked. There are a few small towns nearby, but from the markings on the map, they seem to be more pit stops than cities. We'll try them, but we might have to backtrack west and head toward the town of La Verkin if we want any hope of getting supplies for two of us, and replenishing Jace's pack. It's the only town on my map that looks like it had a significant enough of a population for us to scavenge effectively.

Tracing my finger from our current location to the town, I barely manage to suppress a groan. It's a full day's walk at a decent clip, roughly twenty miles.

For half a second, I debate on climbing down to get my pack back from that runner. But with my luck, those things would be sitting there waiting, or even trying to find their way up to us.

I can't blame our bad luck on the new guy, though he will deplete our resources faster than if it was just Jace and myself. I did lose half of what we had when I played chicken with those runners. I was an idiot not to remove it first. Then again, with the death grip it had on the bag, I would have gone over the edge with it well before Jace was close enough to keep me from toppling over.

Standing, I fold up the map and relay the information to the men.

We'll stick to the trees for the rest of the day, then tomorrow at first light, we will head to town to get a new pack and supplies for me and for Brian as well.

While I talk, Brian looks to Jace questioningly. I try not to take it personally. Map reading isn't a typical skill most people have anymore, and I've met my fair share of guys who don't actually believe I can read one. I half expect him to ask for the map to "double check" my work. But he doesn't. *Good.* We don't need that waste of time.

We walk for a few hours, putting some distance between us and last night's campsite before stopping to eat breakfast. Our portions are a little less than half of what would be ideal, but we don't have a choice if we want it to last us long enough to get to La Verkin.

We walk until the sun starts to set before we venture closer to the outer edge of the trees and make camp.

Sitting around the fire, the three of us eat our meal consisting of barely warmed beans from a can. *I'm so sick of beans.* But we can't risk the pitiful excuse of a fire for more than an hour or the smoke might attract runners. That and our guest, Brian, is looking a little on the thin side. Waiting to make him eat just so his food could be more than lukewarm seemed a bit cruel.

The only sound besides the crickets is the scraping of spoons on metal plates. Supplies we picked up in a camping store on the edge of the city before we left. We'd grabbed two of everything, just in case we lost or damaged something. Part of me had wanted to grab extras in case we found others. That still left us with two plates since I'd lost my pack, and tonight Jace volunteered to eat his portion directly from the can.

Brian sits on the opposite side of the fire. He doesn't look well. A little too pale, even in the dim light.

I glance sideways at Jace. He sits between us, though a little closer to me. It's a move no one but I would recognize as protective. He looks like he's entirely focused on his food, but I know he's studying the man, watching his every move for any sign that he's more than what he seems. He doesn't completely trust him, and neither do I.

I feel a little guilty treating him like this, like a possible threat. But it's just smart if you want to survive. If he notices, he doesn't say anything. I'm sure he'd do the same in our position and I wouldn't blame him.

His spoon scrapes the bottom of his plate a few times before he stops to look up at us with the slightest tinge of embarrassment in his smile. His eyes dart to Jace's pack on my side of the fire. We only have a single candy bar left.

"Here," I say, getting to my feet. "Have the rest of mine." I lean forward, not wanting to get any closer than I have to. Again… it's the trust thing. He hasn't earned it yet.

Brian looks from my plate to my face to Jace and back. He's debating if he should.

"Take it. You need it more than I do right now," I add.

The old habits of manners we had before civilization fell don't apply anymore, but it's hard to not fall back into them when someone new comes around. It's all about survival now, but damn if I'm not a sucker for someone giving me big puppy dog eyes.

"Thank you," he says hoarsely.

I sit back down and Jace offers me the remainder of his. I shake my head. I'll be fine until morning when we have our next meal… if a third of a candy bar can even be called a meal.

I do wish we had found a store that had some canned food left—with labels—on our last looting trip, but we can only carry so much at a time and we'd be stupid to let this food go to waste just because we didn't know what was in it. And not a single can of it was dog food.

"How did you find us? This forest is pretty big and as far as I can tell, we're the only ones here," I ask.

Brian scoops a bite of food into his already full mouth and swallows with little to no chewing before answering. "A little bit of luck." He takes another bite. "Mostly it was the smell of the fire that drew me here."

I frown. I'd known the fire would be risky, but we'd taken the chance starting one anyway, thinking we were far off from any survivors or runners that it wouldn't be noticed.

We wait in silence until everyone has finished eating then Jace scoops dirt over the fire, extinguishing it. I'd be more disappointed but it's not as if it was big enough to provide any heat.

"So," I begin after the long silence has dragged out. "Where are you headed?"

Brian looks me up and down, then to Jace. He sucks on his spoon as if he's trying to get every last molecule of flavor off it. He's assessing us, looking for any signs of sickness after what happened this morning, or perhaps he's looking for weaknesses.

It would be nice to have a third pair of eyes, but the fact of the matter is, we would be stupid to trust him completely so fast. And I hate even thinking that because we do need the extra help. We are always on the move—lingering could be deadly. Neither of us getting enough sleep, and I doubt he was either being out there on his own. Dumb luck could play a part in his survival.

I'm not sure what he sees in us, but his posture relaxes as he says, "I'm headed to Wyoming."

I blink. "Wyoming?"

That could explain why he was constantly looking behind us all day, Wyoming is in the opposite direction from where we're headed. I'd thought he was paranoid and looking out for runners.

We might be in Utah at the moment but heading to Wyoming hadn't been on our to-do list. Call me skeptical, but I don't see the point in heading to a desolate state where limited supplies will probably be even more scarce.

We need the food and shelter of the more populated areas. Which, sure, there are more runners and survivors willing to kill for what you have, but there are more resources. Jace and I tend to avoid cities and towns until we need more, then when we do, we're within a reasonable distance. In Wyoming, there could be a hundred miles between small towns.

Brian leans forward, lowering his voice as if there's actually a chance we'd be overheard. "I heard there was a sanctuary there—a city of survivors."

I snort. "A *city* of survivors? In Wyoming?"

He narrows his eyes at me for my disbelieving tone. Great, I've annoyed him.

"Yes." He's serious then.

"Wouldn't it be more likely that the city is somewhere else… somewhere more people would be? Somewhere easier to get to?"

Jace squeezes my knee in warning, but I ignore it. I don't understand why there would be a city in the middle of nowhere.

"I've heard rumors about groups of them scouting for others." He gestures between us with a finger. "They look for survivors and bring them back to their city. I've heard they even have armored cars." Then he gives me a look that makes me bristle. "They chose Wyoming because there's wide open plains. They can see runners coming with enough time to prepare. But as the state with the lowest population, there is much less risk of those *creatures*," he points his spoon at me as he says the word, "finding them."

Okay… so maybe he has a point. There might be some validity to this rumor after all.

"How are you planning to get to this city?" Jace speaks for the first time. I'm a little more relieved than I should be. I get why he stays quiet. He wouldn't know what to ask about Wyoming, but directions are another matter. Brian seems a little less hostile answering questions from a man, and I roll my eyes inwardly.

He gives a nonchalant shrug and hands over his plate and spoon to me, which I hand to Jace to store in his pack until we get to a place with water to clean them. "I don't know, walking

I guess."

"Is it safe?" I ask.

A city of survivors. It had taken a few minutes, but the implications finally sink in. We wouldn't have to be alone anymore.

"It's safe," he says, nodding to me then turning his attention back to Jace. "It's located near the eastern border—they call it the Tower."

Jace furrows his brows and frowns. "The Tower?"

"Devil's Tower. There's a small city a few miles east of it, only a few blocks in any direction. They managed to wall it off before the runners made it there. But that's not as safe as the compound, mind you, just a small place run by civilians."

"What is the compound?" Jace asks.

At some point, I'd grabbed his hand and was squeezing it. Jace clears his throat and I try to lighten my grip. He doesn't complain, though glancing at his blood deprived fingers, I can't imagine it feels good.

"The government compound. Not all who go to the Tower choose to move on. Though I can't imagine why. The compound is military run, so you know they have ways of protecting you."

I finally let go of Jace's hand and rub my arms. At least there will be choices. After how everything went down in the back home in the city, I don't know if I'd be comfortable having the military in my business.

"Then, there's the rumors," he continues. "Some say they are doing experiments in there. But no one's ever made it there and back to confirm any of them."

"How far is that from the Tower?"

"About thirty-six hours on foot. Less if you can get your hands on a car with fuel. It's located in Mt. Rushmore."

I scoff and lean back, using my arms to prop me up. This guy is heading for a rude awakening if Mt. Rushmore is his ideal safe place.

Making bases was logical, but Mt Rushmore's "secret" room was just that. A room about the size of a hallway. It sure as hell couldn't fit more than a handful of people comfortably, fewer if people chose to call it home. Not to mention, it was *far* from secure. If an uninfected human could get in there, so could a dozen runners. And it would be a death trap.

"Look," I say, trying my best not to be condescending. "I know you can go inside Mt. Rushmore, but it's *just* a room." I bite down on the inside of my cheek. "I'm sorry, I think whoever told you that was lying, or maybe misinformed."

Brian gives me a hard look for a long moment. "If you don't want to come, then you're free to stay out here fighting off runners every night."

Shit. I'd messed up. "Sorry, I didn't mean to be insulting, I just find this all hard to believe. It sounds like some kind of X-files conspiracy."

He sighs in an exhausted way and slumps his shoulders. My chest aches because it's so similar to what Toby used to do after he'd get back from track practice.

I wish Toby was here now. I miss him... and mom and dad

so much, my chest aches. My eyes prickle as tears work their way up.

I blink away the thoughts. I can't allow myself to think of them now. I'd only succeed in crying in front of a stranger.

Our guest gives a half-hearted chuckle and rests his forearms on his knees. "Yeah, I suppose it does." He leans forward and says, "I've been thinking on this a lot today. I think we should take another look at your map. Head east tomorrow and find another town."

"No," I say firmly and without hesitation. "We're less than twenty miles from La Verkin. With my pack gone and you without anything in your small bag, we don't have enough food to make it farther."

"All right," Brian says after a long moment. "I do need supplies. I just hate to backtrack. Anyway, you two should come with me. There's nothing for you out west."

Jace squeezes my hand and nods. I don't miss the spark of hopefulness in his eyes. He'll follow me anywhere I go. He made that clear the moment we left the barricades. He trusts me to make the right decisions for us because he doesn't know this world like I do. I don't have the heart to tell him I don't know much about the world outside my city, other than the places my family and I went to on vacation. It wouldn't make a difference anyway. We have maps and that's good enough.

I loathe the idea of walls… but I know Jace will never feel safe without them. We've spent the better part of two years out in the open. It's time he had some semblance of comfort.

"We'll go with you," I say.

Brian looks at me with a raised brow, then to Jace.

"Even if it turns out to be nothing, three sets of eyes are better than one or two. We'll be safer together." I say, then I chance a side long glance at Jace. "We can take shorter watch shifts and get more sleep."

"You do have a point." He reaches into his bag and pulls his canteen and takes a long draw then wipes his mouth with the back of his hand. "I agree with you—and not to look a gift horse in the mouth—but how do you know you can trust me?"

That question has me second guessing everything. Though in all fairness, I could ask him the same exact thing.

"That is a risk we'll have to take, and it's a risk you have to take. You will benefit from this as much as we do, if not more," Jace says. Though, if I'm not mistaken, there's a hint of a threat in his words.

Chapter Four

Gone Shoppin'

We walked a good distance toward the town yesterday. It's not until around mid afternoon that La Verkin finally comes into view. It's later than I would have hoped, but then the only thing we've eaten since a cold can of beans—split among the three of us—was a candy bar this morning, also split three ways. The last of our food. None of us were able to summon much energy for such a long walk.

My legs are week and shaky. I am starving, though I keep that to myself since we are all thinking it. Complaining wouldn't do any good. We are on a mission to get more, and at this point in time, that is all we can do. I just hope I was right about the size of the town, and I hope there will be enough to loot still. Honestly I don't know what we'll do if I was wrong.

Brian made it clear last night how he felt about heading

west, but I just can't see taking the risk on a walled sanctuary on the far side of a wide expanse of nothingness. What if we run out of food or clean water and there's nothing around for close to one hundred miles?

A grumble halts all three of us in place. I turn to look over my shoulder at Brian who's holding his stomach and grinning sheepishly.

"Sorry, I can't help it. I'm starving."

I shake my head and stifle a laugh as I turn away.

"Come on, we only have another two miles or so before we hit the town. It looks relatively clean from this distance, so there's a good chance that it hasn't been scavenged to the bones yet," Jace says squinting into the distance.

I can barely make out little more than the buildings, never mind if they are trashed or good condition.

"You can tell that from this far out?" Brian's face scrunches in a skeptical look.

I'm glad he can't see my expression right now.

"Yeah." Jace runs the back of his hand across his forehead. It is unseasonably warm today. "Let's not stop now, the town is close and I want to find shelter before the sun starts to set."

We talk more during this stretch than we do anywhere else since we can see in all around us. Still our trek toward the town is filled with mostly silence.

Every once in a while I find myself wondering about the time even though that concept holds no meaning anymore.

When we reach the edge of town the sun is passed its zenith already so I'm guessing it's somewhere between two and four in the afternoon.

The second we reach the edge of La Verkin we go completely quiet even though none of us could see any runners as we approached.

We walk along the middle of the streets and I can't suppress the shudder that runs over me, chilling me to the bone, despite the heat of day. I will never get used to how eerie it is to walk into a deserted town. It's not natural. There's always a lingering feeling of what I can only describe as haunted. Then there's always the sensation of being watched. I hate it.

Give me the forest any day, where the only ones who see or listen are the trees and the birds.

"Hey," Brian says. "We should go to that corner store."

Jace and I face the direction he's pointing in. A small gas station store with boarded up windows with small gaps, perfect for looking through between them. The glass is undamaged and there's nothing that screams looted, so I get why he'd want to go but—

"No. Boarded up places are off limits." Jace says as quietly as he can.

"What? Why?" Brian huffs loud enough to make me flinch.

I know what he's thinking. It's the same thing others have thought when briefly traveling with us in the past. *Too many rules.* But it's kept us alive so far and neither of us are willing to change how we operate now.

"Boarded up windows mean squatters. More often than not someone is using it as their base," I explain. "We are all trying to survive here, we don't take from others, we only take the places already broken. Risking a confrontation isn't worth it and if they want to extend an invitation or help, they'll come to us."

"Or they'll murder you for—" Brian mutters under his breath but he's interrupted by a low scratching sound that makes the three of us turn and look in all directions. I can't see any signs of runners and apparently neither do the guys, though that doesn't necessarily mean they aren't around.

Stay quiet. Jace mouths to both of us then leads us down the street, machete in hand.

On this trip we really need to find a new weapon for me since I'd lost my machete in the skull of a runner last week before we entered the forest. Maybe a bat this time, or a golf club... something that won't get stuck in skulls.

Jace leads us through the streets. It's oddly quiet. I would have expected there to be a good number of runners around but there hasn't been one. We haven't even seen a single body down any of the streets. It makes me wonder if the entire town had managed to evacuate before the virus hit.

To my dismay this town is even smaller than I thought. There's no sporting goods stores. However there is a grocery store and that is just as important right now, if not more so.

Brian tries to run forward but Jace stops him by holding his arm out. We are currently in the shadow of a building and there's nothing but a street and a wide open parking lot between us and our destination. The store we have our sights set on is small, like *really* small… barely bigger than a gas station.

Jace sticks his head around the corner of the building and scans the area before turning back to face us. "I'm not complaining, but it seems weird to have a lack of runners in this area," he says reading my thoughts.

"So does that mean we can go now?" Brian says somewhat impatiently.

Jace considers for a long moment, a muscle in his jaw ticking. "Yes, but stay quiet and move quickly. We'll fan out, but not too far from each other. That way if any runners do come out of nowhere, the others will have time to think and react. We wait to go in until we all reach the store."

I don't need to be told twice. My mouth is already watering at the thought of food. Even picked over, there's always something.

Jace heads out first and veers to the right, seconds later I follow keeping my path straight. I scan the area constantly as I cross. Then I hear Brian's shoes hit the pavement as he veers to the left.

I make it to the store first. The guys are only a little behind so I press my forehead against the window to the glass and use a hand to shield my eyes from the reflective glare of the sun. The store inside looks a bit picked over, but no shelves are knocked over, and most importantly, I can't see any movement inside.

My stomach grumbles and I wrap my other arm around it as I pull back and give a thumbs up to Jace.

Once they reach me, we all make our way to the door expecting to have to pry it open as per usual. Instead it slides open. Jace and I look at each other and I know we are thinking the same thing. It's as if this town was somehow untouched by the virus, as if it somehow existed outside what the rest of the world was dealing with.

I feel a tap on my shoulder and I turn to Brian and see him point at a black wire running from the top center of the doors to a decent sized, shining, black panel attached to the roof at an angle. Solar panel.

For a second I wonder if we should go in given our '*don't take from others*' rule. But there's really no way to tell if that solar panel is new or had been there before the outbreak. Then my stomach rumbles again and I push the worries behind me. We won't knowingly steal, but we won't be overly cautious and allow ourselves to die. After all it's easier to ask forgiveness than permission.

Jace, Brian, and I head in, each of us taking a different direction looking for runners or other survivors then meet back up at the registers.

"All clear," I say.

"My area was clear as well," Jace says.

"Same," Brian adds.

We all smile at each other.

"Happy eating!" I say then take off down the isles not even waiting to see where the guys are going. I spotted some canned fruit when I was clearing my section and while it isn't nearly as good as fresh fruit, I am dying for whatever I can get my hands on.

I'm not ashamed to admit I practically slurp it out of the can using my fingers like an animal. *So not dignified.* But then dignity died when the world fell apart. It's not long until I'm stuffed, managing to stop before I feel heavy and gross. I do have some will power. Then I make my way toward the back and stare slack jawed at the refrigerated section. There are *still running* fridges. I press myself up against the glass, reveling in the chill of it, then reach in and pull out a soda.

Not wasting any time I open it and take a long drink. The bubbles of carbonation tickle my nose and make my eyes water. Gawd, I'd forgotten how refreshing that could feel. The syrup is so much sweeter than I remember.

My hunger satisfied, I find Jace. He's sitting in the middle of the cereal isle eating handfuls out of a box.

There's still so much food left in this store and I wonder why the citizens didn't buy it up before they left. Maybe they expected to return back soon?

It doesn't matter. This place might as well be paradise.

I sit on the floor next to Jace and lean on him, my back against his and let out a contented sigh. I feel full for the first time since… well, I don't actually remember how long it's been since I've felt this way.

"We could stay here," I whisper. "There's enough food to last us for a long time."

"We could."

It's a nice thought, but I'm not sure he'd go for it. I know either way Brian will leave here and go to that compound. We'll probably at least try to find him a pack and a bed roll before we say good bye.

When Jace finishes, we stand and wander through the isles in search of Brian, taking mental notes of what the store has to offer as we walk. A few shelves are empty but it's still far more than we've seen at any place to date. As we round the front I see a stand with a bunch of reusable grocery bags and grab several. Jace being the only one between the three of us with a pack, he can only hold so much food in his, and a little extra carrying room would be nice. Brian and I can haul extra food in these until we can get new packs for us.

Brian is in the junk food isle downing some chocolate cakes.

"The Twinkies *do* have an expiration date," he mutters through a mouthful.

I grab one and laugh. They had expired long before the world ended. I open my mouth to respond but am interrupted by a long yawn. Exhaustion has grabbed hold of me and refuses to let go now that my hunger is no longer a painful distraction. Apparently the idea of relative safety has allowed me to finally relax enough to let my body tell me what it needs.

"Let's find somewhere to sleep for the night, we'll fill up the bags Ray found in the morning." Jace looks to me and smiles. "I think we all could use with a little extra rest."

We head toward the back and find the managers office. I try the door but it's locked. *So much for that.* That leaves… the bathrooms. Gross. This room would have been perfect, we could take turns looking out the window incase any runners follow our scent in here.

"Hold on," Brian says and takes off before we can question him. He comes back a minute later with an eyeglass repair kit.

"What are you going to do with that?" I ask.

"Just watch," he says giving me a cocky half smile, then drops town taking out the tools and doing something to them I can't see, then he brings them to the lock and picks at it.

After a few minutes I'm about to tell him to give up so we can go in search of somewhere else to stay when the door swings open.

My jaw drops. "Where did you learn to do that?"

"I didn't." He shrugs. "I just figured it would be worth a shot."

We pile in. It's a tight fit but there's a plush leather couch. I can't help the tiny squeal that escapes me and I throw myself onto it. I sink in and snuggle into the cushions.

"I may never move from this spot again," I say sleepily.

Jace chuckles then says. "Here, help me push the desk against the wall."

I open one eye to look at him and pout before getting up. Thankfully he wasn't talking to me. I watch the two guys shove the desk and I want to help, I should help, but the pull of sleep is too strong.

"Wake me when it's my turn for watch," I mutter.

I stretch my arms and legs letting out a long sigh, delighting in the delicious feel of waking up after a good night's sleep. My muscles are sore but I don't care. It was so nice to sleep on something other than hard, unforgiving ground for a change.

"Good morning," Jace's soft voice whispers. His warm breath brushes across my cheek right before he places a soft kiss on my lips.

I blink open my eyes and smile up at him. Movement from the corner of my eye catches my attention. Brian stands and stretches, his fingers almost reaching the drop ceiling. His presence hits me and I remember where we are. I sit up frowning at Jace. "You didn't wake me for my shift."

He shrugs unbothered by the accusation as if it's not a big deal and says, "You seemed so tired yesterday, I thought you could use a little extra sleep." I open my mouth to argue how that isn't the point but he continues talking. "Come on, we should get what we can and look for a place where we can get you a new pack."

Brian peeks out between the blinds. "The coast is clear, we should move. Maybe we can find a phone book somewhere and see where the nearest sports store is."

I look to Jace. I was serious when I said I thought we could stay here but I'm not sure how he' felt about that. Jace reaches out his hand to help me to stand. I don't need the help but I take it anyway. I use it as an excuse to put my back toward Brian and give Jace a stern look as I mouth, *we need to talk... alone.*

He nods slightly. *Soon.*

While having to wait isn't ideal, I know we'll find time.

And we do. Brian and I split up the reusable grocery bags I found yesterday and Jace repacks his pack to leave optimum room, then the three of us head out into the store together and loot as much as we are able.

As I'm weighed down and not sure I can comfortably carry much more, I find Jace in the next isle over.

"Jace," I whisper.

He jerks his head in a motion indicating he wants me to go to him.

"I think... I think it would be smart of us to stay here... at least for a while. There's still electricity, the town seems to be void of all runners and other survivors. We could live comfortably. I don't think there's any reason for us to trek across almost two states for a rumor."

Jace finishes packing his bag and looks at me, contemplating what I said. He looks around taking in the lights, the amount of food, everything. If we play our cards right, we could stay here for at least a year or two, maybe even longer.

"While you're right, I think we should at least find Brian a pack and a bed roll, you too, just in case of an emergency. Then we'll come back and decide."

I don't know what I would have said to that because before I can even process his words, I hear the sound of not one, not two, but *three* shotguns being cocked.

CHAPTER FIVE

Three Guns

"Drop the bags and turn around," a deep voice booms.

Jace looks over my shoulder and slowly sets his pack on the floor, but I hesitate.

"I said, put the bags on the floor and turn around," the man repeats his command, slow and measured.

I take a deep breath and lower the several bags before turning around. We have run into more people in the last few days than we have in months. We can usually avoid them better than this.

I stare up into the light blue eyes of an older man with a nasty scowl on his face. His skin is weathered by years in the sun and unruly, white hair sticks out from beneath a padded and worn ball cap. A thick mustache that's a bit too big for his features graces his upper lip.

He looks every bit the father who's been through too much in the past two years turned leader of an old west type gang. Beside him, a younger man, a little older than me, stands motionless with the barrel of his gun also aimed at us.

Jace clears his throat and I flick my eyes to look at him. He gestures with a quick expression that he hears something in the direction of the aisle Brian was in.

Both of the armed men hold sawed off rifles. One trained at Jace, the other on me. The fact that they aren't both trained on Jace is of some comfort. They don't seem to hate the Vor'onins enough to shoot first and ask questions later.

"Found another one," a third man says as he rounds the corner, shoving Brian toward us and making him stumble a step as his rifle pushes into his back.

I take a small step forward, my hands up in front of me in a sign of surrender, trying to cover as much of Jace with my body as I can. My first instinct is to protect him… that and a short girl is less intimidating than a tall man so I assume they will be less aggressive toward me.

With all three of the men lined up, I can see a family resemblance. Two brothers and their father.

The father shifts the barrel of his gun and narrows his eyes on me. I'm the least threatening person here, so I take the lead in trying to communicate. "Look, we didn't know anyone else was here," I say slowly, my hands still raised in the air. "We lost most of our supplies yesterday and just need a few things."

"Well, you won't find them here."

"Okay," I say, retreating until I bump into Jace, hoping the guys get the hint to back up. "Okay, we didn't mean any harm. We needed food." I have to admire his sons, stone faced and detached. It's almost like they have a lot more training than their scruffy faces and thread bare shirts give away. "If you'll let us pass, we'll just be on our way."

"Are there any others with you?" the man asks.

"No, it's just us."

His eyes roam over me, then Jace, then Brian, sizing us up. His gaze lands on Jace's bag. "Is that all you got?" he asks with a jerk of his chin.

"Yes," I say, hoping like hell he doesn't try to strip us of the one pack we have left.

He grunts then thankfully lowers his gun, so it's aimed at the ground rather than my head. His expression is still hard and angry, but I take this as a sign that they'll let us go and we can find another place to grab supplies. At least we have full bellies.

The son to his left, the one who looks like he maybe just entered high school when this all began, leans toward the man and says something too quiet for me to hear. Whatever it is, it earns a glare, and he meets it with one of his own, not backing down.

At this point, I'm grateful we didn't act like animals and go crazy making a mess of this place. Even if that reason was because I wanted to stay for a while and we wanted to preserve as much food for the future as possible, but it might have served us well.

Brian starts to talk, but before he can even get his first word out, Jace silences him. I don't know how but, judging by the grunt issuing from behind me, I'd say a sharp elbow to the ribs.

"You can go," the old man says, and they all back up against the sides of the aisle, him on one side and his two sons on the other, to let us pass. He nods to Jace. "And take your bag with you."

I give him the brightest smile I can, doing my best to infuse it with as much gratitude and innocence as I can. He did say bag—*singular*—but that doesn't stop me from plastering on the sweetness as much as I'm able to as I reach for the bags we've filled. "Thank you so much."

I bend down and pick them up, not taking my eyes off him. I see Jace and Brian following my lead from the corners of my eyes. I might be glad they are letting us leave unharmed with our haul, but I'm not stupid enough to trust them completely.

"I said *your bag*," he snaps, and I freeze, but I don't drop the two I've picked up. "I didn't give you permission to steal from us."

I bite back a remark about how this store probably doesn't even belong to him since it's more likely that the *real* owner fled with the first wave—or was part of it. And that calling something yours doesn't make it so just because they have guns and we don't.

But I stay silent. Getting on his bad side won't help us here.

I draw my eyebrows together and widen my eyes in the most pathetic puppy dog expression I can summon. It always worked on me when our old dog looked at me like that, so I figure it's worth a chance. I think about that dog now, and about the day Mom and Dad told us he went to go live on a farm and how even then I knew it was a lie to spare us… and I let my eyes water, stinging with the tears brought forth by that memory.

I hate this, but survival is survival. And if looking weak to this band of good ol' boys will allow us to walk away with some much needed food, then I'm not above using these tactics.

Clasping my hands in front of me, I look to the bags at my feet then back to him, letting my lower lip quiver, just enough to be believable. "May we please take the few bags we packed? We didn't take much, I promise, and we only took them because we lost almost all of our supplies when we were being chased." My voice wavers as I plead with him, weaving in enough misery with our story as I can manage while keeping it real. Though if he doesn't let us take the bags, I might actually start bawling anyway. "We haven't eaten in a day and a half."

He looks at me, his sons exchanging a quick glance behind him. I can tell he's not thrilled, but that little spark of fatherly instinct is there, though he does hide it well. He grunts as though he lost a battle of wills, and maybe he did. He glares, his mustache twitching to the side as he contemplates my request.

Then the noise of the doors opening at the entrance draws all six of our attention. Two guns swivel toward the entrance, while the third remains trained on us. We listen, but it seems that there is something keeping them from being closed.

The three men don't call out and I'm glad. They're smart. The leader jerks his chin toward the older looking son, and he slinks out of sight to check out who—or what—has entered the store.

I can feel the warmth radiating off Jace at my back as he inches closer and takes my hand. It feels like we stand there for hours, though I'm sure it's only been seconds before the son screams. A shot rings out, there's the sound of stuff being knocked over, then silence followed shortly by the eerie sound of pain filled groans that can only mean one thing.

My gut clenches. *Unarmed.* I am *still* unarmed.

"Billy…" the man says in a strangled voice, but he doesn't go to help him, knowing that it's hopeless. His inability to save his son shatters him, I can hear it in his voice. My heart breaks for him.

Somehow, it's worse for me knowing the guy's name. I hate knowing anyone's name in these situations. It feels more real. It reminds me too much of my own family.

I swallow hard and push my feelings down. I can't do this here, can't do this right now. There's only room for focus, only room for staying alive for the next few minutes, the next hour. There will be time enough for emotions when we have silence again.

The father and the youngest boy ready for the things that

would come around the corner, as the clumsy movements and groans of the runners echo through the store.

They are ready for a feast, and we are on their menu.

"Shit," the man swears then starts to fire. One round then another then another, reloading when needed. His son follows suit, aiming in the other direction.

I stand in place, frozen. I have no weapon, nothing with which to defend myself other than boxes of cereal, but I don't think those will help at all.

I'm quickly shoved into the metal aisle stand by Jace, and then he's gone.

He hacks away at a runner at the far end of the aisle. A wave of dizziness almost knocks me off balance. I'm surrounded and helpless and it makes me… angry. I refuse to let those things eat my brains without a fight. I look around, cursing the soft foods in this confined space.

I bend down and grab the bags of food. Canned goods I can work with. Though possibly denting them isn't ideal, surviving the hour is just a tad more important at the moment.

I chuck a can at the next runner to turn into the aisle… and miss.

It lands behind him and rolls. My aim leaves a lot to be desired. I throw another and another, until the ground around Jace is nearly covered in cans. He has his hands full dealing with one runner, when another turns the corner heading straight for him. Taking a deep breath, I lob one of my last few cans and it strikes the thing in the face with a solid thunk and sends it falling to its back. As more runners come they begin to trip on the cans and each other. Soon it's a tangle of growling, foaming at the mouth runners. Jace dispatches the one he's been fighting with then starts hacking away at the ones on the ground.

I'm all out of ammo—save for one can.

Jace is almost finished. The mound of bodies grows, slowing the remaining runners down. Until no more come.

I turn at the rude silence of gunshots. The boy and his father are walking toward us. Then, my heart skips a beat as one more runner turns into the aisle.

I don't even think about it. I wrench back my arm and lob the final can at the runner, striking it in the chest. It stumbles a step, the father whirls around, shoving his son out of the way with his arm as he crouches and takes aim. The shotgun blast makes my left ear ring this close up and I wince.

The runner falls with a spray of black goo exploding behind it.

We all stand and listen for a long moment, taking in the scene around us. The sheer number of runner bodies, all oozing, makes my stomach curdle. Save for the dark, rotted color of their blood, they look almost human, their faces no longer distorted.

No one speaks for a long time, the only sound that fills the space is our breathing as we wait, with our backs against the shelves. When no more runners come, we all relax. At least as much as we can considering we just survived a massive runner attack in one piece, then I flinch as I remember that's not entirely true.

We are down one… It's only then I notice I'd completely forgotten about Brian.

I take a deep breath and force my racing mind to slow and take stock of what damage has been done. I remain clean, as do the two remaining strangers, but looking to Jace, I see he's splattered with flecks of runner goo from his close up fights.

Brian steps up to his side, slightly behind him, also speckled in goo. I don't remember seeing him at all during the fray. But then again, and as much as I hate to admit it, even if only to myself, I hadn't cared in the slightest what happened to him, I only wanted to keep Jace safe. He's the only one here who matters to me. He is my family and I won't let anything happen to him if I can help it.

"Thank you," the man's son says flatly. "I'm Blake, this here is my pa, Todd."

I smile at him the best I can, but it's strained, so I let it fall. Smiling now just feels wrong. "I'm Raylinn, this is Jace, and Brian," I say, pointing at them with my thumb over my shoulder.

The father, Todd, turns to us, that angry frown still on his face. "I think it's time for you to leave."

I couldn't agree more. I want to get as far away from these runners as I can. But my eyes flick to the now depleted grocery bags of food. We needed those.

"Pa," Blake says in a half scolding, half begging tone. "They did help us."

"Fine, take what you can fit in those bags, then get," Todd grunts. He's no longer aiming his shotgun at us, but his unwelcoming scowl doesn't instill much comfort in me.

My face brightens but I'm careful not to look too pleased. I am sorry about his loss, but it's hard to be upset when you know that you can make it through the next few days alive—incidents with runners aside, starving won't be the reason we die at the very least.

"Thank you," I say, giving him the best half smile in acknowledgment of his gesture as I begin to inch forward. It doesn't reach my eyes, nor do I mean for it to. I'm tired. We are all tired, and even though the five of us are alive, one didn't make it. And that in itself is a huge loss.

"Don't thank me, just don't come back," he harrumphs, and I don't miss the unspoken threat in his tone. He's upset he lost his son, yet I know he's thankful that we were there to help. He knows that the two of them would have been swamped from the front and back if it weren't for Jace, and I suppose Brian.

As we walk between the two men, I hesitate, letting Jace and Brian pass me as I stop to look at Todd.

This might get me killed but... a girl's gotta do what a girl's gotta do, and asking a question is worth risking his further upset. Besides, I don't think they would have shot us unless we attacked. They don't seem the type. They are just a family trying to get by. The guns are more for their safety from runners.

The food they're allowing us to take will go a long way in keeping us alive, but it's not all we will need.

"Could you point us in the direction of a sporting goods store? We lost most of our things."

Todd presses his lips tightly together and just looks at me, not with anger, but with a volley of emotions he's trying to hold back.

"Just head south for about two—two and a half miles, then you'll hit one." Blake steps forward, pointing toward what I assume is south, but his eyes remain downcast, locked on the one hand gripping his shotgun tightly to his body. "There's a uh," he clears his throat. "Another one about a mile west of that." Then Blake lets his arm fall limply to his side.

I shoulder the two bags I emptied a few minutes ago and half turn. But in a move that I think surprises him as well as myself, I take his hand in both of mine and squeeze. Slowly, he lifts his eyes to finally meet mine.

"Thank you for everything," I say. His jaw tenses and he gives me a quick nod. Then I hesitantly I add, "And… I'm sorry about—" I can't finish.

Blake presses his lips together, understanding my meaning.

I turn back toward the front of the store. Jace and Brian are waiting for me just past the end of the aisle.

Silently, the three of us hurry to refill our bags. I try to fill the bag with a variety, careful not to take the last few of any one item. I'd hate to take advantage of them.

Jace, Brian, and I meet up near the end of the aisles, near where the old deli used to be. It's long since been emptied. Probably the first of the food to be eaten.

Brian turns toward the door, but I hesitate and close my eyes. I feel Jace's hand slip into mine and squeeze. He knows what's bothering me and offers to help lead me around the scene while I keep my eyes shut. I take a few breaths and give him an appreciative smile, but shake my head no.

I can't deny what that guy did for us. He put himself in danger—he gave his life—so we could have a few seconds warning, so we could have a few moments to prepare for the onslaught.

Chapter Six

Like a Thief in the Night

The walk to the sporting goods store is filled with a heavy silence. We move slowly, quietly, using what we can to stay hidden. A walk that would take only half an hour at most, takes us nearly twice as long. None of us have much to say as we focus on keeping an eye out for more runners, scanning the distance as far as we can see, not staying too close to anything that could be shielding them from view. We all take turns looking behind us.

Finally, we see the first sporting goods shop, Over The Edge. I want to run in and hide so I can breathe and ease the tension from my shoulders, but that would be foolish.

I feel so exposed, though the second I step foot in the store I know I'll feel trapped. There's nowhere I feel safe. Not anymore, especially not after the attack this morning.

Safe.

That feeling is so foreign to me now. It's hard to remember exactly what it is anymore, other than a concept that is impossible to obtain or feel.

The three of us split up and scout the outside to get the all clear before making our way inside through the broken front window. Our boots crunch on the broken glass and I cringe. After the silence of the past hour, it's incredibly loud, even to my ears.

It takes a moment for my eyes to adjust to the dim light inside, and the instant they do, my hope deflates. Bikes. Bikes are everywhere.

It's not quite what I'd been hoping for, but Blake had told us there was another one about a mile west of here. So, we aren't completely out of luck yet, there's still a sliver of hope. There are some assorted clothes and some shoeboxes to one side that look like they were already picked through and knocked over, though there are quite a few that remain untouched.

"I don't think he understood what you were asking him," Brian says dryly.

I rub my temples. A pounding headache is starting to build behind my eyes. I set my bags down on a polished wooden bench. "We'll look through what they have, maybe we can at least find some new clothes or something while we're here."

Jace crosses to the far wall and looks over the scarce selection of men's tops. He selects several simple ones and holds them up then puts about half of them back. I plop down on the bench beside the two bags of food and just watch him for a while.

I think I need water. I'm not sure I've had any since yesterday, and it's hot out already even though it's still early in the day.

Jace sets his pack down and replaces the old worn out clothes with the new ones he's chosen from the selection. He stands again and grabs the edges of the shirt he's wearing and peels it off. My stomach tightens at the sight of his abs. Damn, that boy is beautifully built.

Even after all this time, I still can't control how my body reacts to seeing his. I force myself to look away before I start drooling like a fool. Instead, I focus on the mound of shoeboxes to my right. Many are empty or knocked over onto the floor. I slide off the bench and tuck my legs under me as I pull out boxes from beneath the bench to check the sizes.

It takes a little searching, but I finally find a pair in my size. I quickly untie my worn-down boots and slip them off. I wiggle my toes, letting myself enjoy a few moments of freedom before I have to shove them into the new pair. Before I do, I get up and grab one of the few remaining athletic socks hanging on the wall.

New shoes call for new socks. I slip into the new boots and walk in a small circle.

I frown down at the old pair only now realizing how worn they'd become and how uncomfortable. Of course, replacing them also means having to break them in, which will most likely mean acquiring a blister or two. But those will heal quick enough and the new socks will help with reducing blisters as I break the new boots in. Perhaps the next store we go to I'll be able to find bandages just in case. For now, I pluck up the remainder of the socks and stuff them into the food bags.

I sit back down and sort through the shoes again, looking for a pair in Jace's size. About the time I find a pair, a hand appears in front of my face, clutching several shirts. I glance up to see Jace's smiling face.

"I found these for you," he says quietly.

Holding up a box of shoes, I say, "How fortunate, because I found these for you."

We exchange our finds as Brian collapses onto the bench with a heavy groan. He's wearing new clothes as well.

"I didn't know what size you were," I say. "So I picked a few different sizes for you to go through." I point to a short stack of varying boxes. By looking at his current boots, I guessed his shoe size was somewhere around Jace's so I chose a range of them.

"Thanks." He nods and bends over without getting up to scan the selection and picks one from the middle.

Jace sits next to me while we rest as Brian replaces his shoes. Resting my head on Jace's shoulder, I sigh. I'm so tired, but it's not just in my muscles, it's bone deep and encompasses my mind and soul. I can see the exhaustion in all of us. The fight this morning, losing a survivor to those runners, and surviving for the past two years in a nonstop battle against runners, exposure, starvation, and anyone willing to kill us—it's drained us.

The smell of our new companion's feet hits me, and I turn

my face away. *Oh man, I'm going to get sick if I don't move.*

Without looking, I snatch up one of the shirts Jace picked out for me and I walk around the nearest partition to change. The softness of the material, the clean scent… it makes me a little sad I can't take a shower first before putting it on. I'm a little more aware of the dried sweat on my skin than I'd like to be.

I go back to where the guys are waiting. We're done here.

Brian and I drape our new clothes through the handles of our reusable grocery sacks. *Yeah. We need to find new packs soon, because this isn't going to work for long.*

"Shall we?" I ask as we head toward the broken window.

It seems a little stupid to avoid the door that is literally only a few feet away, but there appears to be some kind of chimer on it, and we don't need that kind of noise alerting whatever runners may be in the area to our location.

Heat hits me in the face as I step out into the sun. I blink as my eyes water, trying to adjust to the light. I wouldn't complain if some clouds formed in the sky right about now, I think toward the heavens, but the only thing above us is that blinding ball of light in an endless azure sea.

We walk faster this time as we head west. I don't miss that Brian keeps looking over his shoulder with a permanent scowl as though he resents the fact that we are still heading away from his goal. Or maybe I'm just tired and reading him wrong. It's hard to tell, I don't know him all that well, yet.

At least this trip was only a mile out of the way.

None of us are surprised to find the windows at the second sporting goods store broken out as well, or that it's been looted. I am, however, glad that there is still quite a bit to choose from.

Packs, bedrolls, and first aid materials. I mentally run through the list of things I want from this place over and over, adding one or two things to the list as I glance around.

We can see through the whole of the store from where we stand, but still we are wary of possible runners that could be inside. We pile our current supplies behind the counter that's situated in the center of the store. I don't look to see where the men are headed.

I duck down and rummage through the items beneath the cash register. It's full of dust under here, thicker than two year's time could bring. Seems as if the employees slacked on cleaning before the end of the world came about.

It only takes a minute to find the first aid kit, practically brand new, though perhaps only a single bandage has been used. I stuff it in one of my grocery bags between my shirts and the food for safekeeping. My hand goes to my shoulder and rubs the spot where the straps had dug in, making the muscles already sore.

The two guys are together in the back, talking quietly over which bedrolls would be suited for our needs.

"What about these really thick ones?" Brian asks.

Jace shakes his head, throwing a quick smile my way before answering him. "Those would be too cumbersome, they're best suited for colder weather. It's the start of summer so these thinner ones will do." He pinches the material. "They are dense but are light enough for what we need them for."

I reach between them and pluck a bedroll for myself. I am a little more excited over this than I ever thought possible.

Their conversation dies off. Though I suspect they were most likely discussing them because they craved a small sense of normalcy. Having a simple conversation these days that had nothing to do with runners was rare. At least in this, we could pretend we were just three friends heading out on a weekend camping trip.

I'll feel better when we are away from civilization again, where we will have the cover of trees in the wide open space—where runners and other survivors are scarce. I don't like this area. I don't like how we could enter the little town of La Verkin and not see a single sign of runners, only to get hit with a barrage of them the next morning. The family guarding their store were caught unaware as well, and they lived here.

It was almost as if the runners had planned the attack. As if they were somehow capable of devising a strategy.

I shake my head. No, that is stupid. Runners are pulled by one thing, and one thing only: finding prey to rip apart and devour, human and Vor'onin alike.

Jace reaches forward and picks out a new bedroll for himself, bending down to untie his old one and replacing it as Brian still stands there considering which one he wants. I drop mine off onto the register counter and go in search of a new pack. I pause halfway to where they are and flip through a rack of rain gear, selecting three long ponchos before moving on.

Maybe I'm a bit emotional, but I could almost cry in joy at the selection they have here. I quickly pick one out that will fit me, not bothering to try to get one for Brian, he'll need to try them on to get a good fit.

I hurry back toward the counter, rushing past the two of them as they go to find a pack for Brian. I'm excited to get my new things together.

Before I'm halfway finished packing, both Jace and Brian, who is now carrying a metal baseball bat, join me in wordlessly packing and repacking. It's nearly noon by the time we finish.

"We should eat before we go," Jace says, and Brian and I agree whole-heartedly without hesitation.

I stand and stretch my legs and Jace picks through his pack. I hand him mine and ask him to find something in it. There's one thing left I want to do. I've been so preoccupied with my new pack and bed roll that I almost forgot.

I take off toward a side wall and return a few minutes later holding a golf club, swinging it around to get the feel of it. It's strong enough to cause some damage with the heavy end but has more reach than a baseball bat would provide me, giving me more space to work with, and light enough that it wouldn't tired me out as fast.

Now, I feel more prepared.

Three cans are sitting out and opened by the time I return. *Beans*. I do my best to avoid grimacing. I may have picked them off the shelf, but that doesn't mean I'll ever look forward to them again. I also didn't think that we'd be eating them again so soon.

I join the guys and grab my can. We eat in silence until Brian loudly scrapes the inside of his can near the end, only stopping when he sees our wide-eyed stares.

After we all finish, we each take one last glance around the store before heading out. It's a much later start to our day than we try to make, but it can't be helped. If I had to guess, I'd say somewhere between late afternoon and early evening. But we all agreed that we didn't want to stay in this area any longer than we had to. Perhaps there was a reason this little city hadn't been completely looted by now.

We walk for days, stopping at gas stations to scavenge whatever food we can find, even though we still have plenty. There will come a time when looting spots will become few and far between, and we'll be glad we did this.

The farther east we travel, the more I realize how lucky we've been. Some stops have been so picked over that there was literally nothing edible left.

As much as I hate to admit it, deciding to go with Brian was probably for the best. There's no way we would have been able to survive like this much longer. Canned goods and junk food have made for a poor diet the past two years. And now with the pace we've set to get to the compound as fast as possible, I'm really feeling the effects of it.

Being in a hurry when you've been eating like crap is a lot harder than wandering slowly and aimlessly.

The ground has evened out, and it's mostly flat now since we left Utah. And maybe it's my imagination, but I'd swear I'm having a harder time breathing.

If Jace and Brian feel the same, they don't say anything, so I don't either.

I am beyond thankful when we call it quits for the day and make camp early. At this point, I'm not the least bit interested in food. All I want is to lie down and sleep. I hadn't realized how worn my other sleeping bag had become, and I can't say I'm sorry I had to replace it.

I let my bag fall to the ground with a thump and loose a deep sigh. I just stand there staring at it, wishing I could just plop down face first like I used to be able to do when I had a bed, a home... before all of this.

"Ray, you look tired," Jace says.

You look tired is code for you look like crap, but I'm too worn out to even pretend to care. I feel like a giant bag of crap so it stands to reason that I look like it.

"Yeah," I say. "I'm exhausted today for some reason. I'll take the first sleeping shift if the two of you don't mind."

"Of course," Jace says kindly.

Brian doesn't say anything, so I take that as him not minding then drop to my knees and untie my bag and roll it out. I grab my golf club and lay it down in front of me, wrapping my hand around the cool metal.

Among the soft sound of their boots against dirt and the soft cracking of small twigs, I feel myself drift off in no time.

I dream for the first time in almost a week. I know it's a dream because the lighting is soft and seems to make everything glow. But it's not just that... I'm standing outside my house, and when I walk inside, Dad is on the couch watching the news, Toby's music is thumping through his closed door, and I can hear Mom in the kitchen.

I smile and just stand there taking it all in. Remembering the warmth of moments like that, the sounds, the smells... When I open my eyes, Dad is looking at me and frowning.

"Ray..." he says. When I don't answer, he says my name again, though I can hardly hear him. It's as though I have cotton in my ears. "Ray!" he says sharply this time, though there's no anger in his voice.

I open my mouth to answer but I can't remember any words or how to use my voice, and even if I did, I don't know how to respond.

"Time to wake up, Ray," he says. "You have to open your eyes."

I go to say that my eyes are open, but before I can, I blink and I'm looking at the canopy of branches above my head, pale light filling the patches of sky between them. Brian should have woken me hours ago.

I jerk up, gasping for air, and look around. Jace is beside me sleeping soundly. The coals of our fire pit have long since died. My gaze sweeps the area, but I don't see Brian.

Normally, I would just assume he's off peeing behind a bush… except I can only spot my pack next to Jace's, the clothes we both packed now strewn about.

And no sign of any of the food that we'd packed in them.

"Jace, Jace!" I hiss roughly, shaking his shoulder.

He mumbles and sits up. It's only a few seconds before he takes everything in as I had and comes to the same conclusion.

I scramble to my feet and drop down before our packs, looking to see what Brian had deigned to leave for us.

Brian had taken all the food, the first aid kit, and—

I ball my hands into fists, my nails biting into my palms.

He'd taken Jace's machete, leaving us only with the bed rolls we slept on, the clothes we'd found, and my golf club. I'm pretty sure the *only* reason we even have that singular weapon is because I slept with it at my side.

I swear I will kill that bastard if we ever cross paths again.

CHAPTER SEVEN

Intergalactic Spaceport

I can't help the stinging tears that force their way to the front of my eyes. We have no idea where the nearest food source is now. It's been days since we left La Verkin, and we haven't seen anything but sparse gas stations since, let alone something useful like a sports store where we could backtrack a little.

We'd crossed into Wyoming a few days ago, so going back into Utah is not an option. I don't want to go back to the highway, trapped between those mountainous hills for miles on end.

"Jace, what are we going to do now?" I ask, utterly defeated. I know the answer… of course I know the answer. There is only one thing we can do. But I need to hear it. I need to hear him tell me that it's not impossible.

I don't even know where we are. I was too tired last night to mark it on the map before I passed out. My heart skips a painful beat and I'm dizzy for a few seconds before the world rights itself. *The map.*

I grab my pack and dig through it, becoming more frantic as I go. I dump what little was left inside onto the ground. He took the map. That bastard had stranded us after everything we'd done for him, welcomed him, shared everything we had with him—and he thanks us by stranding us with little more than the clothes on our backs.

I should have known something was up when he'd been eyeing the packs, the food, as we ate our meals… I should have known he was planning this when he packed the reusable grocery bags back at the sports store.

"Aarrrg!" I growl to the sky above. *That little weasel!*

Jace places a hand on my shoulder and couches down at my side.

"We keep going. There are signs for everything here. We'll just have to stick close enough to the road to read them." He presses his mouth in a tight line. Then lifts a hand and swipes at the tears that streak down my cheeks. "We will be okay. We can still get into any ships we pass, remember?" Jace shows me the palm of his hand to remind me of the glowing symbol that appears whenever he uses the implant there to manipulate his people's technology.

I rub my forearm across my eyes, wiping away the remaining

tears. Then together we repack our bags and bedrolls then begin our walk eastward. At least I can remember most of this state. There's not really much to it. It's square and stretches out toward the east for several hundred miles. There are a few small towns coming up. Perhaps those will hold something for us.

———

We don't reach a town by nightfall, but we do manage to come across a rest stop. A brown building with several flag poles outside still flying the now worn and tattered flags. The building is just a fancy public bathroom with a lobby that houses two vending machines behind iron gates. There are gaps for us to push buttons and collect our selections from the bottom—which would be useful if there was electricity running in this forsaken place.

Without Jace, I'd be dead a thousand times over from a thousand different reasons. Today though—*today*—we won't die because he somehow is able to use the electromagnetic charge from his palm implant to short out the vending machines. Packets of chips and candy bars fall to the bottom. As I kneel to pull them out for us, he moves on to the next, shorting out that one until it drops several bottles of soda.

We shove all of it into our bags, splitting it up evenly to keep the weight equal between the both of us, then we make our way into the ladies' bathroom and sit on the floor with our backs pressed against the door and eat.

Yeah, it's far from ideal, but we make do.

After we finish, we stand and brush ourselves down then go back to the main lobby. There's a huge map on the wall. I study it. I don't know why we let that thief talk us into heading this direction. There's so much empty space here. This is either going to be a good idea, or a really, *really* bad one. From the look on Jace's face, I suspect he feels the same.

"This is stupid," I snap. My voice echoes through the lobby. "We should have let the runners have him."

Jace's brows dip in a frown. "We both know you would never have allowed a runner to take anyone if you could help it. No matter how deserving."

He takes my hand and pulls me into his arms and holds me. Jace runs a hand down my head, stroking my hair rhythmically. The betrayal makes me angry. I hate that I didn't see it coming. I'm mad at myself for allowing it to happen. I let his presence soothe my anger until it's simmering and manageable again.

Even after all this time, we are still doing this—keeping our negative thoughts to ourselves. Sharing only hope and speaking of what we need to do to get by. Even *I love you,* has become a silent communication between us.

"I think we're close to the next town," I say after a while as I pull away. "About fifty miles, give or take."

"We can make that in two days if we keep a decent pace."

Twenty-five miles a day for two days straight. It's not impossible, it just won't be fun. And that's if we don't run into any problems.

Jace and I stand at the foot of the off ramp and look out at the beginnings of a small city. A train yard nearly full is directly to our left, and a long road straight into town is ahead, with a ramp that travels up and over the street we walk. Right about now, I'd give anything for a car. Everything in this freaking state is so spread out.

We cross under the bridge and nearly run into the tiny gas station on the other side. I'm so sick of junk food, but at this point we just take what we can get.

After we clear the immediate area and the inside, I run to the refrigerated section in back and throw open the glass door, reaching for the bottled water. I thrust one at Jace then chug an entire bottle. Splashing the last bit over my face to somewhat wash it. We shove as much water in our bags as we can, removing the leftover soda and putting it in the fridge for whoever comes here next. We don't need it with the water, but someone else might want it.

The sun begins its final descent and with it comes the chilled winds of the plains. It will be dark in another hour or two. We still need food, but I'm so tired of walking after the grueling pace over the past two days. And I'm tired down to my bones of needing things.

"There looks to be a small room in the back," Jace says, pointing to a red door.

It takes a while, but we finally pick the lock. It's a small cramped space full of janitorial items.

So much for a manager's office, I think bitterly.

We walk in and close the door behind us, settling down on the floor. At least if runners come into the store, we'll at least avoid being eaten in our sleep. Just for good measure, Jace grabs an old mop and stuffs the stinky old strings under the crack of the door to help hide our scent.

It's not the worst in terms of comfort but, at this point, that means nothing. I close my eyes, but I can't even tell if I sleep at all. Time passes differently in the dark. The cold floor is far from comfortable, my butt has long since gone numb. I turn my face toward Jace, trying to guess if he's slept at all or just sat here quietly in the dark.

His warm breath brushes across my face, then he places a kiss on my nose with eerie accuracy.

I strain to listen, but it's my left ear that's closest to the door and I don't trust it. Snaking my arm up his chest to his head, I guide him closer. He leans in, not resisting my pull. "Can you hear anything?" I ask.

He stills and I try to hold my breath, then he shakes his head no. "Are you ready to go?"

"Yes," I whisper.

He stands and takes my hand, helping me up to my feet. It's awkward and my muscles are cramped from sitting in such an uncomfortable spot for so many hours, then he slowly turns the doorknob and opens it a small crack to look out at the store. We can never be too careful. After all, any place we can enter without breaking windows or destroying locks, there's a good chance that runners could be there, or other looters.

It's blissfully void of runners.

We shoulder our bags and pause at the four short aisles for somewhat decent food. There's honestly not a whole lot left that hasn't already expired. And I don't think I want to risk botulism on top of all the other issues we have to face, so we stick to snacking on the dried goods.

I want to just walk out the door without a care in the world. I'm tired of always sneaking around, of hiding. I just want to go home—to not feel like an escaped criminal in my own world anymore. I want the comfort of my family and friends. I squeeze my eyes tight, pushing back the wave of emotions that seemed to come from nowhere.

"Raylinn?" Jace's worried voice whispers against my ear. His fingers caress my cheek and, when I open my eyes, he's frowning down at me. His amber eyes glitter with worry.

"I'm fine," I say, stepping around him, but my words are raw and even I can hear the lie in them.

Here's the thing, we've done our best to avoid areas with large populations, opting to try small towns for supply runs while sticking to remote areas in between. It's not just the fear of runners sniffing us out, but also the bodies of fallen runners, of those who never even made it as far as to change into one—I'd rather not refer to them as survivors, given their ultimate fate. The destruction is hard to stomach. La Verkin was unusual in its lack of fatalities and gore. But I suppose that was most likely in part to the family we saw there.

Jace and I head farther into town, walking on the street along the railroad tracks. There are fewer barricades here, and fewer cars, opting to avoid the main road one block up. Along the stretch of road, several cars had crashed into other cars, some into street lamps. But the sight of rotting corpses was too much. They either become sick and died instantly or had crashed due to the scene of runners attacking others, then attacked in turn.

We meander around, looking for something that might point out where the nearest grocery store might be. The junk we've been surviving on since Brian robbed us is eventually going to slow us down. Eventually we see a small building overlooking the train yard with a footbridge crossing over it.

Not that we have unlimited hours between now and when

we should find shelter for the night, but my stomach is starting to gurgle from hunger. It's too bad nothing we have with us is appetizing at this point. The only thing that even sounds halfway appealing is a home cooked meal. *Maybe someday.*

We cross the street and stop at the building near the ramp that leads to the bridge. A small patch of grass surrounds the east side of the structure. Every window is broken from the inside, and there is a far from pleasant stench emanating from it. I don't think we'll be venturing inside.

Up against a wrought iron fence that borders the edge of the property is a plaque that looks out over the train yard. I wonder if it will have some small nugget about the train yard that seems to be taking up a huge portion of this area, or maybe even the river it's named after.

We never stopped to discuss what we'd do after Brian stranded us. Finding our way to the compound he talked about was not something I even wanted to do in the first place, yet, even after he left, we stayed the course. I'm not sure if it was my doing or Jace's. Perhaps neither, and it was simply just the path we'd already been set on and after losing our map it was the only one that we'd had in our minds. I chew my bottom lip thoughtfully. I suppose it doesn't really matter either way.

Setting my pack down, I stretch my back and arms, crossing to the placard. I brush my arm over it, wiping away the layer of dirt with my sleeve so I can read the words. It takes a few moments before I can process them, but when I do, I snort.

"What is it?" Jace asks, stepping up next to me, handing me a bag of chips and a small bottle of water.

"Apparently this town was always expecting the Vor'onins." I grin up at him as I take the offered food.

Jace cocks his head as he studies my face.

"This city—" I make a sweeping gesture with my arms. "Is home to the intergalactic space port." A smile forms across his lips and a thought occurs to me. "Do you think we'll see many ships here?"

"It's worth looking into. We'll start with the local parks," he says as he opens his bottle of water and drinks deeply.

I watch him as he does, nearly forgetting my own drink. With the sun gilding his hair and highlighting his tanned skin, he looks like he belongs in a commercial.

I find myself contemplating, for perhaps the millionth time, how we could become so attached to each other within moments of meeting. That intense attraction brought us together and somehow kept us alive when we got sick. But now, I know it's not the attraction that keeps us together—though it doesn't hurt. It's long since faded into the background, becoming nothing more than a slight buzz of want hovering at the edges of consciousness, no longer a distraction.

It's the need for survival, the trust we've built since we began this aimless journey. It's the genuine love that grew between us regardless of the magnetic draw we feel for each other. It's everything.

I shrug off the thoughts and take a swig of my own water then force myself to look away.

Over his shoulder is the building with that horrid, rotting stench. It seems like a place where we could easily find a map.

"You can stay out here—watch for runners—I'll go in and grab a map." His words take me by surprise even though, at this point, they shouldn't. We are in need of a map.

When we first started out, we had discussed how to go about numerous situations. Our plan for survival has been updated every time we've run across other survivors and runners, and a million other issues. Now we are always on the same page. I suppose that was one of my main objections to heading toward a compound that and the likely loss of power over our lives—what to do and when we do things. We would have to assimilate into new rules that may not be something we are comfortable with. Then where will we be?

I hate to have him go in there alone, to be surrounded by the decay and the possible runners that could be lurking on the inside.

Before I can open my mouth to protest that I would be going inside with him, Jace presses his mouth to mine in a kiss that turns my knees to jelly. Then he snatches the golf club from my pack in a swift movement and jogs toward the entrance, only stopping once he reaches the door to look back at me.

I debate whether or not to go after him, but in the end, I stay where I'm at, I can see several blocks in the distance. I would have time to run to the building and call for him should any runners approach, with more than enough time for him to get out of there.

Still, the feeling of being alone like this is unsettling. Standing in the sun, a barely there breeze making wisps of my hair sway. It's easy to feel as though everyone has simply disappeared from the face of this planet, easy to imagine myself fading into the wind.

It's quiet. Much as it was the morning after Jace and I woke up in that abandoned building, surprised we had not died, or turned into mindless runners. No birds sing here, no squirrels scrabble around nearby trees.

I'm no longer hungry, so I shove the chips into my bag as quietly as I can, not pausing my constant scanning of the area.

It feels as though Jace is gone for a long time, and I begin to wonder if I should join him. Biting down on the inside of my cheek, I grow nervous that he might have been surprised by a runner—but he would have called out if he had.

My heart beats erratically in my chest, and I don't make it more than a few yards from the door before he emerges from the shadows within.

I run to him, throwing my arms around his neck.

"Were you worried?" he asks with a smile in his voice as he kisses the top of my head.

I pull back and make a face at the scent of decomposition that clings to his hair, clothes, and skin. "You stink," I say.

A devilish grin crosses his face, and he wraps his arms around my waist, holding me tightly against him, and proceeds to rub his cheek on mine.

"Bleh, let me go!" I say between fits of giggles.

After a minute, he finally relents and loosens his arms. "There, now *you* stink as well."

I narrow my eyes at him but the smile on my own face lessens the effect. "Now, I need a bath."

He ticks his chin in the direction of the river. "I'm sure we can spare a little time for a dip in the river. What do you think?"

I pretend to consider, because of course my answer is yes. "I suppose that wouldn't be *terrible*. But first we take a look at that map and try to find a few places that ships are likely to have converged."

"Deal."

Chapter Eight

I Don't Think We're Alone Now

Jace and I stay off the roads, opting to cross through properties in order to avoid them. For a town so small, there were a lot of parks in one area. And all but one was home to a small fleet of Vor'onin ships. We end up at a small island park the river forks around. The ships here are mostly untouched. We take our time scouting out the ones that look the least disturbed and mark them to check out once night starts to fall.

Once our plan is in place, I look at Jace as be kneels down to stash our packs in a bush as he continues talking over the plan. I narrow my eyes, barely holding back a smile. "Race you to the river!"

I spin and take off running toward the rock and sand bank of the river, pulling my top off as I go. He reaches me as I kick off my second boot at the same time I'm pulling off my pants, until

I'm only in my bra and underwear. I turn to laugh before running into the river, but all that escapes my mouth is an, "Oomph!" as he grabs me around my waist and hauls me over his shoulder and wades into the water.

"Cheater," he mumbles.

"Put me down!" I say, flailing and laughing as his fingers graze over the ticklish spot on my sides. "Ja—" But I'm cut off as he throws me into the water.

I resurface sputtering and shoving my hair out of my face. Jace grabs his stomach as he laughs too hard to see. I take my chance and use both arms to send a wave of water up at him that takes him by surprise. I launch myself forward, wrapping my arms around his neck and knock him back in the water. I submerge with him and we both come up for air at the same time, coughing and sputtering and laughing.

Jace smirks. His dark hair is plastered to his head, but in a way that is still ridiculously attractive. Especially when he's looking at me like that. He holds his hands above the water in surrender as I stalk closer, stopping a few inches in front of him.

"I deserved that," he says. Then he moves too fast for me to react. He pulls me to him with one arm, his other hand cups my cheek as he kisses me deeply.

After a few minutes, a cool breeze kicks up, sending goose bumps racing painfully over my exposed skin. Jace pulls away. "Cold?"

"Mm-hmm," I say, clenching my teeth to keep them from

chattering.

We walk out of the river and put on clean clothes. It's no hot shower with soap and shampoo but, compared to earlier, I feel refreshed and clean. As we dress, I stop with my shirt halfway down as a groan carried on the wind reaches us. *Runners.*

I quickly finish dressing and look to Jace. He grabs our packs and hurries back to me to lead me to a covered area.

The swim in the river had been refreshing. Ignoring the temperature dropping, I was tempted to stay there all day, and I think so was Jace. It is tempting to try to live our lives as though every day wasn't a fight for survival. As though there was no reason to stay quiet or to hide. It's exhausting to live this way, to always be on guard.

We sit behind one of the large trees that border the river's edge and crouch down, eating a small meal of dried cereal bars. Jace and I take turns peaking around the trunk to see if any runners are coming our way. We ready our packs and put them on and wait for night to fall. A few more groans float our way, then a movement from the corner of my eye has me whirling to face the opposite shore.

Several runners have converged, having spotted us. We have a river between us, but it still doesn't give me much comfort. The ones in the back of the horde push forward until the ones in the front are forced into the water, and the current washes them away. This continues until the last few stare us down, groaning pitifully.

I shiver but not from the cold.

Eventually, the runners quiet and stare at us, watching.

I'm both relieved and freaked once darkness falls. Jace leads me away from the shore and places a bush between us and the runners, hiding us from their view.

Jace places his mouth against my ear. "We need to get to a ship."

I nod and follow him between the trees. The scent of the river still clings to our skin as we stand under the cover of low hanging branches and look out at the ship in the middle of the field. The others surrounding it have their entrances open, but this one is closed. I'm just glad it's one of the closest ones to where we are.

We learned a long time ago that the open ones are usually already scavenged and picked clean. Though sometimes they provide decent shelter for the night when there's no other choice. The risk is too high for other scavengers, ones who wouldn't have a problem slitting our throats in our sleep to take what little supplies we have, and for runners to accidentally stumble into.

A shiver runs down my spine at the memory of the first time we slept in one of the ships. A runner somehow had the wherewithal to stumble up the steps and inside... and *we* had been stupid enough to camp in the docking area. We'd thought we would be safe, that it would be smart to be near the exit in case we needed to make a hasty escape, or to see if anything was happening outside.

Whoo boy, were we wrong. That was also when we realized we needed to start sleeping in shifts. Half the sleep and double the stress.

The closed off ships are a blessing and a curse. They mean a chance for supplies but also a chance for calling attention to ourselves if there are any Vor'onin runners in the area.

We stay hidden for an hour at least, just listening and scanning the area for others and waiting for it to be dark enough to hide us when we are exposed. We want to be sure we are alone before Jace opens it.

It's late now, and I stifle a yawn, rubbing my arms slowly to ward off the goose bumps that still haven't gone away. I have to make a conscious effort not to swat at the bugs biting at me, but if this ship is loaded like we hope, then it wont matter.

I look up at Jace, his eyes are narrowed on the ship, darting to the sides. He seems to sense my stare on him and meets my gaze, giving me a small yet strained smile.

I raise my brows in question. *Is it safe?*

He nods once then steps out in the open, motioning for me to stay hidden.

He advances slowly and stops halfway there and waits a few beats, turning in a circle and scanning the area one last time before motioning me over.

I adjust the straps of my bag over my shoulders then jog through the grass toward him. Even though he's standing there waiting for me, I don't stop looking around, trusting he has my back as I watch his. We both need to keep a lookout at all times. I reach him and Jace slips his hand into mine, and together we slink toward the ship, trying to stick to the shadows of the surrounding ones.

I want to breathe a sigh of relief once we reach it, though I restrain myself. I will wait until we are safe inside, with the hatch closed. We are almost there. I have to keep telling myself that.

Jace lifts his hand toward the ship, but I keep my eyes peeled for anything that moves in the dark. I wish I was able to see as well as Jace can at night. From my side, I see the light emanating from his hand. The field around us lights up with the glow, it's dim, about as bright as a regular flashlight, but its enough to call attention to ourselves should anyone be near.

My fingers tighten on my straps, and I hear the soft whirr of the ship hum to life. Then the metal of the front of the ship moves and reforms into steps making both a metallic and a soft sloshing sound at once.

"We're in, let's go," Jace says as the light in his hand dims and fades. If I hadn't seen it with my own eyes, I would never be able to tell that there was a small implant in his palm.

I turn and follow him up the wobbling steps. I've always hated these. They were meant for someone with perfect balance, not someone who could fall over standing on solid ground. The thought triggers an automatic reflex and my hand goes up to my left ear. I cup it slightly, then wiggle a finger on the outside as if trying to dislodge water.

Ever since we got sick and I thought we were going to die, my hearing from that ear has been lessened to half of what it should be. It would be a mild inconvenience if it wasn't for the fact that runners have infected the world. Though I've learned to keep a sharper eye out because of it, noticing things I might have missed before.

The one thing I haven't adjusted to yet is the ever so slight change in my balance. I know I'll adjust... eventually. It's not as if running from what are essentially zombies is the ideal adaptation situation.

Zombies. I refuse to call the runners that, not seriously at least. This isn't a movie and it's not a game. This is real, and it's dangerous. I won't give what they are that added bit of power from some fictional, supernatural fear.

We board the ship and the dim lights flicker to life on the backup generator setting, which gives my eyes time to adjust just enough. I take stock of the bridge as Jace works to close the door.

My eyes water as I take it all in. This place looks practically immaculate. No sign of runners, and no sign of previous looters.

Jace takes my hand and says, "Come, let's look around. I want to check the med bay."

I nod. "Can we check the galley next?" My heart speeds up in excitement. Food... *real food*. "Then the showers? I would die for a nice hot shower with soap and shampoo right about now."

He smiles, then wrinkles his nose slightly as he leans forward and sniffs. "I think I might die for you to have a hot shower right about now," he says, using my own words against me.

I know he's kidding, since we no longer smell like death but river water. And though it's an improvement, it's nothing compared to the scent of soap. My jaw drops and I playfully swat at his arm, he steps to the side out of reach and laughs. His sense of humor has really come through this past year.

"You're no spring flower yourself," I say, sticking out my tongue. I think I like this town, despite the few dead and the horde of runners we've come across. Perhaps there's something to this place after all, even if I still hate how spread out everything is.

It feels good to be playful and joke around. Neither of us have been this relaxed in so long. Life has been nothing but a series of events that threaten to steal what little sanity I have left, and heart break I can only push to the side until I dream when I can manage to sleep.

"I'll wash your back if you wash mine," Jace says with a devilish grin.

My jaw drops, then a warm heat floods my veins. I miss moments of peace with him. They are so few and far between. We are always together, yet I miss him and crave him all the time. I meet his grin with a devious one of my own and say, "We should get going then."

I drag him through the hall toward the med bay at a hurried clip.

All the ships are exactly the same. The layout is identical, which I find to be helpful. We walk quietly toward the back.

I swallow hard and remind myself this is a different ship. Doctor Lar'ruk is not here. Even if he were, there's no way I'd let him use me again. My blood still boils at how he treated me as a lab rat for testing.

We enter the med bay and the low lights flicker to life.

Jace presses his hand to the pad on the wall, but after a long moment, nothing happens. He frowns and shrugs, then says, "The ship seems to be running on the power saving mode."

We move forward in the dim lighting and search cabinets and rummage through them. I still can't read the Vor'onin glyphs, but I've memorized a few that Jace taught me to look out for. Things that symbolize the supplies we need.

I start on the lower cabinets under the counters, in search of notes that pertain to a cure or anything that might help protect us against the runners, maybe even cure them, or anyone who might be falling ill.

I find a small knife at the bottom of one cabinet. It's made out of some strange metal I have never seen before, I suspect it's a Vor'onin metal from their planet. It seems to almost glow blue where the light hits it, but by tilting it, the color changes to red, purple, and even green. I strap it to my leg, making sure the black curved handle is exactly where I need it to be, then I return to sifting through the contents before me.

We need a cure and, even though I know we are looking for

supplies to help us survive for another few days, I can't help but hope that we'll stumble upon something that will be world altering. It would help if I had some medical knowledge. Jace has a great deal more than I do, having apprenticed under Lar'ruk before we met, but even he needs something to work with.

One of these days I'll have to make a point to drag Jace into a library and research diseases, just to have a better idea of what we should be looking for. Or find a doctor… or both.

There's not much we can use. I am a little relieved to see a lack of files. It means experiments weren't done on this ship. But that also means that there probably won't be a vaccine we could use.

A deep sigh to my right makes me pause. I look to Jace and he has both hands resting on the counter, his head drooping. I stand and walk quietly to his side, placing a hand on his shoulder.

He faces me, his mouth drawn in a tight line. He shakes his head and opens his mouth to speak, but before he can, we hear a clank echo through the ship.

Crap, we are not alone. Though I can't tell if Jace opening the ship alerted a runner, possibly several, in the area, or if there are looters or runners currently *in* the ship.

We hurry and shove what little we've found into our packs then move toward the door, sticking close to the wall. Jace motions for me to stay behind him. Then we move out into the passage, careful to keep our footsteps silent.

A shiver runs along my spine. I hate this part. I hate searching for an unknown. Because I never know how to prepare, survivors and runners require very different strategies. We make it to where the hall splits—the way we came, to the exit on our left, and the remainder of the ship straight ahead.

We wait for another sound, but there isn't one. Several minutes pass and we need to make a decision. Jace looks conflicted. Then he motions for me to stay here in the shadows. I shake my head no. There's no way I'm letting him go alone to possibly get attacked.

I can't decide if it's heart warming or infuriating or both that he's always so willing to put himself in harm's way to protect me but never wants me to do the same. I finger the knife strapped to my thigh. *It's a bit of both.* I am still not putting up with it.

We have a silent battle of wills as I step out toward the hall leading to the barracks. I make a motion with my hands indicating that we should split up, each taking a different route. He gives me a pleading look, but I will not have this overprotective crap, especially when it puts his life at risk.

Jace looks over his shoulder once more, trying to look into the dark. When I don't say anything, he motions again for me to stay, but this time it's more of a request. I hate this. I hate splitting up. But in the end, I nod, because I know he won't be able to really search the hall and beyond if he's worried about me.

He's relieved—I can tell in the quick but passionate kiss he presses against my lips. His fingers trail down my arm and he squeezes my hand once before turning and sprinting past the crossway.

He heads straight. Great. The lighting is even worse in that section and it doesn't take long for me to lose sight of him. I suppose it makes sense that whatever we are looking for is more likely to be this way.

I silently pull my knife from the sheath and grip the handle as I strain to listen.

Long seconds pass, until it feels like hours. The light flickers down the hall and I see Jace's outline, he's nearing the first turn, moving slowly and staying tight against the wall. Then a shadow moves. At least, I think it does. It's hard to tell with the lights flickering on and off.

I hear a rustle, a brief flash of light, something small, then a soft groan.

Crap, crap, crap! I don't know if that was Jace reacting in self-defense or if that was someone or something else attacking Jace, I can't just stand here hiding. I have to go help him.

I open my mouth to speak then think better of it. I need to stay hidden if I can. Flattening my back against the wall, I slowly peek around the corner, but the bridge has gone dark again from lack of movement. I hurry across the intersection of hallways, hating the open space.

I'm almost back to being under the cover of shadows when the light flickers to life once more. A dark shape hovers in my peripheral, and as I start to turn toward it, I open my mouth to yell out to Jace.

My jaw snaps shut and a blinding pain courses through my body. A flash of light, and I hear the clink of my knife hitting the metal flooring before I can process that I'd dropped it. Every muscle in my body seizes. I have no control over my muscles, though my mind remains aware of the pain that leaves a metallic tang coating my mouth.

Then the world tilts as I crumple to a heap, my head smacking against the metal flooring and stars burst before my eyes. The dark shadow steps up to me until it stands over me, crouching down. Light flickers in their hand.

But before I can make out their features, black encroaches in on my vision, swallowing it up.

Chapter Nine

Friend or Foe

I wriggle and stop immediately. Everything hurts. Every single muscle in my body feels like I ran a marathon, only I have no recollection of it. My eyelids are heavy, and I just want to go back to sleep, but I'm cold and uncomfortable and that has made my muscles even more sore. I reach to my side to pull my blanket to me, but the slightest movement hurts far too much.

The dull pounding in my head kicks up and I wince. I try to grasp my head to still the constant beat and my eyes snap open when I can't move my arm. I look around, struggling to focus on what the actual hell happened. My arms and legs are bound and I'm on the cold metal floor with a gag in my mouth. I push my tongue against it, trying to dislodge it but it's too tight. It's actually cutting into the corners of my mouth.

Shit. How am I so out of it I hadn't noticed that right away?

It's dark and I can hear voices. Voices that don't belong to Jace or Brian.

Then it comes rushing back to me as my vision slowly comes into focus. I'm on the ship—Brian is long gone and I'm here with Jace… we were walking down the hall when—

I freeze when I hear footsteps approach. I crane my neck to look but there's a crate in the way. I've been shoved into a dark corner, with boxes stacked up on one side and behind me, the wall of the ship on my other side. All I can see are crates that weren't there earlier when we boarded. If Jace is anywhere around, I can't tell because whoever did this made sure I can only see the hatch of the ships door that leads outside.

My heart threatens to beat out of my chest. What have they done to Jace? For all I know, they blame the Vor'onins for the virus and Jace is lying on the other side of the crates, dead. My thoughts spin further out of control until my breath comes too shallow and black spots dance before my eyes.

A dark figure stops at my feet, with hands on their hips.

"Well, well, well. Look who's finally awake," the girl says in a gravelly voice.

I curl into myself a bit at her tone, there's something vaguely threatening in the way she speaks. She looks behind her and with a jerk of her head, she calls out, "Hey, Des, she's awake."

The low talking in the distance ceases, then there's a whirr then the light on the bridge brightens enough to see a girl standing over me better.

I try to reach for the knife I'd strapped to my thigh, but the smug look on her face stops me. With one hand, she reaches behind her back and pulls out a knife, twirling it around. *My knife.* "Looking for this?"

I scowl. She can't be much older than me, if at all, but the sneer on her face gives off the impression that the last two years have been very unkind to her. Thick black hair is held back by a bandana wrapped around her forehead. Her arms are crossed over her surprisingly clean overalls. If I'm not mistaken, she's even wearing... *eyeliner*?

"Bring her over here, Garcia."

She huffs in annoyance, rolling her eyes. "Yeah right, Scotty, I'm not lifting her all by myself. She looks heavy."

Ignoring her jab, I strain to listen past their words to hear any sign of Jace being alive... but damn it my good ear is against the side of the ship and everything has a muffled edge to it.

"So, have her walk," another male voice says.

"What?" She drops her arms and turns away, storming back toward her group. "Nu uh, no way. You remember what happened the last time we *'let someone walk.'"*

Two of the guys laugh.

"What are you laughing at, Desmond? It was you who got a swift kick in the junk," she retorts hotly.

One of the guys stops laughing and mutters under his breath.

I pull my knees to my chest. *What is happening? Where did they put Jace?* I want to call out and demand they cut us both loose, to demand they return Jace to me… alive. I try again to push the gag out of my mouth but no luck. *Why couldn't I have been blessed with a loose gag like they have in movies?*

The girl, Garcia, appears in my vision again. One of the guys, a ginger, walks into view and bends forward, grabbing me roughly by my shirt and jerking me up until I'm sitting. He gives me a look that says *yikes* as I growl at him from the pain it causes. The freckles splattered across his face, the unkempt hair, wide blue eyes, and his overall features make him look younger than he probably is. It's hard to take him seriously, even in this situation.

In this cramped space and being tied up as I am, this position is more than a little uncomfortable.

She dismisses him with a head tilt then takes his place crouching in front of me. He stays a few steps behind her, leaning against the wall with his arms crossed. He looks like he could be chatting with an old friend for all the casual demeanor he holds in his posture and expression.

The others continue to stay out of view. No doubt to keep me from guessing how many they are and unable to size them up.

"If you scream, yell, call out, et cetera—my friend in the other room will gut your friend like a fish." Her gaze narrows. "Do you understand?"

I can feel my eyes widen at the threat, but I'm also elated that they haven't killed Jace. They couldn't possibly mean to kill either of us or they would have already. It was one thing for

survivors to be hostile and defend what they claimed as theirs…
But this was something we'd never encountered before.

"I said, *do you understand?*" she repeats herself through
clenched teeth.

Hastily, I nod.

"Good." She plays with the knife, pressing the tip of one
finger against the sharp point hard enough to draw a tiny bead of
blood. "I'm going to take the gag from your mouth now."

It takes everything in me not to move as she inches forward,
the light glinting off the knife. When she's in reach, she brings
the blade to my face, dragging the flat side against the skin of
my cheek. I close my eyes thinking she might slice my face open
while she's at it.

The cold metal skims along my skin as it slips beneath the
gag.

With a sharp tug of her wrist, I feel the cloth loosen then fall
away. And when I open my eyes, I can see her all but laugh at
my reaction.

My gaze flicks to the guy at her back and a little bit of his
demeanor has slipped away to something a touch more worried,
even if it seems like he's trying to hide that. I don't *think* he was
expecting his cohort to threaten me quite like this.

"What are you doing here?" Garcia demands.

I glare at her. It's obvious what Jace and I were doing here.
Any idiot could see that. The best I can guess is that she's trying
to gauge how I lie versus how willing I am to tell the truth.

I opt for the truth. It's easiest, and we weren't doing anything that the rest of civilization hasn't already been doing. I refuse to apologize for trying to survive. "Trying to gather supplies."

She eyes me a long moment then looks over her shoulder before turning back to me. "You don't seem to be well prepared at all. Where's your base located?"

My brows scrunch together. "We don't have one."

"Bull," she snaps. "No one comes out here with so much garbage and so little to sustain them. Tell me the truth or your mate is going to pay."

"Garcia…" the ginger protests quietly, but clamps his mouth shut as she cuts him a glare.

Blood drains from my face and my skin goes cold and clammy. She knows what Jace is to me—either having experienced the same kind of bond herself, or just as likely putting it together because we're a single human and a single Vor'onin traveling together.

"Answer me."

"We don't have a base," I bite out.

Her eyes narrow. After a beat, she pushes herself up to standing and I panic that she's going after Jace.

"I'm not lying!" I snap before she leaves my view. I have to keep her in my sight to protect him. "We had another survivor with us—but he stole all our supplies."

Garcia contemplates me for a while before saying, "Stay quiet."

She doesn't need to add *'or else'* for me to know the threat is there. Then she motions for the ginger boy to follow her. The sound of their footsteps don't go far, then the murmur of voices—three I think—it's hard to tell and I curse my inability to make out anything they are saying.

I lean to the side and rest against the wall, trying to get a little more comfortable. It doesn't help. Finally, several minutes later, Garcia returns and looks down at me with her arms crossed.

"So, let's say you're telling the truth. What brings you out here?"

"What makes you think we aren't from here?" I demand.

Garcia scoffs and rolls her eyes. "Whatever you think, we aren't stupid."

There's something in her expression that makes me snap. I'm done with this. I'm not a criminal and I refuse to be treated like this any longer. "Let me go, and let me see Jace, or I'm not going to answer another one of your damned questions."

Though I'm pretty sure she's about to say no, someone clears their throat from the other side of the crates. She looks sideways at them then drops her arms to her sides.

"Fine," she huffs. "Scotty, go get him."

Garcia stomps off, leaving me in my little corner. Though I don't have to wait long before the owner of the third voice comes to get me. His black curly hair is cut short and his warm brown eyes hold no hint of hostility, as Garcia's had. He's taller than the other two and his muscles are more defined. He gives me an apologetic smile before lifting me up by my arm.

My muscles ache, but it's a welcome ache. He lets go as soon as I catch my balance, but his eyes follow Garcia as she makes a hasty retreat down one poorly lit passage way.

When she's fully out of sight, he takes my wrists and undoes the bindings. "Don't mind Garcia, we've been burned in the past by trusting other survivors too quickly."

I rub my newly freed wrists. "Yeah, I know the feeling," I mutter.

"I'm Toby Desmond, but you can call me Des—everyone else does." He offers his hand to me.

The feeling of 'good cop, bad cop' is strong with these people, but I take his offered hand anyway. I'd rather be grilled by *'good cop.'*

"Raylinn," I say, not trusting them enough to give my full name. Not that it matters—the internet is gone and technology is pretty basic. It's not like he can look me up.

"So… what *are* you two doing out here? Most survivors stay away. There's not a whole lot of looting for this state and it's pretty spread out."

I glare at him. "Like I told your friend, I'm not answering any more of your questions until I can see Jace, *alive*." I emphasize the last word.

He reaches up and rubs the back of his neck, giving me a slight laugh. "Yeah, sorry. I was just making conversation, but I don't blame you. You can't be too careful."

I'm a little taken aback that he doesn't push me to answer. Maybe I read him wrong.

I look up as the ginger rounds the far end of the passageway with Jace at his side. I take one step then stop, looking to the guy who is essentially guarding me. He gives me a slight nod, and I take off, running toward Jace and throwing my arms around his neck. He scoops me up in a hug and holds me tight.

"Are you okay?" he whispers in my good ear.

I nod and take a step back, examining him. "Are you?"

He smiles at that and says, "I am now."

A movement behind him catches my attention. A Vor'onin stops several paces behind Jace, his face emotionless. He still wears the traditional Vor'onin garb with the high collar and clean lines. I am beyond relieved. If they are working with a Vor'onin then they don't blame them for the virus. I'm beginning to wonder if anyone besides Jace and me *do* know the origin, or if it's just widely assumed that the government was to blame.

I would hate for every Vor'onin to be blamed for the actions of a few corrupt men.

"This is Scotty," Desmond says, gesturing to the ginger, then points to the Vor'on. "And that's Mon'te."

Neither Jace nor I say anything.

"Are you hungry?" Desmond offers. "We can get you something to eat, but we do have a few questions we'd like to ask you two."

I cut a glance to Jace to try and gauge how he feels about

these survivors we've run into—if he thinks we can trust them or if we should be wary. Though, other than Garcia, none of them have been threatening or overly hostile. Jace blinks slowly at me, one of our signs to each other. I squeeze his hand in agreement.

Neither of us had eaten much today. We had planned on making a decent meal out of whatever we could find here, or at least once we were sealed inside this ship.

"Okay," I say.

Desmond leads us toward the galley with Scotty and Mon'te following at our backs.

Less than an hour later, Jace and I are sitting side by side at one of the white, smooth edged tables, shoveling a warm meal of bread and pasta with sauce into our mouths. It's the best meal I've had in longer than I can remember. Though the bar for that couldn't actually get any lower. That doesn't change the fact that right now, it is the best thing in the world.

The three survivors don't question us while we eat, which I appreciate since I don't think I could talk with the amount of food in my mouth and I'm not capable of slowing down. I could choke to death on this spaghetti and I would go to my grave a happy woman. Instead, they make small talk among themselves.

Scotty takes our plates away when we finish, leaving Desmond and Mon'te sitting across from us. It takes me a moment but then I see it. The way they sit close, their body language toward each other, they are the same as us. They feel the same bond that Jace and I do. Something about that puts me at ease.

"How long were we out?" I ask. Not even sure Jace was out at all, but that's not the point.

"The rest of the night and most of the day." He checks his watch. "It's about five in the evening now."

My eyes bulge. No wonder I'm so hungry.

"Most people left this area within the first few days of the virus. What brings you two out here?" Desmond asks.

"Just trying to survive. Same as everyone else," I say.

He smiles, knowing my answer is technically true, but still a pure crap, non answer. Of course, we're trying to survive, everyone is—but that's not what he's asking.

"Okay. I'll give you something first." He folds his arms and rests them on the table, leaning forward. "We are out here scouting for supplies and survivors to take back to our base."

I hold my breath. There's something to his words that makes me think there's more to his meaning than what he says.

It's tempting to ask about their base, but I want to feel them out a little first. "We were in Utah when we ran across another survivor... we looted a store then about halfway here, he took our supplies, leaving us stranded while it was his turn to be on watch."

"We were betrayed by one we picked up several months back," Mon'te speaks for the first time, but he keeps his voice low. He looks over his shoulder before saying, "We lost one of our own to the virus. *We* had to put him down."

I'm curious about the details now. It makes me wonder if this incident is the same one Garcia had referred to earlier where Des here got a swift kick to his man bits, but I recognize the need to share information equally in order to get the details I want.

I'm not sure how much to say but I'm not sure if it can be worse than being left high and dry again. I know Jace and I will be able to survive.

"We heard about a place east of here." I lean forward. "Do you know of it?"

I know the answer by the narrowing of Desmond's eyes and the twitch of his lips before he speaks. "Perhaps... Tell me more about this *place* and how you came to know about it."

Well... here goes nothing. I straighten my shoulders and lean a little closer. "We heard there was a sanctuary called the *Tower*, from the guy who left us stranded. Do you know of it?"

He leans back, his face an unreadable mask. Mon'te shares a look with him but, rather than answering, they both stand in unison.

"Come with us, I think this is a conversation that requires the rest of the team."

Jace squeezes my hand gently. Then we stand and follow them as they walk out of the galley doors without saying another word, heading back toward the front of the ship.

Chapter Ten

A Threat With a Smile

Jace and I stand in the middle of the hallway, our backs toward the interior of the ship, as the four of them create a crescent before us, essentially blocking all exits.

Garcia leans against a nearby wall, closed off, with her arms crossed and keeping her gaze locked on her feet.

"These two are looking for the Tower," Desmond announces.

The others are quiet for a while.

"You're a fair distance from it," Scotty says. The abrupt end to his words makes it seem like he has more to add, but after a few seconds I realize that's all he's going to say. Something about that makes me bristle.

"We figured as much from what our map said," I say flatly. While I don't mind giving information out little by little, I'd rather not delay more than we have to. If they are going to sit around and talk about how "interesting" our destination is and have nothing of value to offer, then I want to leave here and get back on the road. "So, if you don't mind, we'd like our things back now so we can be on our way. " I glare at Garcia. "*All* of them."

Desmond lifts his hands up in a calming gesture. "Hold on a minute, we may be able to help you."

"Oh, hell no!" Garcia snaps. "I'm not going to deal with this crap—*not again*." She cuts her hand through the air. "Let's just dump them and their crap outside and let them find their own way."

"Excuse us for one moment," Desmond says, walking up to her and pulling her by the arm down the hall, with Scotty following after them.

I can't help but notice Mon'te stays with us. Either to watch that we don't do anything they don't want us to, or because he doesn't want to be part of that conversation and knows his human counterpart will be able to speak for him. Honestly, if it's the latter, I don't blame him one bit. Life is hard enough without that kind of attitude.

This new world will breed hardness where there was none. It has in me, in Jace, and everyone else we've met. The moments between the hardness are few and far between. But you have to know when to use it and when it will only cause problems.

Jace and Mon'te stand still in a military-like fashion, as though hanging out in a passageway is an everyday thing for them. I couldn't feel more awkward having to listen to the murmur of voices that is—judging from the tone alone—clearly an argument.

I try to avoid staring at their backs, but as I look around, there's not much to look at. Everything from the walls, the lights, and the floor is all functional and void of any decor or design. I focus on my nails as if they are the most fascinating things in the world. *Oh, nails, those things are new.*

It's about the time that I begin to feel a little antsy that the three of them return. I can't help but breathe a sigh of relief that I don't have to pretend I didn't notice their little disagreement anymore.

Desmond stands before us with Scotty at his side, Garcia glaring daggers from several paces behind makes it clear that she did not get her way when it comes to their offered help. Though I'm not entirely sure any help they could give would be worth the headache of her unwillingness.

"We'll take you with us," Desmond says with a smile the apocalypse hasn't been able to dim.

"Excuse me?" I frown, not understanding where he wants to take us.

"Right, I got a little ahead of myself." He laughs, rubbing the back of his neck. Mon'te gives him an affectionate look. "We were sent out as scouts from the Tower to find supplies as well as other survivors. We were nearing the end of our assignment and about to head back anyway, so we will take you with us."

"You're serious?" I ask, raising an eyebrow. "You're from the Tower? What are the chances of that?" I scoff.

He nods. "Pretty good I'd say. There aren't many people wandering this state who aren't from the Tower." He takes a step back and hops up to sit on the crates that I was once stuffed between when I woke up. "It will be nice to have two more sets of eyes on patrol, we'll be able to get a few more hours of shut eye at night," Scotty says, earning a groan of disgust from Garcia.

I can't seem to form a proper response to that so I stare on, slack jawed. *Is this really happening?*

"Thank you," Jace says, stepping forward.

I'm not usually one to look a gift horse in the mouth, but this all seems a little too easy. Too neat and tidy.

Then there's the fact that the last survivor we ran across took everything we had and left us for dead in the middle of nowhere.

"You don't even know if you can trust us," I blurt. I'm thankful that Jace understands me and doesn't look at me like I've lost my mind. Though, he wouldn't be wrong if he did think that.

Mon'te laughs gently and Desmond gives me a smile that's more humoring me than amused.

"We checked your bags when you two were unconscious," Mon'te says. "You are not a threat. But if you were, we are better armed and could kill you both before you had a chance to try anything." All of that said with a smile. Mon'te's eyes darken as he speaks the last few words soft and low. "We have learned what precautions we must take."

"Okay," I say slowly. "But how do we know we can trust you?"

"How about because we didn't slit your throats after we captured you?" Garcia mutters to herself, but she makes sure it's loud enough for me to hear.

"Do you mind if we talk it over for a minute?" Jace asks.

"Take your time," Desmond says.

Jace and I walk to the far part of the hall, keeping them in sight.

"Jace… we just trusted Brian, and he screwed us."

"I know, but these people are not like him."

"Yeah… but *how* do we know that?"

Jace presses his lips tightly together. "We don't. We have to trust that they aren't. We both stay vigilant and watch out for any signs. If they so much as do anything to make us question their motives, we'll take off and go in any direction you want."

I think about the offer for a moment. It's not ideal but it's all we can do. "Okay. Let's do this then."

Once we rejoin them, Jace says, "We will go with you."

"Great!" Desmond jumps down from the crates and claps his hands loudly before rubbing them together. "We'll show you to your quarters for tonight and we'll leave first thing in the morning. But first, we'll fill you in on all the important aspects of how we work."

Within a few minutes of listening intently to Desmond explain what to expect, I feel a little more comfortable that they are the real thing. After we are filled in, Mon'te shows us to where they expect us to stay for the night, stopping before a solid door with no doorknob or keypad.

Jace places his hand on the slat and a soft glow emanates from it for a second before it slides open.

"Scotty will be by to return your packs to you shortly," Mon'te says. He dips his chin, a gesture Jace returns without hesitation, then he's off down the hall, stopping a few doors away to enter into the room I can only guess is the one where he's staying.

There's only one bed in our room, but thankfully it's wide enough for both of us. A thin door leads to a small compartment room with a standing shower and a toilet on the left, the sink and a mirror are on the wall next to it on the outside. To the right is a small doorway that starts about one and a half feet off the ground, which turns out to be a closet. Other than that, there isn't a whole lot to these slightly cramped quarters. I don't care, there is safety here and I have Jace. I don't need anything more.

I debate throwing myself on the bed and just passing out for a solid eight hours or whatever I can get. But then there's the promise of a hot shower waiting for me, and after the week we've had, *hell, after the year we've had,* I need it.

"Do you mind if I go first?" I ask, gesturing to the bathroom.

"Go ahead." He walks over and places his hand on the glass

shower door. Immediately, the water inside starts. The glass turns from a crystal clear to an opaque frost.

I enter and the door to the room slides closed behind me. Steam billows out from the opening into the shower. Shedding my clothes, I'm completely naked in seconds and stepping under the fall of water. The warmth of the water elicits a groan of happiness from me.

Heaven... this is heaven. I've forgotten how good a real shower feels. I stand, not moving for several minutes as the heat soaks into my muscles. Pulling in a shaky breath, a shudder works its way down my spine as tension leaves my body inch by inch.

I hiccup as a sob wrenches from deep within my chest. Too late I realize the tension has been the thing keeping my emotions at bay as they crash into me like a tidal wave of bricks, and sobs rack my body. I lean back against the cold tile and slide down, wrapping my arms around my knees as the water continues to rain down.

I don't know how long I sit there letting the tears flow down my cheeks, hot and burning, even through the barrage of hot water. The loss of my family, of my friends, of the future I would never have, and the world I'd only begun to know, threatened to crack my heart in two.

It isn't fair. I've always known life wasn't fair... but this is different in so many ways. This wasn't something like losing the top spot on varsity to someone else, this wasn't as simple as being passed over for a promotion... my entire world—everyone's world—had been ripped away by a force completely out of our hands. And we are still powerless to stop it.

I stop fighting the pain and cry until I'm hollow on the inside. When most of my remaining energy is sapped and I have no more tears to cry, I manage to pull myself up and wash myself with the various soaps available. My body moves on autopilot with motions it learned long ago.

I step out onto the floor that seems to absorb the water as it runs off me. Reaching for a towel, I run it over my hair, getting out as much water as possible, then drying the rest of my body off before wrapping it around me. I glance up and catch my reflection in a small mirror I hadn't noticed until now. My eyes are puffy with dark bags under them, even my nose is a little red from all the crying. My first hot shower in a long time and I manage to look like crap afterward.

Turning away, I kick my filthy clothes off to the side, content to just sleep in the towel for the night if need be. I don't feel like putting on the dirt and sweat covered clothes again. I hope we get a chance to wash them before we go.

Returning to the main room, Jace is crouched down in front of our bags, digging through them. He pulls out a clean tee from his bag and hands it to me. It's the closest thing we have for sleepwear, as we tend to just sleep in our clothes in case we need to make a fast get away. It's gross, even washing them as often as possible, but I try not to think about it too much.

"Is there a laundromat on this ship?" I ask, pointing toward the bathroom.

"It's in there. I'll throw your clothes in with mine." Jace stands and places a kiss on my forehead. If he notices my puffy eyes, he doesn't say anything.

I toss the towel on the floor near the foot of the bed. It's sloppy, but it seems my manners over the past two years have gone the way of civilization—to hell. That thought angers me a bit as I slip the large shirt over my head. I walk over to my towel and pick it up then hang it on one of the two wall hooks next to the bathroom.

"There," I mutter. That one gesture is almost enough to make me think that perhaps one day humanity will overcome this disaster and rise again, becoming better than it ever was before. Not quite... but almost.

With that, I climb into bed, my eyes are already heavy with sleep and exhaustion from crying.

I'm halfway to oblivion when Jace emerges from the bathroom, drying his hair with a towel and wearing a pair of shorts that don't quite fit the personality of the man I've come to know. I smile sleepily at him as he hangs his towel over mine and presses a hand against a spot on the wall. The lights dim to about fifty percent.

He crosses the room then crawls into bed next to me. I scoot over to make room for him.

"Our clothes will be ready in the morning," he whispers as

he wraps his arms around me, pulling me to his chest.

I don't think I realized how much I needed a moment like this until just now. Pure affection without worry or fear. We had something close in the river, but it wasn't like this.

I look into Jace's eyes. I run my fingers over his forehead, the bridge of his nose, his cheek and jaw, then finally through his hair. That same undeniable pull is there. He's the only one I have left, and I owe him everything, even if he didn't already own my heart, and I his.

"Good," I say. I tilt my face up to his and place a kiss on his mouth.

This quiet man, who stole my heart, would risk his life to save mine—and though he hates it, I would risk mine to save his too.

I'm tired, exhausted beyond what I thought possible. But I need a moment where life isn't just about survival but about the parts worth living for. I want to enjoy focusing on every detail of his face, the weight of his hand on my hip as he gently glides his hand down my thigh to hitch my leg over his hip.

I want to forget that everything outside this room even exists.

The dim lights continue to darken until they almost fade entirely, with only the soft glow of the barest light that runs along the edge of the bed frame on the floor. It's as though this small room is our world and we are the only inhabitants.

Jace caresses my cheek with his knuckles, taking me in before his hand glides to the back of my head, his fingers tangling in my hair. With his grip, he tilts my head back slightly and places his lips on mine.

He melts into my embrace and kisses me back almost desperately. I open up to him and his tongue flicks against mine for a moment until he pulls away. Then he leaves a trail of kisses along my jaw and neck, nipping gently.

I wrap my arms and legs around him and let myself get lost in his scent, his touch, and his body.

Chapter Eleven

To the Tower

A knock on the door startles me awake. I sit up gasping for air, feeling around for my golf club as I try to remember where I am. It's so dark I can't see.

Jace's hands fly to my shoulders, gripping me firmly but not hard enough to hurt. "It's okay—we're on a ship."

It takes a second for the words to sink in, and I relax against him.

The knock comes again, and this time, I'm ready for it.

"Be ready to leave in sixty minutes!" Garcia's voice comes through the door.

I groan and flop back down. I want to keep sleeping. The mattress shifts as Jace gets up and turns on the lights. I hiss at the sudden brightness and drape an arm over my eyes as I mutter, "Just ten more hours."

He snorts but doesn't push me to get up. I can hear his shuffling around and, eventually, guilt and anxiety get me to sit up. I let my legs dangle off the edge of the bed and scrub my face with my hands. I almost feel more tired than I did before I fell asleep, but I'll have to push through this feeling.

Jace enters the bathroom and emerges a few minutes later looking as put together as the day he first set foot off his ship, albeit in less formal attire.

"Here," he says, handing me a bundle of clothes.

I can hardly recognize them. The clothes I wore yesterday that were covered in a mixture of sweat and dirt now look as good as new. Now that I think about it, his clothes are the same as yesterday, only freshly washed.

It's more than a little messed up how accustomed to dirt we've become. We try to be as clean as we can manage, but it's as though we are living in the camping trip that won't end. There's always a layer of something, be it dust, sweat, blood, runner guts, or some combination of those things.

"Why can't we just live on this ship?" I ask as I yawn and stretch my entire body.

Jace doesn't answer, only giving me a placating smile, because I already know the answer. Resources are finite and the risk of others helping themselves to the ship is too much of a risk.

Reluctantly, I get dressed and we are ready to go with time to spare. Our bags are packed. But of course they are. They are always packed. We learned long ago that it's a bad idea to unpack. Take out what you need for the moment, then once you're finished, pack it back up immediately.

Lazily, we make our way toward the main hall of the ship, heading to the exit.

"Hey, we missed you guys at breakfast," Scotty says. "It was over an hour ago. We're getting ready to leave in about twenty."

I give a side glance to Jace and we both know why we weren't at breakfast. Our wakeup call came over an hour too late. Part of me doesn't mind and is actually grateful for the extra hour of sleep. I know I needed it and by extension, Jace needed it as well.

"Yeah," I say, "We opted to sleep in a little longer."

"Well, if you're hungry, there are some fresh biscuits left in the galley."

We hurry to the back of the ship and swipe up a few rolls as Mon'te is gathering all the food into the packs that he can fit. It seems like a bit more of a burden, even split evenly between everyone, than is practical for such a long trip. Jace and I add our bags to the mix and help finish packing sustenance that we will need down the road.

Afterwards, we return to the room we stayed in with just enough time to make sure we didn't leave anything behind. I glance longingly at the bathroom, saying my goodbyes to the indoor plumbing—that sweet, glorious, indoor plumbing, with its warm, clean water and the bed that feels like a cloud—then

I turn away.

If there's not running water and electricity at the compound then… I don't know what the point of all this will have been. If nothing else, I'll take Jace and we can find a working ship to call home. At least for a while.

Together, with mouths full of bread, we head out toward the front of the ship. The exit is already wide open, and as soon as we get to the steps, we can see all of them waiting on us. I'd blush from embarrassment of making them stand there in the wide open, except Garcia's glower just irks me. She mutters something under her breath, but no one seems to notice, or at least they pretend they don't.

The sun is barely cresting the horizon, casting golds and vibrant pinks and purples across the deep azure of the sky and chasing away the last of the stars. I squint at the line of gold and white on the edge where the land meets the sky. This isn't any earlier than Jace and I try to be up and ready to go… but with the comfort of the ship I'd managed to fall back into the comfort of life as it used to be.

It was only marginally safer inside. Vor'onins who've been infected by the virus could easily infiltrate the ship before they were too far gone. That's a terrifying thought. I shake my head and push it away, focusing on the here and now.

"All right," Scotty claps his hands together and is promptly slugged in the shoulder by Garcia.

Desmond shakes his head as he tries to hide his laugh.

"Everyone ready? We have a few days of intense walking ahead of us."

"Where are we headed?" Jace asks.

"Rawlins," Scotty says, quieter than before.

I frown, not able to recall how far it was. Either I was too tired to absorb anything, or I hadn't looked that far ahead on my map when I was plotting our route.

"Eh, yeah, it's pretty far." Scotty grins.

I raise a brow. He must really like walking.

"It is approximately one hundred and twenty-five miles," Mon'te interjects.

If I had a drink, I would have choked on it right about now. One hundred and twenty-five miles in a few days? That would take Jace and me at least a week to a week and a half at our normal pace, and that's if everything goes right. I can't imagine the pace we'll have to set to get there in just days.

"And," I start slowly, "it will just take us a few days?"

"We'll aim for under a week."

I don't know how we'll make it, but they're the experts I suppose. They did manage to make the trek here from the Tower.

"It's a grueling pace, but you'll get used to it soon," Desmond says.

He gives us the rules they live by, the plan of travel, how long we'll be walking before we break for the day, all down to how many times we'll stop for rest—only when we stop to eat, which will be a maximum of thirty minutes, give or take five for relieving ourselves. He goes on to discuss how long the night watch shifts will be, how many will be on each shift, and how long we will each get to sleep before we better be ready to move again. Desmond ends his speech by complementing us on being prepared with our packs.

It's all a bit daunting to take in, and I begin to almost regret wanting to be part of something so strict. My hand reaches for my golf club but comes up empty. That's right, I'd given it to Jace. Not because I couldn't defend myself, but he has a much longer reach than I do and is far more lethal with blunt objects.

"If you don't have any questions, we'll move out." Desmond waves a hand and starts walking east. The others follow. Mon'te waits for me to pass him before he starts walking at my side.

"I got this back for you," he says, holding out the dagger and the thigh holster.

"Thank you," I smile up at him, taking the blade and quickly strapping it to my leg, then scramble to catch back up with the group. I'm out of breath by the time I make up the few yards.

There is way more food than normal in my pack. The extra weight will take some getting used to.

It feels like we have been walking for a year by the time we stop for the night. My legs ache and I think if I had to walk for five minutes more, they would have fallen off.

Dinner is a quiet event, at least on our part. Desmond and the others chat quietly, joking around for a bit. I spend what's left of my energy trying to make sure I get the limited amount of food I have in my mouth, rather than down the front of my shirt. Jace sits on my left, also wordlessly eating his own meal.

The food is better than a cold can of beans—bread and canned stew, but it's half of what we're used to. I am still hungry when I finish. I think the extra weight I carried in addition to the intense pace we set made my apatite soar.

After we are all finished, we clean and store our dishes. Something I'd forgotten in our time on the ship, but Jace had remembered and grabbed a set of utensils and two metal plates that could also serve as shallow bowls.

Mon'te stands and addresses our little group. "I will take the first watch, who will join me?"

Two sets of eyes per watch will feel worlds safer than what we are used to. Even though I'm exhausted to the marrow of my bones, I think to volunteer but Jace places a hand on my shoulder before standing and accepting the first watch. We made a deal to take opposite shifts until we know if we can trust these people or not.

I'm woken sometime in the middle of the night to take a shift with Scotty. He gives me the run down and shows me the perimeter we will walk on opposite sides. When our two hours are up, I eye my bed roll longingly, ready for another two hours of sleep. Except, Scotty informs me that it's time to wake everyone up.

"But the sun isn't even up yet," I protest under my breath, my words bordering on whiny.

Scotty only pats my shoulder sympathetically. "By the time we pack up and get back to the road, the sun will be rising, and we'll need to get going. Des wasn't kidding about making it to Rawlins in less than a week."

He just gives me a smile and goes to pack up his roll.

I hang my head then trudge over to Jace and squat to gather my own things.

"Are you all right?" Jace asks, kneeling down at my side, and finishes strapping my bed roll to my pack for me.

"Yeah," I say, then glance at the others from the corner of my eye. "I'm just wondering if this is such a good idea after all."

He cocks his head to the side in silent question.

"I mean, we are traveling out in the open and as far as I can see, we left all trees and cover behind in the first part of the day yesterday."

He cups my cheek with one hand then pushes a loose strand of hair behind my ear. "Raylinn, we will be okay. With or without them—I will keep you safe."

He's giving me an out. Permission for me to say I want to keep wandering as we had been, to have it be only us.

I consider carefully for a long moment, but I don't miss the way his eyes flicker toward Mon'te. Of course, he is homesick and misses his people. We both are, but while we both lost everyone we've ever known or loved, he also lost his world, his culture. We've seen few Vor'onins along our travels—none who weren't with an established group or turned. Then there's the fact that we've been living in the wild this entire time for me, and I know he wants to at least try something like the safety of the Tower.

"No, we will stick with them."

I don't know how he does it, but he manages to give me a look that is both grateful and doubtful at the same time.

He has done the same for me for two years. I love him and he's done everything to make me as happy and comfortable as this world will allow. Now's my chance to do the same for him. It's time to give him what he needs.

We rise to our feet and Jace helps me put on my pack, along with my extra burden of supplies. Then we walk to meet the rest of the group at the edge of our camp and prepare to walk on the long trek to the next town.

Chapter Twelve

A Scream in the Night

Life goes on like that for days, and the more we keep this grueling pace, the more worn down I feel. My mind and body are working on autopilot. I try not to think of the discomfort and soreness of my muscles. I try to welcome the pain as something to keep me somewhat alert.

With only five or six hours of sleep, if we are lucky—sometimes we only manage four hours depending on how generous whoever first watch was. I've been woken for watch over an hour or two early by Garcia several times now. I manage to keep my mouth shut about it each time and just deal. Cooperation is key right now, as Jace keeps reminding me. I'm pretty sure she's just doing it to see how far she can push my buttons anyway. Well, I refuse to play her game.

I only talk when I have to because I feel nothing but irritation or complaints try to burble their way up. And that's the last thing any of us need. The others grow quieter as well, mostly speaking only when the situation requires. Though they are still more talkative than Jace and I ever were. I guess with numbers comes the feeling of safety and a certain amount of confidence and ease.

It isn't more than three days into our journey before anyone even notices that Jace and I have a silent way of communicating. Scotty drills us about it for a good hour when I end up just shrugging him off and telling him we developed it as we went because it was necessary and there are only so many runners two people can fend off. There must have ben something sharp in my tone because Des tells him to fall back into line and give it a rest.

We walk straight ahead on the edge of a long-abandoned highway, going out of our way to skirt any crashed vehicles we see. The road stretches on straight ahead for what seems like an eternity. There are few trees or brush at all, and nothing in a reasonable distance for shelter. Only wide-open plains on either side, or the occasional mountainous hills that border the road. We do have deep ditches on the outside of the road, which we keep close to for a '*just in case*' spot. Those are better suited for hiding from other humans rather than runners.

Any threats we happen across, we can see miles ahead of us and therefore are able to avoid the runners well in advance.

We avoid survivors too, at least for the most part. Mon'te told us it was because there was no way to get the high ground with groups as they were able to with individuals or couples.

While it's their main goal to find as many as possible, they must make sure they aren't a threat first. Which I suppose is why they knocked us out and hog tied us before attempting to talk.

There haven't been many survivors on this leg of the journey. We came close to other survivors only once. As soon as we heard the sound of several motorcycles revving in the distance and heading toward the highway, we quickly got off the road and did our best to stay out of sight in the lower trench area next to the pavement until they passed. The sharp rocks and brambles of some dead and dried plants poked through my clothes. It felt ridiculous hiding from other survivors, but I suppose it was better than a confrontation and possibly having our supplies stolen… or worse, being killed for them. Thankfully, it's been a quiet journey ever since.

Today marks the sixth day and even the vocal Scotty has stopped talking until we stop, except for the occasional observation here and there.

Glancing sideways at Jace, I frown. He looks tired, even for him. Though his posture is still perfect, despite the extra weight we are all carrying. It's only slightly annoying how put together he looks. Meanwhile, I can feel a bead of sweat drip down my temple, piling onto the dried sweat already streaking my face.

I feel like a bag of garbage next to him, and I'm sure I look it. My shoulders started to slump days ago, and while Jace offered to carry my pack for me, I refused. I *will* pull my own weight through this trek, and always. I keep my head down and focus on putting one foot in front of the other. Left, right. Left, right.

Today. We'll reach the city today. I chant the words over and over in my mind, hoping that we'll get a chance to rest when we get there, or at the very least slow our pace. It's this stretch climbing up the continental divide that is a killer. My legs burn.

But as night falls, I wonder if we'll have another day of this torture ahead of us.

I don't look up from the pavement after we stop for lunch. I concentrate on putting one foot in front of the other, again, and again, and again, and again, trusting Jace or anyone to correct my path if I begin to stray. It's a dick move, but I am struggling more and more during the day. I'm tired and I don't think my body was ready for the combination of the weight plus the unforgiving pace.

Jace places a hand on my shoulder and pulls me to an abrupt stop. I look up in time to see Garcia's back a few inches in front of my face.

I almost ran into her. Gawd, that would have been a whole new headache if I had. Small miracles.

"Isn't she beautiful?" Des asks, way more cheery than he has a right to be.

I list my head to the side and peer around Garcia. The edge of a city is only a few miles or so out—and while it's far from what I would consider to be beautiful—the promise of buildings, cover, supplies, and beds *is*.

I want to slump down in relief and shoulder this weight off

my aching shoulders, but I can't. We aren't safe just yet, but we *are* oh, so close!

Jace and I grip each other's hands and exchange quiet smiles that are so much more than just a silent *yay*.

"Let's keep moving, we'll get to the temporary stop in less than an hour." Des waves an arm and leads us away from the city to the opposite side of the highway.

Jace and I let our hands fall to our sides and follow behind the others. My heart sinks.

"W-where are we going?" I ask. My throat burns. I need to drink water, I can feel dehydration coming on.

Scotty bumps Desmond on the shoulder and falls back to walk between Jace and I. "We can't stay in town. Too many, what do you call them? *Runners* in the area. We'll scout tomorrow at first light."

Oh. I suppose I'd hoped to sleep in a bed tonight, but if our options are a town full of runners or off road in the dirt—then in the dirt away from runners is the preferred option.

We make camp about two miles or so outside of town, forgoing any shelter. As soon as night descends, I start to shiver, so Jace takes the opposite watch from me to let me use his blanket on top of mine when it's my turn to sleep.

We are splitting the night in half tonight, upping the watch from two people each to three.

"I don't trust her to have my back. I'm not taking the same watch." Garcia snaps in a whisper that I'm pretty sure everyone in our group can hear.

"Garcia…" Desmond grinds out.

I turn my back on the conversation and face Jace. I'm not sure what her problem with me is exactly, but I wish she'd let it go. I am not all that fond of her either, but no one hears me complaining.

"Don't take it personally," Jace says quietly as he looks over the top of my head at them. I wonder if he knows something I don't. Either way, it's her issue to work through. There's no room in this world—this life—for that.

She ends up on the opposite watch as I do, as does Jace. Which means that Scotty, Desmond, and I take turns walking in concentric circles for half the night.

I am nearly dead on my feet and counting down the minutes as they pass, hoping with each step I take that our shift ends soon.

A mournful wail in the distance rips through the still night air. The sound slithers down my spine and freezes my feet in place. I stop breathing entirely for a long moment, until my lungs begin to burn. Then the cry comes again. Followed by a high-pitched scream that's cut off abruptly, leaving it to echo through the night.

The noises seem to surround me from all sides and far too close for comfort. I know it's not possible and that it's only the plains letting the sounds travel unhindered, making it seem as though they are much closer than in reality.

By the time I am able to get my body to respond to my brain's commands again, Des is approaching me. I don't shout to him but run as fast as my legs will carry me.

"Ray, what's wrong?"

"There… there was this horrible sound. Runners. I think they got someone." I pant, pointing toward the city, where I think the sound came from.

He takes a few steps forward and listens. I can barely make out his outline in the dark. He's so quiet that if I hadn't seen him walk out into the night, then I wouldn't know he was there. Which makes me ever so thankful that runners are not the sneak up behind you types.

After a few moments, he returns, shaking his head. The look on his face is sympathetic. He knows my left ear is messed up. "I didn't hear anything, are you sure?"

Perhaps it really was all in my mind. I shrug. "I think so… I'm not sure. Maybe I'm just tired."

"It could have been an animal," he offers. "I've learned to tune them out in this area." When I don't respond, he continues. "Come on, just another hour then we can wake the others for their shift. I'll have you wake Jace first, you…" he clears his throat lightly, "seem a little tired lately."

A little tired? That's an understatement. Everyone in this group seems to be fairing better—the others because they have probably done this several times now, and Jace because he is in perfect shape. Meanwhile, while I could run well enough to make the track team, I was a soft high school student.

"Yeah," I say. "Let's keep moving before we all end up on this side." Then I walk away at a slightly quicker pace to catch up on my loop before he can say anything more.

I push the thoughts of what I think I'd heard far from my mind. My tired brain was probably messing with me, making the noises seem to be something other than what they actually were.

With that worry out of the way, I keep my mouth shut for the rest of our shift, but I keep my eyes and ears peeled. Runaway thoughts or not, I'm left with a feeling crawling its way up and down my spine.

My focus is starting to wane when a hand grabs my arm and pulls. I spin, wide-eyed and pulse hammering like mad in my head, and swing. Scotty pulls back, taking his face just barely out of my reach.

"Whoa!" he says, letting me go and taking a few steps away. "It's just me. Des asked me to let you know that our shift is over now. Go brief Jace, then get some rest."

"Right… sorry about that," I say, ducking my head. I can't believe I almost decked poor Scotty. "I'll see you when the sun comes up." I give him a half-hearted salute with my index and middle fingers, then run off.

I kneel down and gently shake Jace's shoulder to wake him. He wraps his arms around me and pulls me to him. His hold on me is comforting and warm, and I damn near fall asleep immediately. Jace places a kiss on my head and gives me a light squeeze before adjusting me onto the bedroll and getting up all in a smooth motion.

"Anything happen tonight?" Jace asks.

I roll to my side and give him a shrug.

"What happened?" he asks more seriously this time. He doesn't move until I finally meet his eyes.

"Nothing. I just thought…" I take a deep breath then blow it out. "I just thought I heard something, but Des didn't so, I think I just let the exhaustion get to me." What I don't say is what we both know. There's nothing I can hear that others wouldn't. After all, I'm the one who only has one good ear.

"Rest, I'll stay alert and see if I hear anything. I won't let anything happen to you."

The slight weight of a blanket glides over me, and then I'm too tired to stay awake any longer. I'm too tired to whisper goodnight or say thank you… much less think the words. My eyes close and everything turns fuzzy, even the dull ache in my feet and legs.

CHAPTER THIRTEEN

Pit Stop

We lay in a row on our bellies alongside the edge of the highway. Rocks, or sun hardened clumps of dirt, dig into my stomach as we look out toward the edge of the city. There's no movement so I'm not sure why we aren't walking in yet.

"All right, we need to get to the ATVs behind that big building over there," Desmond says in a loud whisper, pointing straight ahead... toward nothing. "They are hidden in the brush over there." He explains this for Jace and my sakes, because of course the others in our group already know this. "We'll draw straws now, then each group will take turns filling up the gas canisters until each vehicle is filled and we have full canisters for later. We only have four ATVs, so Jace and Raylinn, you'll have to double up with someone. Ray you'll be with Scotty, Jace you'll ride with Garcia."

I prickle slightly to think of Jace having to ride with her but quickly stamp down the uncalled-for emotion. As if sensing my feelings that I would like to remain unnamed, Jace reaches his hand to mine and gives it a squeeze.

"Each group will take turns running to the gas stations—" Desmond points east. "—over there."

With that, he gets up and everyone follows suit. We don't really need a more concrete plan than that. It's straight forward enough.

Scotty pulls out a small matchbox and hands Desmond six matches. He lights three and extinguishes them, then holds out his fist with the tops hidden within his grasp. We take turns plucking one each until the teams are divided. Jace, Mon'te and Desmond on one team, Scotty, Garcia, and me on the other.

I ignore the sound of disgust coming from Garcia as we shoulder our bags and head toward the ATVs. I would think a car would be more beneficial, but I'm sure they have their reasons. Besides, cars—working cars—have been harder and harder to come by after the first few months of this new world.

We get to the spot where they had hidden the vehicles in minutes. I wasn't entirely sure what an ATV was, but it looks like a motorcycle with four wheels—not exactly something that is meant for more than one person at a time, not for the distance we still need to cross. Not wasting a second, Desmond and Mon'te throw the brush used to disguise them to the ground and we all begin loading up our supplies as evenly as we can, with just a little less on the two where Jace and I will be doubling up.

Jace wraps his arms around me from behind and places a kiss on my neck. Instantly, I melt into him, but before I can really enjoy the moment, he pulls away, picking up two empty gas canisters that have been painted a camouflage green to hide the red-orange color of the plastic.

"I'll be back soon."

I nod and then the three of them are off at a brisk jog.

The entire time he's gone, I keep my eyes on the horizon as if I could still see them even through the buildings. I roll my shoulders, trying to ease out the nearly cramping muscles.

It feels like hours have passed before I see them emerge from behind a building as they head back, each of them holding two large containers. They are moving slower now, but the weight that had settled on my heart eases, only to be replaced with an uneasy pit in my stomach at the thought of having to go into that town. The memory of the noises from last night comes back, and I swear I can hear them just as clear now as I did then.

I quickly shake off the feeling as they reach us. Des, Mon'te, Garcia, and Scotty, all fill up one of the ATVs each. Scotty waves me over so I can see how it's done alongside Jace.

Now it's my turn. Jace hands me the two empty gas canisters and kisses me on the head.

"Any sign of runners?" Garcia asks Desmond as he walks with us for a few yards. She leads the way and I'm more than happy to follow.

"No, but there were some noises in the distance, so be careful. Also, you'll need to pass the first gas station—it's all dried up, go to the next." She nods and starts off at a decent paced jog.

I follow, not far behind. Though I could catch up to her, I opt not to, just to keep what peace I can during this mission. Scotty matches my pace and throws me a few questioning glances.

I frown. *Do I have something on my face?* "What?"

"You all right, Ray? You seem… upset." True concern shines in his blue eyes.

Crap, my thoughts must have been plastered all over my face. "Yeah, I guess I'm just tired."

"You'd tell me if there was something wrong?" He looks doubtful. I'd be insulted except he's reading me correctly.

I think about it for a long moment and come to the conclusion that my answer would probably be *not really*, but I don't tell him that. He considers me for a moment and seems to be about to speak again when Garcia looks over her shoulder and gives me a death glare. I take that as my cue to shut up. It's a look even Scotty doesn't miss. So, I just shake my head at him, and do my best to give him a reassuring smile.

Garcia stops just before we reach the city and holds up a fist, signaling for us to stop. We all strain to hear for any sound that might indicate runners are around. With only one good ear, I know the two of them are more likely to hear something than I am—I do my best to listen anyway.

When Garcia deems it clear, we move out, passing the first gas station as Desmond had instructed. Even though the storefront is most likely ransacked, I eye it dreaming of cold water bottles in a running fridge as it had once upon a time.

Sweat drips down the side of my face by the time we get to the second gas station. Each of us silently taking a gas pump after Scotty locates the transfer switch and moves the power to a generator. I stare at my pump.

"Ray, is something wrong with yours?" Scotty asks.

I feel my cheeks flame. "Uh, I don't know how to pump gas."

Garcia curses from the pump on the other side of me.

Scotty snorts. "Seriously?"

"Hey, I grew up in Oregon. We don't pump our own gas there," I mutter somewhat defensively.

He finishes up with his canister then comes over to where I stand and shows me how. It's way easier than I expected. It only takes a few minutes for us to fill up our canisters.

I lift one in each hand and let out a grunt. *Geez, these are heavy.* I hope my arms don't fall off before we get back to the rest of the group. *Note to self: workout your damn arms.*

"You two go ahead, I'll go turn the gen off and catch up," Garcia says.

"Let's go," Scotty says, jerking his head toward our destination and starts off at a brisk walk.

The heavy canisters of liquid slosh around out of rhythm

with his steps, making him slow his pace. I pick mine up and follow. I wobble as I try to jog, but anything faster than a walk threatens to send me so off balance I'm worried I might trip and break an ankle. To compensate, I lengthen my stride as much as possible.

As we move, I take several glances over my shoulder. Garcia should be catching up to us by now, but I don't see her—but that's when I see *it*—down the side street is a large reddish-brown spot marring the pavement with chunks of…

I barely hold in a gag as bile rises quickly up my throat. Dried blood, still somewhat fresh and pieces of flesh scattered around. Unrecognizable body parts.

Shit… I've never seen an attack so violent before. Is it possible the runners are getting worse?

The sound of large metal objects clattering as if knocked down echoes through the streets.

"Damn it, Garcia," Scotty hisses under his breath. I've never seen him so much as utter a grumpy word, much less be angry at anyone. He sets his canisters down and runs back the way we came.

I curse, not knowing if I should stay with the gas, or go with him. A second's hesitation and I decide to follow. Gas can be replaced—as limited a resource as it is—Garcia is more important.

I run as fast as I can, catching up to him after a block and nearly running into him when he stops abruptly. A horde of runners turns a corner a few blocks from the gas station.

Garcia sprints from a pile of hubcaps and metal pipes to the pumps where she left her canisters. We jump up and down to get her attention as she walks away from the gas station. Does she even know runners are on her tail?

My heart leaps up into my throat as the runners scent her location and begin their charge. It's then we give up our silent attempt to get her attention.

"Run!" I cry.

"Move your ass, Garcia!"

She looks up at us and we point toward the runners gaining. It's like watching an avalanche. A violent, gory avalanche. We can't go to her—it would be suicide. There's far too many of them and we have no weapons. I see the look on Garcia's face, and I know she's not thinking logically. Panic is clear in her expression, even from this far away.

"Ray, I need you to go back and take whatever gas you can carry and head back."

"What?" I ask in dumb shock. "What about Garcia?"

"I'm going to get her."

"You can't, that's suicide!"

"Please," he says. "We need the gas to make it to the next stop point. We can't do this without it." He's never been one to take charge that I've seen, so I'm a little thrown.

"Okay." He's right. We have to save whom we can. That was one of the rules Desmond set down: save the majority.

I take off back toward where we left our gas and somehow manage to pick up three containers. I situate them in my arms as I spare a glance behind me.

"Go, now!" Scotty yells at Garcia who's nearly to where I am.

He continues past her, screaming and making noise, leading them away from us.

"What are you doing? Get back to the meeting point!" Garcia snaps.

Then she looks behind her at the same moment, realizing that Scotty is no longer behind her. I see the change in her posture, the expression of frustration on her face falls, replaced with one of pure fear.

Scotty runs toward us but... he has a limp and the runners are closing in on him. I don't know when or how it happened but, his injury is slowing him down. The closer he gets the more it's clear, it's not just a twisted ankle, he's bleeding. A bright red line trails behind him.

I set the gas canisters down, ready to make my move. Garcia is about to run in after him and they'll both get killed. I grab her arm as she starts to move and jerk her back. We fall to the dirt on the side of the road.

"Get the fuck off me!" she screams in my face, pushing me as I continue to cling to her.

"We can't help him. We need to run!"

Her dark eyes burn into me. She knows I'm right and hates me for it. That's fine, she can hate me all she wants as long as she doesn't get herself killed.

We pick up our gas canisters and, before we run, Garcia yells, "Scotty! Hurry!"

Scotty waves us off and I see him veer off in another direction. He'd never make it to us in time. He knows it. It's why he waited until Garcia turned her back on him before leading the runners away from us and away from the rest of our group.

We'd never make it with all of them chasing us, not bogged down as we are with the several gallons of fuel each. I take one last look behind as we leave the town behind.

Most of the runners have followed Scotty, a few have stayed on our trail so we can't slow. I try to keep my eye on Scotty, hoping against hope that he'll get away.

My heart sinks when a few seconds later, he's swallowed up by the horde.

Chapter Fourteen

Left Behind

The gas canisters slow us as we race toward the group, but we manage to make it with still a decent amount of distance between us and the runners. Garcia sets the canisters she's holding down on the ground, even as Mon'te and Desmond try to take them from her.

She spins and looks behind us, tears have left streaks in the dust down her cheeks. Her eyes dart frantically around as she cries out over and over. "Where is he? Where is he?"

Jace helps me with my canisters as I set them down, when I straighten, I barely have time to blink before Garcia shoves me with both hands as hard as she can. I stumble back, avoiding being thrown to the ground thanks to Jace's close proximity and his fast reflexes. Mon'te rushes over and grabs Garcia by the waist, pulling her back so she can't come at me again.

"What the hell happened out there?" Desmond demands.

Garcia pushes Mon'te away and swivels to face Desmond, pointing her finger at me accusingly. "Her, *she's what happened.*"

My jaw drops. "What the hell did I do?" I snap before I can think better of it.

"You stopped me from helping Scotty, and now he's back there with the infected and for all we know, he could already be dead!"

That last word came home like a serrated knife to the heart. She doesn't know. She didn't see him limp, didn't see him turn and lead them away from us, she didn't see him being overtaken by the runner... I can't say anything, only look away.

"Oh, god... oh god!" she wails as understanding of what my silence says hits her. She falls to her knees. "I knew we couldn't trust them! Every time we take someone in, we always lose one of our own."

"Damn it," Desmond mutters, "Why didn't you tell us infected were on your trail? Everyone get on—we have to go now!"

"What about Scotty?" Garcia asks, but she sounds so young when she speaks. So broken. It's a pain I understand, one that resides in my heart.

Mon'te and Jace strap the full canisters onto the ATVs and mount them. I climb on behind Jace as Garcia stands without another word. Desmond doesn't need to spell it out for her. They live by a set of rules they all agreed on long before Jace and I joined them.

We were lucky to have had the few minutes we did. Hell, Garcia and I were lucky to have made it back at all. Scotty had bought us the time we needed. That thought churns my stomach as the ATV four-wheelers growl to life and take off. I cling to Jace's middle and bury my face into his back.

Scotty didn't deserve that fate—no one does—but least of all him. He was sweet and too good for this harsh world.

For a second, panic overwhelms me, and I want to go back for him as much as Garcia. But I know we can't. Several runners now swarm where we had been standing moments before. Scotty had known what he was doing, he understood the risks, but even knowing that doesn't make it any easier to swallow.

Ten minutes into our ride, when we've lost the runners, Desmond swings his ATV in front of us all and forces us all to a stop.

"What the hell happened out there?" he snaps.

Garcia looks him dead in the eye but says nothing. Of course, *now* she chooses to stay quiet.

I shrug and shake my head. "I don't know. We were on our way back when runners came around the corner. He—" I swallowed the lump in my throat. "He tried to lead them away. He told me we needed to get the canisters back to you guys. I thought he'd catch up."

Desmond takes in my words for a long moment and sizes me up as if he knows I left out some details, like what attracted them in the first place. Details about who was where and doing what. But I told him the important parts. It is up to Garcia to fill him in on the rest, if and when she's ready.

Mon'te and Desmond exchange a look over her head. They too are upset, but Garcia is upset on a whole other level. There's something more going on than what's on the surface. I'm more sure of that now than ever. I don't expect answers or explanations, Jace and I aren't fully part of the group, not yet. We're essentially rescues they picked up and are taking home.

"We all knew the risks of these missions before we accepted them. This kind of thing has always been a possibility. Scotty leading them away so you two could get back to us was exactly what we outlined to do in that situation," Mon'te spoke low and soft, making his words gentle. "Sacrifice one to save the many— It's how we survive."

Garcia doesn't move for a long time, only sits on her ATV, head bowed.

After giving her a few moments, Desmond restarts his ride and taks off, expecting us to follow and knowing we will.

"We must go, we need to cover as much ground as we can before we have to stop again," Mon'te says, then he too takes off.

Jace and I follow. I glance behind to make sure Garcia is

also following, which she does after giving us all a bit of a head start. I don't blame her for wanting space. Scotty meant something to her.

It's not long into the ride before my butt hurts from the rocky terrain bouncing us. We stay off the road but not so far as to lose sight of the highway. There's less chance of crossing paths with runners or other not-so-well-intentioned survivors.

I tighten my arms around Jace's waist and rest my cheek against his back. I let out a shaky sigh and hot tears roll down my face as I let the afternoon sink in. Scotty wasn't the first person we teamed up with that we lost... But I've never seen anyone sacrifice themselves like that. I didn't think it was something people would do for anyone.

In this time I have to sit and think, with zero expectations of having to be on the lookout for runners, my mind rolls over the few memories I have of Scotty. I don't have many, but all of the ones I do have are of him being a bright spot, smiling and unwilling to dim even with the hard, unforgiving place this world has become.

Jace pats my leg in a comforting gesture, giving my knee a gentle squeeze before he returns his hand to the handlebar.

When night begins to fall, we drive a little farther away from the highway before we stop to make camp for the night. It's business as usual, splitting into groups for watch, making dinner from our limited supplies, and settling down for when we get to rest.

Jace takes the first watch shift, letting me rest. Tossing and turning, I barely get any sleep. My backside hurts and I can't get the image out of my head of the horde swallowing up Scotty. It plays over and over in my mind in a morbid, nonstop loop. I'm actually a little glad when it's my turn to take a watch shift.

The only light in the pitch-dark night is the small fire we have going. We're far enough away from the highway that we can take the chance. It's quiet out here. And while I'm pretty sure we could all sleep the full night and be fine… after what happened only hours ago, it's something to keep us busy, to think about Scotty in private. And anytime there is an attack, it's easy to think another could come at any second.

A twig snaps to my right, and I spin, ready to call out to the others to get up and run. But it's only Garcia walking toward me. I wonder what she is doing up. I pretend I don't see her and continue walking my circle. Fighting with her is not on my list of things to do tonight.

A few seconds later, she catches up and walks silently beside me. I'm too shocked that she hasn't tried slugging me that I can't bring myself to say anything. She obviously has something on her mind, but she'll speak in her own time.

"Why didn't you say anything to Desmond?"

"About what?" I ask, actually confused about which detail I left out that she's referring to.

"About why Scotty went back toward the infected. If I'd been with you two… if I hadn't made all that noise… all three of us could have made it."

Oh.

"It wasn't my story to tell. And…" I say, slowly continuing quieter than before, "We don't know if we would have made it without him drawing them away like he did."

"I should have gone back for him. I shouldn't have let you stop me."

"No. He did that to save you so you had time to get away. If you'd gone back, that would have wasted his effort."

She swings her head toward me and glares, though she doesn't argue. We lapse into silence again and continue to walk.

"I don't like you," she says after a while.

Normally that kind of confession would shock me or maybe even hurt my feelings a little but, coming from her, it's not the least bit surprising—it's actually almost amusing.

"I could tell," I say dryly.

"Do you want to know why?" she asks, but this time, her words are soft, and I know she wants to tell me but for some reason she wants me to ask.

"Only if you want to tell me," I say.

"About three months back, we picked up a small group of survivors—just like you two. Things were fine for the first few days, then when we went out on a scouting trip with them,

Tris'an… my mate," she whispers the name so quietly, I wasn't sure if I'd heard her right, "and two of the newbies, we were sniffed out by a horde of infected. Long story short, they made sure to sacrifice Tris'an so they could get away, then they took off. We didn't know what happened until we found what was left of him…"

That explains a lot. I can't say I'd be trusting anyone at all if someone used Jace or myself as fodder so they could get away. I mean, I get instinct to survive—but only to a point. Using others as zombie bait is a whole other level of messed up. There's that stupid word again…

"They were human, not Vor'onin?" I asked.

She nods. "Jace reminds me of *him* sometimes, more than Mon'te."

At least now I know why she has had an issue with me from the start but was always civil to Jace. "Not to ruin the moment we're having right now, but… why are you telling me this?"

She narrows her eyes at me for a long moment before her features soften. "Because Jace was right."

I start coughing, choking on nothing. *Smooth.* Garcia pats me hard on the back until I can catch my breath again.

"You talked to Jace?" My brows furrow. "When?"

"He found me during our shift. He said you cried over Scotty, and then he lectured me about how you weren't the person I assumed you were."

I don't know whether to be embarrassed he shared such personal feelings with the one person who couldn't have hated me any more, or if I should be grateful he did something that led to a sort of… truce between us.

"I don't know if we can trust you yet." She looks at me long and hard, as if her thoughts are leaving a bitter taste in her mouth. "But he made me see that you holding me back was probably the only reason I'm alive right now, and it's what Desmond would have ordered—even if I am having a hard time seeing it that way. So, I guess, thanks… you know, for saving my life and… whatever." Garcia huffs and crosses her arms.

Screw it. I know those words are leaving a bitter taste in her mouth as her thanks still sounded more like, *I still hate you,* than appreciation. But whatever. I'm tired and it's good enough for me.

"Uh, any time… I guess… whatever." I scowl back at her, using her words.

She meets my eyes, and I'm not sure if I just messed up whatever peace we came to until the corners of her mouth lift up into a reluctant smile. Garcia runs a hand through her hair. "Anyway, I'm beat, I'm going to bed. I just wanted to get that off my chest."

As she's turning away, a thought hits me. "Hey, Garcia? Can I ask you something, about the compound?"

She faces me again and tilts her head, which I take as a yes.

"How are they with…" I glance over toward camp. "How are they toward Vor'onins?"

"What do you mean?"

"I mean," I start and swallow hard. I've never voiced this concern to anyone, not even Jace. But every time we run into other survivors, I worry they'll know what Jace and I found out about the experiments that Thral'el and Lar'ruk were doing. I worry they will take Jace away from me and I'll never see him again. "Do they blame them for all of this?" I sweep my hands wide. "I mean, considering the timing and all…"

She frowns. "No. Why would they? As far as any one can tell, their immune systems mixing with ours is the only reason why any of us survived, why we weren't all infected."

Relief floods through my veins. My worries over the past two years, the wanting to avoid other survivors as much as possible, is over. Well, I don't know if I'll ever get over wanting to avoid other survivors, seeing as in a world like this, the law means very little anymore.

"Oh, okay. Thanks. That's good to know."

Garcia gives me an understanding smile then heads back to the inner most circle of our patrol without so much as a wave or a look over her shoulder.

"Goodnight," I call, only loud enough for her to hear.

"I still don't like you," comes her answer, but there's not even a hint of hostility in her voice.

Our chat doesn't make what happened to Scotty any less horrific, but I feel as though I can breathe a little easier. I understand where she's coming from now and the animosity between us is cracked and fading.

That's all I can ask for. That alone will make the rest of this trip easier.

Then I frown. Without her hate to distract me, the uncertainty of going into a compound, living in what is essentially a large cage—and under someone else's thumb for the first time since this world went to shit is a whole new level of unsettling.

We've been doing things our own way all this time that it's hard to know if we'll be okay following a whole new set of rules, and a leader who we know nothing about.

CHAPTER FIFTEEN

As My World Turns

There's little talk from anyone for the rest of the trip. The landscape makes it impossible to judge distance, all flat and nearly barren as it is, save for the mountains in the far distance as we drive north east through the state.

If I thought a few hours on one of these was hard on the butt, well, three hundred miles is enough to make it fall off—or at least that's what I could have sworn happened two hundred miles back.

The long ride gives me time to think. A little too much if you ask me.

The two years since we walked away from the only home I've known my entire life, my family, my friends… from the girl who called out for help—has changed me more than I ever thought possible. It broke me, losing everything and everyone, even with Jace by my side to pull me through those dark times. I can feel the jaded edges it has left behind almost as if it were something physical. Eventually survival instincts kicked in and I had to learn how to push my feelings away until it was safe to deal with them.

I thought I loved Jace the moment I'd met him, but I know now that was infatuation and extreme attraction. The time we've spent together just trying to live for one more day showed us the ugly side of each other, but it also showed us what love actually is.

It's hard to believe now that I was once the cowering girl in a dark, dank cell. Now I've somehow managed to keep my wits about me long enough not to let a member of our group run head-first into danger, that I don't think twice about fighting for my life, or Jace's. He's the one light left in this dark world—the light that guides me and keeps me safe as a lighthouse guides a ship in the night.

Jace's hand falls to my leg and he gives my knee two squeezes. I squeeze his hand back once. I don't know what tipped him off to my train of thought, but the fact that he noticed and checked in on me warms my heart. He's so attentive to the small details.

A few minutes later, Jace taps me, trying to get my attention. I lift my face from my nearly permanent spot in his back—

windburn is a bitch—and look up to see a large lake coming into view over the horizon. I gape, unable to look away. The blue green of the massive body of water is surrounded by lots of vibrant green. After staring at the brown, barren land for so long, it feels like I'm seeing color for the first time in my life.

Several miles later, Des pulls us all to a stop. Dread pools in my stomach at the grim expression he wears. "We need to stop for gas one last time. We won't make it as is on this tank, and we'll want extra for the next time we head out." He half turns in his seat and points east. "The lake horseshoes around a town, the body of water means it's less likely to have many infected, but it also means that while we're there, we'll be surrounded by water on three sides, and if there are any infected, they'll be able to corner us."

We all fall into a silence that seems unnaturally loud. My mind immediately jumps to what happened the last time we stopped for gas, and Scotty. I have no doubt that everyone else's does as well.

"We'll ride in together, fill up directly, and fill the canisters—in and out fast—no time for anything to go wrong. We start slow and try to keep quiet. The first sign of even just one runner and we get the hell out of there. Got it?"

We all nod in understanding and set out together.

My heart hammers in my chest. We've stopped to fill up a few times since that first time, but there's something about being surrounded on three sides from the start that makes unease roll over our group.

Driving slowly through the town, like many of the ones we've been in since the start, is eerie in the abandoned feel. Ghost towns used to be rare, now it's the norm. But it's the way they were abandoned that make them feel haunted. Signs of life remain as though people just vanished into thin air in the middle of everyday tasks. A few cars are crashed on the side of the roads. While there is usually signs of struggle or the occasional body, this was a small town, so signs are few and somehow that frightens me more.

Not having to drive gives me the chance to look in as many directions as I can, looking out for any sign of runners.

Desmond leads us to the first gas station in town and we stop. Mon'te jumps off and immediately goes looking for a switch to the generator. We all stand with our backs to each other, facing out as we wait.

A few moments later, Mon'te jogs back toward us. "No luck, the gen is dead. We must find another."

Desmond grinds his teeth in frustration. "Let's go, there's another station further in town."

Jace and I exchange a look. No one likes the idea of venturing any further into town than we have to, but we keep our feelings to ourselves. Voicing them won't help the situation.

Thankfully, as it is a small town, the second station is

relatively nearby. Mon'te has no problem starting the backup generator this time.

"You can stay seated," Jace offers.

I shake my head and dismount, grabbing my golf club from the seat. "I'll keep an eye out."

While they fill the tanks and canisters, I circle the pumps giving them a wide berth. It's quiet, not even the sound of birds singing or cicadas chirping. The light breeze would have once been refreshing in this heat, but now it makes me jumpy as things flutter in the wind, making me feel as though we are surrounded.

I gaze down the street when a larger than normal movement to my left catches my eye. I glance back at Jace. He swipes the back of his hand across his forehead, wiping away a layer of sweat. They are all still filling up, so I inch toward the side of the gas station, my golf club ready to swing.

"Ray?" Jace whispers, but I just hold up a finger, not looking toward him. He knows I'm just being overly cautious. I just want a minute to make sure the movement was just my overactive imagination. At least, that's the hope. My pulse quickens and the familiar prickling of adrenaline courses through my system.

I peek around the corner and see a flap of a tarp moving lightly. Turning back to him, I smile and give a thumbs up, letting him know it's clear. I move forward to go tie it down, leaning my golf club up against the side of the building.

My shoes crunch over broken glass. I cringe, the sound is

loud to my ears after the silence. I bend down and catch the loose string and try to find something to secure it down to.

The glass behind me crunches. "I'll be there in a second, Jace, I'm just trying to tie this down really quick," I say without looking over my shoulder.

That's when I smell it—the scent of raw meat that has just turned. My fingers stop their movements and I stand, spinning to face a runner. The thing that used to be a man looks at me through milky eyes, his jaw hanging open at a slight angle. It grunts in a low growling way.

Shit. Shit, shit, shit. My back is to a set of crates covered with this stupid tarp. I reach out to my side for the golf club, but my hand comes up empty. My eyes dart to the side—it's just out of my reach.

And in that second, I know I made a huge mistake.

He shambles one step closer, sniffing the air. I back up automatically, not wanting this thing anywhere near me, and my heel comes into contact with a piece of wood, sending it scraping across the pavement.

The runner growls at the sound and lunges for me. I throw myself back and to the side, hitting the crates. The wood digs into my back and scratches at my skin through my clothes as I bounce off and hit the ground hard. My left wrist wrenches under my weight and I know it's injured, but how bad, I'm not sure. The runner crashes into the crates hard after me. Large shards break and rain down.

"Ray!" Jace calls, rounding the side of the building. His warm amber eyes meet mine as I lie helpless on the ground.

The runner growls again and throws a crate down at me, I cry out and barely lift my arm in time to shield my face as the wood hits. My eyes squeeze shut on reflex just as the wood cracks against my arm painfully. I can't keep the whimper of pain from escaping.

I wait for the inevitable, but nothing comes. It's as if time freezes for several minutes. Then there's a crack of something hard against flesh, followed by a dull thud. I peel my eyes open. Jace stands over the runner with my golf club in hand, dark ooze on the metal end. He reaches a hand out to me to help me up as the sound of mournful wailing fills the air.

"Are you all right?" he asks, looking at our surroundings. It's rare for a runner to be alone, they hunt in packs, so why I wasn't surrounded is a mystery, and a miracle.

"Yeah," is all I manage to say before Des cuts me off.

"Get your asses out here now, we're leaving!"

Jace takes me by the hand and drags me back out to the ATV. We mount and he shoves the golf club into my hand then starts the engine. The others are already maneuvering out of the station lot and runners are closing in from down the street, and to the east.

Shit, shit, shit. There's at least two dozen all together. It's kind of hard to get an accurate head count when you're running for your life. Several more come out from the other side of the building, nearly surrounding us. *Holy shit.* How did they manage to ambush us like this? It almost feels planned.

We're off, and the sudden movement jerks me back but I grab hold of Jace to keep from being thrown off the back. Five seconds. That's how long it takes me to notice a warm tickle on my arm and a deep stinging. I shrug, trying to push the feeling away but it burns a little. I take my eyes off the runners chasing us and moving a lot faster than I remember them being able to. Or maybe these things we are riding don't go as fast as I'd assumed.

"Faster, faster," I chant under my breath, begging the ATV to put more distance between us and the runners. But they are just as persistent, as if we were running toward them with open arms. "Jace!" I lean forward so he might hear me. "They're still following us!"

"Hold on!" he calls over his shoulder.

I tighten my grip just as he jerks to the side, veering off the path the others took toward a side street. I hold tight, my right arm burning from the strain.

I brush my hair out of my face and hiss at the sharp pain the movement brings. The dead eyes of those walking nightmares on our tail continue to gain.

Finally, I look at my arm. Warm blood drips down from

a deep gash just below the muscle of my right shoulder. I'm bleeding. That explains why the runners chose to follow us. I mean, besides the fact that the other part of our group has a head start so we are the closest, and easiest, prey. Like a wounded animal, my injury calls to them.

"Jace," I call over the noise of the engine and the wind. "I'm bleeding!"

He turns to look at me, concern darkening his amber eyes. "Use your knife to cut strips from my shirt."

I do as he says, pulling the dagger from the holster strapped to my thigh. Then gripping the edge of his white tee, I slice a long strip off, careful not to cut him in the process. I sheath the blade then wrap the cloth around my arm, tightening it with my teeth. It's not great, but it will have to do for now.

As soon as I'm gripping on to Jace with both hands again, he swerves again, aiming for the others so we can rejoin them. It looks like they slowed down to wait for us.

We eventually catch up after a few miles. I glance behind. Thanks to what appears to be a runner traffic jam at the corner, we are slowly gaining distance between us and them, but not enough for my taste. Never enough.

Why didn't this group carry guns? I'll have to ask them once we are safe, because if I could be picking them off as we go, we'd have a lot easier of a time the next time we stop. Jace and I never did for the noise factor alone. It would bring a horde down on us and there's no way just the two of us could take them all on like that.

Then a thought occurs to me. We didn't get a chance to fill up the reserve canisters. I don't even know if they finished filling the tanks on these things. Will we even make it to the Tower on what fuel we have left? Because it doesn't look like we'll be losing these runners anytime soon.

Eventually, we manage to put a decent amount of distance between them. But they're still coming, I can see them on the horizon. They are tireless and single minded. They've locked onto us, got the scent of my blood, and they aren't willing to let us go.

Far sooner than I expected, we crest a hill to see an enormous cylindrical shape rising up from the group. The Tower. Devil's Tower. I can't help the giggle that escapes—whether it's from relief that we're almost to safety or delirium.

"Mashed potato mountain," I mumble, only now realizing I'd never actually knew what it was really called until this moment.

"Huh?" Jace calls back over his shoulder.

"Nothing." I shake my head. I'll explain it to him later when we have a moment. Now is not really the time to go into details about a movie about a man obsessed with UFOs and building this landmark out of his food, or a giant pile of dirt in his living room.

The five of us race down, Desmond in the lead as he guides us. A fence juts up next to the tower, much taller than I expected. Thirty feet at least, it's hard to tell.

The men walking along the top part of the fence stop when they see us. Desmond waves at them with one arm, then points behind us indicating the runners still trailing us.

Nerves settle in my stomach like a bolder as we near the gates and they don't open.

Desmond skids to a halt in front of them, jumping off his ATV and running to the gate, pounding on it with his fist as he yells up. "Open the gates! Now! Can't you see infected are on our asses?"

The two men look down at us, seemingly unworried, but their guns are pointed at the horde behind us.

I look nervously behind me. They keep gaining on us.

Jace takes my hand, leading me to dismount with him, then pushes me behind him, shielding me with his body. His hand in mine is just about the only comfort I have left in the world, so I cling to him tightly as we watch the horde grow closer and closer with each passing second.

We made it to the bunker, to where we should have been safe... only to die at the gates. What kind of sick cosmic joke was this?

"What the hell are you idiots doing?" Garcia snaps. "Let us in before the infected get here!"

"Where's Scotty? Who are these two?" One of them calls down. "That one looks injured, is she infected?"

"How about you let us in then we'll have a chat, now is not the time!" Mon'te says.

We all ready ourselves. Jace lets my hand drop from his as he hands me my golf club and he takes my knife. The runners will be on us in a minute.

Jace's arm bumps mine gently, drawing my eyes to his face. He smiles, but it doesn't reach his eyes. "Together," he whispers. "We go out fighting together, or we get through this together. There are no other options."

Hell, zombies or not, it's the most romantic thing I've ever heard anyone say to me. Something about his words gives me a little extra strength.

I spread my feet for balance and raise my golf club as I steel my nerves. Jace's warm gaze meets mine, and we give each other a nod. We are ready.

Then the most beautiful sound reaches my ears—a high pitched grinding of the gate as it opens. I turn to look at Garcia, Des, and Mon'te, but I'm jerked off my feet and land hard on my back, skidding a good distance before I come to a stop, kicking up a dust cloud in my wake. I cough through the dirt as Jace falls to his knees at my side.

The gate slams shut.

"Raylinn, are you okay?"

But before I can answer him, he's pushed out of my sight and two rifles are shoved into my face.

"Is anyone else hurt?" comes a gruff voice off to the side, and I can't see who it belongs to.

"No, but—" Garcia starts and is immediately cut off.

"Good, take her to the quarantine cells before she turns."

"I'm not going to turn!" I try to sit up, wanting to defend myself, but two men grab each arm and haul me away.

"Ray!" Jace calls out, reaching a hand toward me as I'm dragged away like some kind of criminal. He's stopped by yet another man with a rifle.

"Jace!" I reach toward him, knowing it's pointless.

Then the ground beneath my feet turns from dirt to cold metal and a door slams shut, cutting off the light, and I'm surrounded by sudden darkness.

Chapter Sixteen

The Silence Continues

I sit with my back against a hard wall and damp dirt under me. There's barely enough light to see, but I'm not sure if it makes it worse or not. Cold metal walls line three edges of my cell, floor to ceiling bars line the fourth. After being out in the open for so long, these walls threaten to suffocate me.

I feel trapped. And as unlikely as it is, if runners made it past the gate, and the doors between, I would be helpless to defend myself.

My hand goes to my leg only to brush against my cargo pants. They took my golf club, which I'm not surprised about, but I wish I had my knife hidden in my boot.

I wish Jace was here and that he's okay and not locked up like I am. But wishing is useless. Wish in one hand, crap in the other, and see which fills up faster.

Though, I hadn't seen or heard them drag anyone else down here after me hours ago. My arm throbs, reminding me of exactly why I'm here and no one else.

There's no way to know how much time passes, because the light never changes, and I can't hear anything that's happening outside. All I can hear is my breathing and that of the two guards waiting by the far door. Every once in a while, they shift, and I hear the sound of their rifles tapping against something on their belts.

I'm cold, and tired, and so thirsty. My throat feels like I had sand for lunch.

I crawl my way to the bars and grip them, pulling myself to standing.

"Hey," I croak out toward the shadows. "Hey!" My voice is so dry it burns to utter those words.

"What do you want," snaps one of them.

"Water." The word comes out low and gravelly. And I worry they'll think I'm turning. My legs shake as I'm answered with silence. "Please?" I practically whine. "I've been here for hours."

"You think we'd waste perfectly good resources on someone about to turn?" he snaps, stepping into the dim yellow light. He's holding his gun as if he's ready and more than willing to lift it and shoot me in the head.

I already hate him just by looking at his stupidly clean face, and his shiny blond hair. Ugh, I can even smell the soap he used recently. He just stands there, all freshly washed and wearing clean clothes, while I sit in a cell like some damned criminal because I hurt my stupid arm on a piece of wood.

I wrinkle my nose at him. "I'm not going to turn, you moron. I fell."

Okay, so maybe fighting with the one guy who could give me water isn't the best decision. But what can I say? I've been here for who knows how long, I'm so thirsty I can hardly think straight, and I'm hungry to the point that I can't control my temper anymore. Even the sound of his breathing irritates the crap out of me.

"How do we know you weren't bit or scratched by one of them? You could be lying."

"Because," I say slowly, as if a rock could score higher on an IQ test, which I think is entirely possible. "I think I would know if something bit me or scratched me. This is from a crate I fell on. As far as I know, wood can't turn people into runners."

His face distorts with fury at my mockery, and he steps forward and looks as if he's about to head butt me with the end of his gun.

"Relax man," another voice says. "She's probably not going to turn into one of them. She's still pretty lucid." Then he faces me, his dark eyes sparkling even in here. "I'll be right back with some water."

As he turns to leave, I make sure to give the first guard a smug look, taking a step backward as he takes one toward me. He definitely would have smacked me with the end of his gun if

I'd stayed still, but I know he won't risk sticking it, or a hand, past the bars. He still thinks I could turn into a runner.

It's a few minutes of us glaring at each other before my legs tire. I don't sit down though, or break eye contact. Instead, I lean against the wall with my arms folded, adopting an air of superiority even though I'm in here and he technically has all the power.

The door to the stairs leading to the ground level office opens, and I see a dark figure enter, holding something before the door closes with a near slam, cutting off the bright light at his back. I can't help the big grin on my face to see my other guard with a canteen and a chunk of bread. He walks up to my cell, only hesitating once he's within arm's reach. He raises an eyebrow in question.

"Nope, still one hundred percent human," I say, trying to ease his worries.

Guard number one snickers, which seems to make this one want to prove a point. He approaches and hands the food and water to me through the bars. I accept it and try not to take the slight tremble of his hands personally.

"Thanks," I say, giving him a weak smile.

"Not a problem." He withdraws his hands a little faster than necessary.

I plop down in the corner of my cell and cross my legs, first taking a long drink, until about half of it is gone. Then I eat the bread and sip until both are gone. It wasn't much, but the water makes the bread expand, making me feel full.

The three of us don't talk the rest of the time they are here. Though guard number two—my favorite, who tells me his name is Phillip—brings me water once more before the end of his shift. Two new guards replace them after a while and the silence continues. These ones don't talk to me even though I try a few times. At least they aren't aggressive like guard number one.

I'm relieved when Phillip comes back later on, and this time he's alone.

"How are you doing?" he asks, walking right up to the cell bars.

I give him an incredulous look and snort, not bothering to get up off the floor.

"Right, right... sorry. That was a stupid question." He has the good sense to look embarrassed. "I'm just here to let you out, unless... you feel like you might be turning?"

"Nope, I feel as human as ever," I say, jumping up to my feet.

"Good, because I think there's someone who's anxious to see you. He's been asking about you non-stop."

I can feel my face brighten. "Jace?"

He nods and pulls out a set of keys then unlocks the door. "Yeah, he'll be happy you're finally free." He pauses and his face turns serious. "I'm sorry about all of this." He waves a hand around, indicating the cell and, I'm assuming, the treatment. "We don't get many new people anymore. Not after the first few months. There were a few who were bitten that lied about it and ended up turning. It was almost disastrous, so we don't take any chances. They also tend to give the minimum amount of food and water, depending on how strong they think someone is."

I harrumph. "They must have thought I was pretty strong then."

He laughs then says, "Yeah, actually they did. Most people don't fight on their way to the cells. But if it's any consolation, if anyone who lives here gets hurt on a mission, we get the same treatment."

I shake my head. "Not really, I mean, even people who are about to die should get better treatment than that. Turning into a runner is just a worse death sentence than most."

"You're right, and I agree. Too bad the higher ups don't see it quite the same way." He offers me his arm. "Anyway, let's go get you cleaned up and get you a place to stay, and a real meal."

I take his arm, and he leads me up the stairs and outside. I take in a deep lungful of fresh air, and before I can adjust to the bright light of day, I'm being wrapped up in two strong arms. I would recognize his familiar embrace anywhere—*Jace*. I wish I could say I'd never been happier to see him, but I have felt this way before many times since we met.

"Are you okay? Did they hurt you?" he asks, pulling away and looking me up and down.

"Yes, I'm fine," I say.

Jace frowns and lifts a hand to brush away a tear that had

escaped. *Crap, when did I start crying?*

"Ray tell me—" he glares at Phillip like he's about to murder him.

"No really, I'm just tired and I'm so happy to see you." I give him my best smile. "Phillip made sure I was okay." Just as our reunion is about to get underway, guard number one shows his face again, eliciting a groan I can't hold back.

"Jace, it's time for your training," he calls.

Jace's shoulders slump, and he gives me an apologetic smile. "I'll see you a little bit later?"

"Don't worry about her, I'll make sure she's taken care of and show her around the compound," Phillip says.

The main gate we entered through faces west, but the compound ends up being quite a bit smaller than I'd expected. Not considering the amount of people they claim to hold. During the tour, I hardly see anyone. Apparently, it really only gets busy during meal times. The quarantine area for those who just get back from their missions is in the same building as the cells, only they are above ground and are much more accommodating. I can't imagine many people would be willing to go on missions if they were essentially thrown into those prison-like cells upon their return every time—the ones where I spent a cool three days simmering in. Then to the North is the large dining hall.

When I ask about where people sleep and train, Phillip explains that all of that is underground. I'll get a tour of that area once my living quarters are assigned. He's confidant I'll end up with Jace, seeing as how we are bonded. I am more than okay with that.

Just as we finish, the man I recognize as being the one to order me into the cell comes marching up to us. He is dressed as an average man, around his early forties, but has the air of someone who has had military experience.

"That will be good for now. I'll take care of Miss..." He pauses and raises an eyebrow in my direction.

"Marrow," I say.

"Yes, I'll take over from here and personally escort Miss Marrow to her living quarters."

Phillip doesn't hesitate before accepting the orders and after a brief goodbye leaves me alone with this new tour guide. I can't help the slight sting of abandonment, though logically I understand.

"Miss Marrow, I am Mitch Ross, but you can call me Ross," he states gruffly.

I blink at him. Was that supposed to be friendly? Most people who give you their full name followed by "*call me*" usually insist on first names. I suppose he's settling for more formal.

He leads me to a door with a rounded entrance that sticks up then bends down into the ground. It reminds me of a giant slinky.

"There are no free rides here, Miss Marrow. We operate like a hive here and you will be expected to train, go on missions, and help out with some aspect that helps this place run the everyday functions so we can continue surviving for a long time to come."

I bristle at his tone but remain quiet as we make our way through the doorway and down to where the living quarters are.

The stairs are lit by some kind of industrial lighting, and I can't imagine how they fit so many people in this place… that is until we reach the bottom.

The ceiling is at least fifteen feet high, and the walls and floors are all made of metal. The constant hum of what I assume is a generator buzzes quietly through the walls.

He points as he speaks, "This is built like a big box. If you follow the hall in either direction, it will lead you all the way around. Down to the right is the men's quarters, the back wall is the couples' section, after that is the women's quarters. The training hall is this large section in the center. You'll be assigned a training schedule and a trainer by the end of the night." He drops his hand and points in the other direction. "Over there is the firing range and the ammo room. You will learn how to wield a gun and reload empty rounds—we do not waste things here."

I nod, accepting the terms. I have nothing against guns, not after what happened at the final gas station. In fact, a gun would have come in handy.

Ross gives me a quick tour, showing me each area, starting with the firing range and training room. We don't go in depth, as he said whoever my trainer is will show me the details. I'm not about to complain because he's not exactly a warm individual and the shorter this tour is, the better. We just stick our heads in the door, then we're out. In each area, there are several groups of people training. Target practice is not only with guns but also with bows and knives.

There's even a boxing ring in the main training room where a few people are fighting. I try to find Jace but can't seem to spot him. I do see Mon'te and Des sparing. They almost look like they are dancing, their moves are fast—accurate—they know each other's rhythms so well that they don't pull a single move. Each move is designed to inflict the maximum amount of damage. After spending days and days with them traveling across a state, they never once showed how deadly their fighting skills were. It's impressive.

"Do you have any questions?" Ross asks, pulling back and heading to the start of our tour.

I have so many, but I start with, "Why at Devils Tower?"

"There are compounds at all national monuments. They are hard to miss, and they make good markers for civilians so that they know where to go." He manages to look annoyed even though he's the one to ask if I had any questions. "Anything else?"

I take that to mean that he'd rather I not ask anything more. Which is fine with me. I can ask almost literally anyone else and probably get better answers. "Nope, I was just curious about that."

"Good, I will show you to your bunker in the women's quarters."

"What about, Jace?" I ask. I thought I'd be put with him…

could Phillip have been wrong?

"He is living with the men. Don't worry about him." Then he starts walking away from where I stand.

Reluctantly, I follow, not liking how we have no say about being together. Something constricts in my stomach, making me feel uneasy.

I look longingly at the couples' quarters as we pass the last of them. Ross continues to lead me farther and farther away, until we nearly reach the end of the women's quarters. We could have gone down the hall past the firing range, but he took me this way. And part of me can't help but think he did that on purpose to rub in the fact that he'll be separating Jace and me.

He stops in front of a door with the label G572 in bold block letters.

"You can't split them up," Garcia snaps from the neighboring door. I jump, nearly tripping over my own two feet as I take a few steps to the side. She pushes off the wall and stomps forward. "You know they are bonded. She stays with Jace'el."

She's ordering him. We had a moment the night we lost Scotty, but she's the last person I expected to fight for me. They stare at each other for a long moment. I expect him to dismiss her and pull rank.

After a moment, he grunts, "Fine, go get him, meet us at Delta bunk in five minutes."

She runs off without another word. Then he starts walking again without speaking to me, but this time we are headed back the way we came. I hurry to catch up, keeping a few paces behind him.

Ross takes me to a room similar to the first, only this one is in what he called the couples' quarters. The number on the door reads D42. He ushers me inside then leaves, saying someone will come by with my daily schedule later on.

Not sure what to do, I sit on the bed and wait for Jace to come.

Chapter Seventeen

You Again

It's been way more than five minutes… according to the clock on the wall it's been more like half an hour. At this point, I'm not sure if Garcia knows exactly where to bring Jace. My hands twist in my lap as I wait. I've been stuck in a cell for several days, and once released, I got a quick and dirty tour then unceremoniously dropped off at where I'll be staying.

It's not as welcoming as I had imagined it would be. But I suppose it makes sense as there are too many people to care about feelings. Everything is about survival and necessity.

When Jace comes in through the door, the look on his face makes my heart skip a beat. It's a mixture of worry, surprise, and relief. Sweat from whatever training he was doing glistens on the skin of his face, neck, shoulders, and arms. The tight-fitting tank he's wearing must have been given to him, and I am *not* complaining.

He scoops me up in his arms and holds me tight. "What are you doing here? I thought you were staying with me."

I lean back just enough to look him in the eye. "They didn't tell you? You were staying in the single men's quarters—we'll be staying here together from now on."

Confusion crosses his face for a brief moment. He was apparently a little misled, which I'm guessing it was thanks to Ross. I'm not sure what I did to the man who seemed to hate me on sight, but I refuse to let him get to me. And as long as I have Jace at my side, everything is right in my world, and I know we can make it through anything together.

There's a knock on the door and we both turn to see Garcia standing in the threshold with a bundle of clothes in her arms. She's followed by a tall blonde woman with more grace than I could dream to possess. Her hair has been pulled back into a tight ponytail, and she's obviously been working out. She doesn't even spare a glance in my direction—her attention is completely and solely on Jace. The telltale signs of three lines on either side of her neck mark her as a Vor'onin.

"We must return to training," she says in a matter of fact tone before turning on her heel and striding out.

I glance to Garcia, who rolls her eyes and plops down on the bed, still holding everything.

"I'm sorry, Ray, I will be back soon. We can talk more then." Then he kisses me deeply, but far too briefly, before heading out the door.

Garcia is looking awkwardly at the door even after he's gone and it's just the two of us.

"So," I start, "what is all of this?"

She stands quickly and shoves everything into my arms. "Just some basics. Toothbrush, hairbrush, some workout clothes—I had to guess your size so let me know if you need something different. There's some basic tops and underwear. I wasn't sure what else to grab that you might need, but we can always get you that stuff later."

I drop the stuff on the bed and say, "Thank you."

She looks at me like she has no idea why I would possibly be thanking her. "It's just basic necessities. I give this stuff to everyone that comes in."

"No, I mean for making sure Jace and I weren't split up. I mean… it wouldn't be the end of the world as long as we're both here, but we've spent two years together… alone. This will take some getting used to."

A blush creeps across her face, followed by a look of heartbreaking sorrow, but it's gone in the blink of an eye. "I told you about Tris'an… I know what you two feel for each other, I get the bond—and if he were still here with me, I wouldn't want to be without him. This world has gone to shit, love is all we have left." She rubs her hands over her face then drops them to her sides. "Anyway, I don't know why I'm telling you any of this. Masters is going to be your trainer, he requested you specifically. He'll be here later with your assignments and the rest of your things will be dropped off shortly."

My trainer requested me specifically? My brows furrow. "Sorry… Who is Masters?"

Garcia stops in the doorway, one hand resting on the frame. "Phillip Masters. He was one of the guys guarding you down in the cells. Looks like you made an impression on him."

Those last few words seemed to be a bit miffed. I can only imagine it's her lack of fondness for me shining through again.

"Is everyone treated like that?"

She heaves a sigh. "Basically. Anyone with an injury gets thrown in there. Don't take it personally. Ross is just a good ol' boy with misogynistic tendencies, but he won't do anything to hurt you or put you in danger, he's just an ass who somehow still thinks women aren't capable of doing the same things a man can do. It's irritating as hell, but he has no choice but to allow it. The bonds people have with the Vor'onins helps some." She brushes a thick lock of hair from her shoulder. "Anyway, dinner is in two hours, you might want to get clean."

Then she leaves and I'm alone again. Only this time, I feel more at ease.

I quickly go through the things Garcia brought and pick out

everything I need for the moment then head into the small cramped bathroom. *Definitely only room for one.* All I care about right now is taking a shower and feeling a little bit more like my old self.

It takes us a while to get used to how things run and the rules. Jace has an easier time than I do. For someone so young, I seem to be set in my ways and reluctant to change. But I do. A month passes, then two, then six.

It's the middle of summer when things change.

Around an hour before noon, I walk out of the kitchen and stretch, soaking in the heat of the summer sun. I have a few hours free, so I decide to visit Jace in the med clinic.

I make my way across the open center that everything is built around. It reminds me of those old civil war settlements, only everything here is made of hard metal rather than entirely of wood.

Shouts from the catwalk on the upper section of the fence echo through the hive. They point their guns and voices on the other side answer. I stop to watch. One of the scouting parties is returning.

The men on the catwalk lower their guns and wave them through as the gate opens. Mon'te, Des, and Jos'lin walk through the gate. I raise my hand to wave and stop when I see they are followed by three others, two of them team members I don't know, but the third figure I do know. And I see red.

Ice water seems to run through my veins.

Without thinking, I sprint toward the group.

"Hey, Ray," Des starts, his smile quickly dropping as I shove past him as if I didn't know he was there.

"You again?" Brian says turning to face me, recognition sparking in his shit colored eyes.

"I'm going to kill you!" I spit out and lunge toward Brian.

The smile drops from his stupid face. I don't give him a chance to react before my fist connects with his jaw. My hand hurts like hell the second it connects, but his head snaps to the side and he stumbles back and trips, landing hard on his ass.

I'm jerked back by two strong hands gripping my upper arms.

"Let me go!" I growl.

"Raylinn, what the hell are you doing?" Des demands at my back.

"Keep that bitch away from me," Brian snaps from his position on the ground. He wipes the back of his hand across his mouth, and I smile at seeing the thin trail of blood left behind.

"You two know each other?" Mon'te asks.

"Yes," I say through gritted teeth. "This is the piece of shit who stole all of our things after we saved his ass."

"I'm going to let you go now, but you can't attack each

other." Desmond's meaning is clear enough.

It's the cells again if I kill him. I'm half tempted to do it anyway. It would be worth it.

Brian stands and approaches me, but I can't help but notice he stands a fair bit out of my arm's reach. "Stop overreacting. You are alive, aren't you? Hell, you made it here before I did."

"Is that supposed to make me feel better?" I ask in dumb shock that he's actually acting like it's not a big deal.

"I'm surprised you made it."

"No thanks to you!" My muscles twitch as I force myself to refrain from beating him to a pulp. "You left Jace and I for dead in the middle of nowhere. If you wanted to go it alone so badly, the least you could have done was leave us with our supplies."

He shrugs. "I needed it more. Besides, I didn't think you'd end up coming here after I left."

I blink several times really fast and look around at the confused faces around us. *Am I hearing this douche right?* "Like hell you needed it more. And is that supposed to make it okay that you stole everything from us? We could have died!"

"You know," he says, looking at me and adopting a thin veneer of confidence I can see through. He's measuring me up to see if I'm about to attack him again. "I'm surprised you made it with you acting as leader between the two of you."

A buzzing fills my head and I can barely control my seething.

"Okay, that's enough for now. Jos'lin, maybe you should

take Ray somewhere else for now, we'll take care of Brian."

She nods and approaches me. "Come, I will take you to Jace."

Des and Mon'te position themselves between Brian and me, blocking my view of him. Jos'lin takes my arm and leads me away. I'm still so pissed that I know she can feel me shake under her hand.

I can't stop myself, I call out over my shoulder, "You better stay the hell away from me, Brian, because if you ever come near me again, you will regret it!"

Chapter Eighteen

Dread Settles

I don't see Brian again, though I know he's around. I also haven't seen Mon'te or Des either, which makes me suspect that they are keeping him on an opposite schedule.

Jos'lin had her hands filled with my ranting, and while Jace was furious when he learned of Brian's arrival, his was more of a quiet upset. Eventually, I calmed and swore that if I did run across him that I wouldn't slug him again, even if he did deserve it, but would ignore him instead. I wouldn't risk us getting kicked out over someone like him.

The days soon become monotonous. After years of always being on guard, it's hard to get used to all the walls. Though sleeping next to Jace at the same time, every night, is a welcome change even if I still can't sleep straight through the night. Several times during the first week, I'd sit up in bed and fumble around. And since the one time I fell out of bed and smashed my shin on the metal foot of the bed, Jace has taken to leaving a candle burning all night so when and if I wake up, I'll know instantly where we are and that we're safe.

Our time here is filled with training. Jace is working as an assistant to the doctor here since he has some training in it already, but as for me? I get the joy of being regulated to kitchen duties. Washing dishes and prepping food is mind numbing like I never thought possible. Though I have to say it's managed to make me look forward to training with Phillip. I throw myself into our workouts because it's the mental and physical stimulation I need.

Phillip is impressed with how well I've picked up on using a gun. I don't tell him that the image of Scotty being enveloped by the horde, and that ride away from that last gas station, are my motivators. Soon I'll be considered "ready" to go out on missions as Desmond, Mon'te, and Garcia had when they found us, and I want to be prepared—though no one has explained what exactly ready means, or how it will be determined.

Phillip is training me how to box, which I have not picked up on as well. So we focus mainly on defensive moves and ways to escape if a runner somehow gets too close. Once he learned about my weapon of choice—the golf club—he started having me practice with a sword for an hour a day. Where they got this, I don't know, and while it seems a little odd to use a sword during what is essentially a zombie apocalypse, I am not going to lie, it's kind of cool. It's heavier than my golf club, so I suppose if nothing else, it's strengthening my arms.

I hardly ever see Jace anymore. We try to meet up for meals, but even with Phillip's attempts at moving our training schedule around a bit, we seem to miss each other more often than not.

At least we have the nights together.

On one of the rarer days off we have that match up, we lay in bed skipping breakfast. His arms wrap around me, holding me to his muscular chest. I inhale his scent. God, he smells so good. I listen to the steady beat of his heart as his fingers gently comb through my hair. I'm so relaxed, my eyes drift closed and I can feel the edges of sleep slowly drift over me, covering me like a warm blanket.

I nearly jump out of my skin when someone starts knocking on the door, which is much closer to pounding it down than a civilized knock. Jace's arms tighten around me instinctively before loosening.

He grumbles then moves out from the covers as he calls out, "Just a moment."

I flop back to the pillows, mourning the loss of our quiet morning. Nothing good can come from that knock. With a huff, I throw back the covers and hurry to dress. Jace waits at the door until I'm ready then opens it. Ross's face glowers from the other side.

Yeah, nothing good can come from his visit.

He ignores me, which I prefer over his attention.

"Jace'el?" he says. "You are to report for a mission in one hour. You're heading out."

I open my mouth to protest—not that I have a leg to stand on—but he's gone before my brain can even attempt to make my mouth form words. With a grim expression, Jace turns to me.

"No, it's our day off… you can't go," I pout.

Jace strides over to me. "I must go. You know as well as I that it's part of the requirements of staying here."

I know it's safer to be here, where we have the responsibilities and help of others with the same goal… but I still hate it. I miss the life we had when we were living in the wild. I miss the routine we had together, even if we were constantly exhausted, at least we lived and worked on our own terms and we never faced danger without each other. Here we have to depend on people we hardly know to have our backs.

"Then let's leave," I say, though we both know I don't mean it. This whole thing is a trade off. We lose some of the freedoms we've grown to want and depend on in exchange for walls that, while sometimes feel a little claustrophobic, are probably a lot safer. We get more people with the same mission; keep the runners out and survive another day.

He takes my face in his hands and gives me a sad smile. "Ray, I hate that we hardly see each other too, but once we get used to this, I know things will change and we can be together."

I can't help but frown. "It won't be the same."

"I know, but it will get better. Nothing will keep us apart."

Jace places a kiss on my mouth. "I promise." Then he kisses me again. I sink into his embrace, wrapping my arms around his neck and pulling myself into him. He ends the kiss too soon for my liking.

"I have to get ready to go," he whispers as he lets his hands glide from my face, down my neck and shoulders and arms.

I watch him prepare, and I'm on the verge of being in a full on pout. "I don't like the idea of you going out there without me. How do I know I can trust them with your life?"

He laughs, shaking his head and holds his hand out to me. "Walk with me?"

I'm being overprotective and grumpy because our day off was ruined and I know it. We've been together since day one, it feels wrong for him to go without me.

I take his hand then walk with him in silence through the halls and up and out to the front gate. As we reach the group of people who'll be going with him, Ross gives me a look as though he thinks I'm trying to sneak out with them… not a bad idea, but it wasn't my plan.

I stay by Jace's side for as long as I can. Then he walks through the gates and they clang shut behind him. The noise reverberates through my bones and I can't seem to shake the feeling of dread that settles in the pit of my stomach.

Chapter Nineteen

Other Side of the Nightmare

"I thought they were only going to be gone for a few days," I say quietly to Garcia as I lean against the counter in the industrialized kitchen.

She heaves a sigh and sets down her knife. "Look, either grab a knife or go do some training or whatever."

I walk over to the corner and pick up a knife, then rejoin her. It's supposed to be my free time, but I'm on edge and worried about Jace. They were supposed to be back three days ago.

"I'm sorry, I just… don't know who else to talk to." I pick up a potato and begin slicing. "I have this sinking feeling. I haven't been able to shake it since they left."

"It is strange you two were split up… but I wouldn't put too much stock into it. You have to remember there was some confusion when you two arrived with us. He was brought in right away—you weren't brought in until after you got out of the cell. It's entirely possible you two aren't in the system together like you should be."

I stop chopping for a moment. I hadn't thought of that.

"Once we're done here, I will help you figure it out," she says calmly before I can react.

In the almost three weeks Jace has been gone, I've hardly slept at all, and I can feel it wearing on me. I've also taken to searching out Garcia to talk. Despite her sometimes snarky comments, something tells me she doesn't mind. In all the time I've been spending with her, not many people talk to her. She seems to be warming up to me though.

We continue to prepare food for dinner. The variety we have access to isn't the biggest, but at least it's mostly fresh and locally grown. With whatever the scouting parties bring back.

"Marrow! What are you doing here?" Lilly's cheery voice pops up as she enters the room.

I swivel on the stool I parked myself on and wave to her. "Hey, Lil, I just came by to chat with Xiomara," I say, using Garcia's first name only to get a rise out of her. I also really love her name and wish she'd let me use it.

Garcia glares at us both then mutters under her breath. "Ugh, I really do hate you, you know."

"I'm kidding, I was only playing with you." I stick out my tongue. It's childish, but it still earns me a hint of a smile from her.

Lilly continues to putter around the large kitchen, double

checking to see what needs to be taken care of and making sure the schedule is being followed to the letter. She's very much her father's daughter. Only nice.

I don't know how someone so cheery and energetic could be related to Ross. Lilly is twenty-two and the daughter of the leader of this place. It took me a few days to realize who she was. For the first week I knew her, I thought Lilly was her last name since everyone here almost exclusively uses last names unless they happen to be family or good friends. Which is why I take it as a good sign that Garcia even told me she had a first name let alone what it was.

From the open window, we hear the creek and slamming of the gates, then yelling. It takes a moment for the meaning of those noises to hit home, and by the time I can even think about moving, Garcia grabs a hold of my arm and drags me outside.

Jace is back!

I can tell something is wrong the second we look to the gates. The two tower guards are pointing their rifles down at the returned group, and two of the men are helping another walk. Except, it's just not any man they are helping to walk. It's Jace.

My heart nearly stops in my chest. He's heavily favoring one leg, and everyone seems to be shouting at each other. Then the two holding him up are leading him not toward the infirmary, but toward the cells.

"Jace!" I call, running toward him.

Before I can catch up, Phillip appears seemingly out of

nowhere and catches me with an arm around my middle. "Raylinn, no. You can't go with him." The calm of his voice infuriates me for some reason.

"Let me go!" I snap while wriggling around and try to get out of his hold. Why is he so freakishly strong? "I need to see him, he's hurt!"

Phillip's hold on me tightens and I can barely breathe. He lowers his head and whispers, "Exactly, Ray, he's hurt. You *know* the protocol to this. There are no exceptions."

Though quiet, his words have a finality to them that breaks my fighting spirit. I have to know what happened to him. I need to see him. What if he was bitten or scratched? I can't just let him turn without telling him I love him one more time, without a chance to say goodbye.

"Let her go. I'll take her back to her room," Garcia says from beside me.

Phillip releases me and Garcia takes me by the arm and offers me her sleeve. "Use this to dry your eyes."

I feel like a kid drying my tears on her sleeve like this. I hadn't even realized I was crying. I'm grateful for her attempt at saving a little bit of my dignity. Even though I want nothing more than to tear away from her and run for Jace, I let her lead me toward the underground bunker of this settlement. I trust her.

I can't bring myself to speak until we get back to the small living quarters Jace and I have been staying at, fearing that if I opened my mouth I'd burst into tears. This room feels even more empty and cold than before.

I can't sit still, so I pace nervously around the room then turn on her. "I have to see him… what if—what if—" I can't say the words. Just the possibility is enough to break my heart.

"I know, but defying orders won't help you right now. I'll tell you what, how about I talk to some people and see what I can find out. But I need you to stay here for now, okay?" She places her fists on her hips and gives me a pointed look. "I mean it. There's no way you'll see him if you piss Ross off. You seem to have a talent for it."

I continue to walk from one side of the room to the other, not caring how ridiculous it looks. The space is small, and it only takes about three and a half steps to cross the room. Adrenaline and fear course through my veins, and I can barely feel my limbs. Small pinpricks tingle through my arms. "I feel sick."

"Ray," Garcia says, firmly grabbing me by the shoulders. "You need to calm down, you're going to pass out if you don't breathe. Leave it to me. I'll find out what happened, and I swear I'll tell you as soon as I know anything."

"No matter the time?"

"No matter the time." She gives me a reassuring smile. "I'll see if I can get you out of training today, but something tells me that won't be too hard."

Just as she's leaving, Lilly pops her head in through the doorway.

"Knock, knock!" she announces, earning a scowl from

Garcia. I'm inclined to mirror Garcia's reaction, not being in the mood for anyone or anything upbeat.

Lilly lets herself in and seems to realize her mood doesn't fit the situation. "Ray, I just stopped by to see if you were going to make it to dinner tonight."

I plop my butt down on to the bed and shake my head. "I don't think so. I don't think I could eat."

What's left of her smile fades. She walks over to me and puts an arm around my shoulder. It's a bit awkward, but I allow it, not wanting to hurt her feelings. She is trying to be comforting. Thankfully the embrace doesn't last long.

"I'm so sorry about Jace'el, Ray. I'm sure he'll be okay."

"Do you know what happened?" I ask with a little more energy than I mean to as I spin to face her.

"No, I'm sorry I don't. But I'm sure Daddy would have told me if something was wrong." Lilly offers me a shrug. Suddenly she looks a little nervous as she twists her fingers in her lap. "I hate to say this because I know you're worried for him, but I couldn't get you out of kitchen duty after dinner."

I let out a breath. I thought she was going to say something really awful and hopeless. But dishes? It's fine. I mean, doing dishes while the man you love is locked up and you have no idea if he'll be okay or if he'll turn into a runner… sure. There are a million other things I could be doing instead, like wearing a hole in the ground as I pace, or digging a tunnel with a spoon trying to get to him so I can see for myself. Dishes seem pointless, but

I can do that.

"That's okay," I say, trying to sound as neutral as possible. "Thanks for trying."

The clock on the wall dings the hour. Dinner is over. With a groan, I push up and trudge my way up the steps and out into the open area of the compound, making my way toward the dining hall. Dinner came and went faster than I'd wanted. I'd stared at that damned clock the entire time, waiting for Garcia to return and tell me *something* about what happened with Jace.

No one speaks to me as I pass through the dining hall and into the kitchen at the back. No one in the kitchen even looks at me, not directly anyway. I feel like a leper… Like I exist separately from everyone. They feel sorry for me and don't know what to say, that much is clear when they turn away really fast or avert their gaze as if they weren't staring at me seconds before.

I do my best to ignore them. Was this what Jace went through when I was left to chill down in the cells?

I set to starting on the dishes with the others on the same duty, only they talk and make banal conversation as if life is great. And maybe for them it is, but it's so hard to be here knowing Jace is outside these walls is at this very moment. I push down the sting of tears that burn their way to my eyes. I want my mom and dad… I want them to comfort me. But I'll never have them again… and Jace, the only one I have left, might be taken from me as well.

If that happens, I have no idea what I'll do. Likely lose my mind.

Just as my thoughts start to plummet into a really dark space, I'm hip-checked gently. I take a step to the right and look up to see Garcia settling in at my side.

"Hey, Linn, move over," she says, using the nickname she came up for me based on my least favorable reaction.

"Did you find out anything?" I blurt. I know the answer before she opens her mouth.

"Not yet. I still have some people to talk to. I wasn't able to talk to the rest of his team—they've been in a meeting with Ross since they've returned."

"So then, not to look a gift horse in the mouth or anything, but… why *are* you here?"

"You helped me earlier so I'm returning the favor," Garcia says it like it's no big deal. After a long moment, she glances at me from the corner of her eyes, then adds barely above a whisper, "I thought you might need someone who understands what you're going through."

We fall into silence after that. She's right, I did need her presence. She, more than anyone else, knows exactly what I'm going through and what I may or may not have to face. Her situation ended the worst way imaginable… and I pray mine doesn't.

The lights go out in the underground bunker long before I fall asleep. The soft glow of the overhead red lights that come on at ten every night without fail filters in through the small crack at the bottom of the door. I still know nothing about Jace's situation, and I'm damn near crawling out of my skin from it. I need to do something.

As if on cue to that thought, a furious knocking on the door has me jumping out of bed and stumbling halfway across the room before I realize what I'm doing. Bleary eyed, I open the door to find Garcia standing there like she's been waiting for a long time.

"Wha-?" is all I manage to sputter before she pushes me out of the way and closes the door behind her.

"Get dressed, we are going on a mission." A glint sparks in her eye.

"What? A mission, but don't they leave in the day or—"

She throws her hands up like I'm being purposefully dense. "Not an official mission, Ray, a *secret* mission."

It takes a few seconds for me to get it. But give me a break, I was just about to fall asleep. I don't even wait to hear about the details before rushing to throw on some dark clothes.

Garcia shoves a black ball cap on my head, instructing me to keep my eyes on the ground then leads me through the corridors and out into the central part of the above ground compound.

"Follow my lead," she instructs. She walks with purpose as if she's doing exactly what she should be, and I attempt to imitate her the best I can. I don't know what her plan or goal is exactly, but I trust her.

Though we stick to the shadows as much as possible, we still run into a few guards, but a few choice words from Garcia and they go back to minding their own business. None of them even bother to look at me.

I have no idea where we are going until she stops and says, "We're here."

I look around, but it's way too dark for me to know where *here* is. "Umm, where exactly are we?"

She mutters a curse under her breath and says, "The cells. Where else would I take you in the middle of the night?"

I don't say anything because I don't think I ever expected her to take me anywhere in the middle of the night. Though the cells kind of makes sense now. I must still be half asleep.

"Stay here and try not to draw attention to yourself." Then before I can mutter so much as an *Okay,* she's off.

Garcia goes in through the heavy metal door, closing it quietly behind her rather than letting it slam from its own weight. A few minutes later and guard number one comes walking out the door—one of these days, I should learn his name… but then he's not exactly my favorite person so who cares. Seriously, what kind of person denies water to someone just because they are in a cell for a possible scratch?

He moves to the side of the building and… *oh gross*. He's peeing practically in the open like he's some kind of wild animal.

Garcia pops her head out and waves me over. I crouch and run, trying to stay as quiet as possible, only straightening once I'm inside the door.

"Come on, we don't have much time before Fred gets back. I told him to take a walk and find his girlfriend. He'll be busy for a few minutes at least."

The thought that I never would have pegged him to be able to get anyone to date him flits through my head but is quickly replaced by thoughts of Jace.

She leads me through the dark hall and down several steps I don't remember being dragged down. We come out in a large, concrete square room with a handful of cells lining one wall, and Phillip standing guard across one in particular.

He turns to us, his mouth dropping open. "Ray? Garcia? What the hell? You know—"

"Shut it, Phil, she has every right to see him and know what's going on. I don't care what Ross told you."

His mouth pinches into a tight line, and he looks as if he might object to our being here for a long moment before motioning us forward. "Just make it quick. We don't need Fred in here throwing a fit."

I rush to the cell he indicates, and I fall to my knees before it, gripping the bars so hard my fingers ache. Jace is lying on a cot up against the far wall, his back to us. His body is in a fetal position, so unlike him. It makes my heart ache.

This time I find myself on the outside looking in, but the cells are still very much a nightmare.

His cell is by far less accommodating than anyone deserves, but it has a bed and it's more than what I was graced with, probably due to Ross's tendency to favor Vor'onins. He wants to stay on his good side for their tech or whatever, I haven't figured it out yet, but I can tell there's some motivation there.

"Jace?" I say his name softly, not sure if he's okay or not. He hadn't heard us, and if he did, is he too hurt or too far gone to think of turning around? "Jace…" I say his name a little louder.

For a long moment, he doesn't stir. Then his shoulder twitches before he partially rolls over to peer at me. His dark hair half obscures his eye. It feels as if forever passes between us as I wait for that spark of recognition.

In a flash, he's sitting up and gazing at me with wide amber eyes that, to my relief, are just as clear and bright as they've always been. "Ray?"

I smile and nod, reaching a hand through the bar. He stumbles over to me and drops to his knees, pressing his body against the barrier just as I am. We hug each other as tightly as we can stand to, until the metal digs into my shoulders, threatening to pop them out of their sockets or bruise bone.

"Ray, what are you doing here? They said no visitors."

"It was Garcia, she brought me here. They won't tell me

what happened? Are you all right? What did happen out there?"
I can't seem to stop the volley of questions bursting from
my mouth.

"I'm fine, Raylinn, I promise. There were runners on our
tail as we were gathering supplies, we had to hop a fence to get
away. My leg got caught in some wire as I was helping Jos'lin
over. It cut pretty deep but… no runners came close to touching
me, or any of us. I'll be out soon. I promise." A lock of hair falls
forward over his brow, and I brush it away. He looks so tired.
"You should go," he says quietly, "before they catch you."

I open my mouth to protest—I only just got here—but he
cups my face in his hands and kisses me through the space
between the bars.

I hear Phillip start to say something, but he must have been
cut off with an elbow to the ribs if the *omph* that follows was
any indication.

I try to pull Jace closer to me and deepen the kiss, but he
pulls away.

"I love you, Ray… I'll see you soon, I promise. Now, go
before Ross finds out you came to see me. I don't want you
getting into any trouble before I'm free."

Reluctantly, I nod and push myself up off the floor and let
Garcia lead me out of these horrible cells, my heart a fraction
lighter for knowing he'll be returned to me soon.

Chapter Twenty

Sanctuary

The next two days drag slower than should have be possible. I try my best to behave, making sure I do my job and show up to training, while I spend almost all my free time in my room pacing. I don't want to do anything to risk delaying my reunion with Jace. I take comfort in knowing he will get out and that we will be together again, and most importantly, he will *not* be turning into a runner.

"That is about the thousandth time you've sighed in the last hour." Lilly's voice makes me jump. "What is going on with you, Ray? Are you still worried for Jace?"

Her voice scares the crap out of me and I almost drop the glass I'm holding back into the soapy water. I glance over my shoulder. "Oh, I didn't know you were in here," I say lamely.

The last thing Garcia, Phillip, Jace, or I need is for anyone to find out that I broke the rules, with their help, and went to go see him.

"I'm sure Jace is just fine," she says, walking over to me and patting me on the shoulder. "If he was going to turn, it probably would have happened by now and we would have taken care of it. This is just a precaution."

Her voice borders on cheery, it's almost disturbing. I blink at her for a moment, wondering how someone could look at a survivor possibly turning in such a casual manner.

Yes, killing runners is part of life now. But that doesn't mean they weren't once people. That doesn't mean they don't have loved ones to mourn their loss. They aren't simply a problem to be taken care of. It is a complicated situation. It's easier if you don't know the infected beforehand. Life doesn't come packaged in a perfectly wrapped present like that.

Not knowing exactly how to respond, I just gave her a weak smile and nod.

"I just can't wait to see him again," I offer, and it almost comes out as a question rather than the statement I mean for it to be.

"It won't be much longer now, but you might want to hurry up with those dishes," she says, heading out the door.

I really needed to talk to someone about finding a different "job" in this place, something I am good at, something that is mentally stimulating.

I've had my doubts about this job being randomly assigned

to me when everyone else talked about what they did before, and where their skills were before getting assigned. Everyone else but me. Something tells me it's Ross's way of trying to remind me of where he thinks I belong. I'd much rather be out tending to the gardens, feeling the earth between my fingers and watching my hard work grow into something.

———

I can't bring myself to go back to the underground quarters just yet. I know I have to go to training soon, but Phillip let me know that as long as everything goes as planned, Jace should be getting out today. I expected him to be released this morning, but when the afternoon came and went, followed by dinner, and hours later he still hasn't been released. My nerves grow and tighten in my stomach like a painful knot.

I pace behind the large dining hall building, wringing my hands and not taking my eyes off the door that leads to the cells on the opposite end of the compound.

As I turn to continue pacing the other direction, I spot Phillip headed this way, his fake angry expression in place. Well, it looks like I've been caught. Not that Phillip would actually care that I'm planning on skipping training today, but he'll fake it for appearances since Ross will expect him to rip me a new one.

Before Phillip reaches me, the door to the cells along the south wall open. My legs go weak with anticipation.

First, one guard walks out, and I hold my breath, then another guard who helps Jace walk. He's not as weak as he'd been when he returned, but there's still a deep enough wound that he's favoring his left leg.

They don't lead him toward the underground but toward the small infirmary next door. I rush to follow, ignoring Phillip as he calls my name. They wouldn't tell me anything while he was in there, and if it weren't for Garcia, I still wouldn't know anything, so I refuse to let them keep us apart any longer.

I am closing in on the makeshift clinic when I slow to a snail's pace as Ross descends the ladder from the watch post at the top of the front gate and strides into the clinic.

Damn.

I push forward anyway and enter the clinic without hesitation. Ross's head snaps toward me. It's obvious I interrupted their conversation. Jace lies on a gurney between them as the doctor checks him out.

"Ray," Jace says, lifting his hand, calling me to his side. The smile on his face melts my heart.

The doctor moves to the side and explains to Ross—not Jace—that he'll be okay but needs a few stitches and should heal up in a couple of days.

Jace smiles warmly at me, practically pulling me onto the gurney with him. I avoid sitting on it, but compromise by leaning against it. With his arm around me, it feels like we are in our own little world. Nothing and no one else matters.

"I'm so glad you're okay," I whisper to him.

Ross clears his throat, loudly. "Shouldn't you be *training* right now, Marrow?"

"Let them be," Doctor Vazquez cuts in. "They haven't see each other for a few days. You know how hard it is for bonded couples."

"You have ten minutes, then I expect you to start your training," he huffs then storms out, mumbling, "We won't tolerate anyone slacking in their responsibilities."

The doctor closes his clipboard and excuses himself so we can talk in private. I'm thankful for the peace, and I know Jace is too. I'm glad he's not stuck in that grimy cell anymore and he'll actually be taken care of, and that his injury wasn't life threatening.

With just the two of us in the partitioned off area, I allow myself to sit on the gurney with him, and Jace doesn't hesitate to wrap his arms around me. His familiar scent envelops me and it makes a world of difference to have him hold me again.

A low chuckle rumbles in his chest. "Are you sure you missed me?"

It's then I realize how hard I'm squeezing him. "Oh, sorry."

"Don't be." He places a series of kisses along my cheek, then along my jaw, slowly working his way toward my neck, and I let out a soft, *Mmmm*.

"Knock, knock," the doctor says. I barely have time to put distance between us as he rounds the partition. "I need to give him a shot to fight off any infection he might have developed in the cell."

It's clear from his tone that the idea of putting injured in the cell immediately, and without checking and treating them first, is not something he has a say in. I'm sure we all understand the base reason for the rule, but that doesn't mean it won't cause problems for the injured.

I rub my right arm. The long scar that runs across it is jagged and pale. It could have been much worse, but thanks to Phillip re-bandaging it and giving me a salve to use, I was able to take care of it with Jace's help and not seek out medical attention. It wasn't a bad injury to begin with, but by the time I got out of the cells, it had started to heal.

Doctor Vazquez pulls out a large pen that looks both familiar and foreign and presses it against the side of Jace's injured leg.

"Where did you get that?" Jace asks with a hint of awe to his voice.

"In the first year, they were much easier to find than they are now. We took what we came across and I've hoarded them. They come in handy for those who end up in the cells."

Then I realize what it is. It's only something I've seen on Vor'onin ships in their med bays.

"It's more effective than our own antibiotics, and you'll heal in a matter of hours rather than days or weeks." Doctor Vasquez winks at me. "You should probably be off now, but you can come back after training. I'd like to keep him here overnight. He'll be back in your quarters by the morning."

Reluctantly, I slide off the gurney and mutter a thank you, knowing he's right but hating it all the same.

During training, I get my ass handed to me over and over again by Phillip. He doesn't let up even knowing why I'm distracted.

"Focus, Raylinn! You need to learn to focus no matter what else is going on around you." The words are harsh, but he sounds more frustrated than upset.

"I know," I groan, pulling myself off the ground for the twentieth time, or maybe the millionth—I've lost track.

He offers me a hand, and like an idiot, I take it only to promptly have my feet swept out from under me. I land with an *oomph* as all the air leaves my lungs in a harsh whoosh.

"Low blow, man," I grumble as I get to my feet, swatting his offered hand away. "I'm not falling for that again."

He laughs but it's cut short as his gaze travels around the room. I take the opportunity to sweep his legs. He lands on his back but says nothing, his expression changing from curious to confused. That's when I check to see what he's staring at.

The others in the training room are milling about, whispering to each other and filing out.

"Someone's here, from Rushmore," a nearby trainee I've never seen before says as he walks by.

Phillip jumps to his feet and grabs my hand, dragging me behind him.

We burst out of the heavy metal door and out onto the surface. I could swear that everyone in this hive was out and watching the scene unfold. Phillip manages to get us closer than most—being a guard, people tend to give way to him.

A man in a filthy lab coat stands before Ross. Three guards surround him, each pointing a rifle at his head. He doesn't seem the least bit intimidated as he speaks with muted hand gestures. Ross listens, nodding.

I want to ask Phillip what's happening but from the look of concentration, he's trying to figure that out himself. We both lean forward, as if somehow that will help us hear what's being said.

Ross raises a hand and makes a swirling motion, and that's when the crowd dissipates, as if on cue. The three guards lead the man in the white coat toward the quarantine area. The man, skin darkened and reddened from the sun, with unkempt hair and overgrown facial hair, tries to turn back to Ross as he calls out, "You have to do something—we can't wait!"

But Ross just waves a hand and strides over to the dining hall.

"Come on," Philip says, trying to lead me away.

"What just happened?" I ask. The desperation in the man's voice strikes me, and I don't understand how no one else is bothered by it. How they can just walk away or ignore it.

"He's here requesting sanctuary." He shakes his head. "I can't believe he made it all the way here on his own." He looks over his shoulder at me, then says, "You should get back to the training room, I need to go check in." And with that, he strides away from me.

I make my way back to the training center and half-heartedly punch a bag until my session is officially over. I strike the bag and it barely moves. If this guy really is from the government compound and he's here telling us that his reason for being here is an emergency... why wouldn't Ross listen to him? I mean, protocols, blah, blah, blah, but that shouldn't stop him from *talking* to the man. I hit the bag again and again, gaining a little more movement from the one hundred pound monstrosity. Ross went to dinner, acting as if this happens every day. But in the time Jace and I've been here, this is only the second new person to arrive.

If it's an emergency, I think it's worth noting, even if I have to find out for myself. Sitting back and waiting to be told anything just feels like a bad idea.

I land a resounding, yet still weak, punch.

Tonight, before I see Jace, I think I'll pay a short visit to the new arrival.

Chapter Twenty-One

Breaking the Rules

With a firm click, I close the door to my quarters quietly behind me. I make my way through the corridor, smiling at anyone I pass as if I haven't left nearly twenty minutes earlier than normal for visiting hours. I'm thankful no one stops me to make small talk.

I blow out a breath as I climb the metal stairs. *This will be easy.* I mean the quarantine and med bay are literally next door to each other, so no one will suspect a thing. I will be fine. *Just pretend you're exactly where you are meant to be and no one will question it.*

The pep talk does little to ease my nerves.

Cool air hits my face as I step out into the open. I breathe in sharply, not expecting the wind to be so strong. Clouds of dust kick up and swirl around the entire above ground part of the hive.

The night sends a chill crawling down my spine, but I don't think it has anything to do with the temperature. Something just feels off...

I press a hand to my forehead and laugh, silently shaking my head. The way I'm acting, you'd think walking around after dinner was forbidden. I'm being ridiculous. Paranoia caused by knowing I'm about to break the weird rule of no talking to those in quarantine.

Even so, I move back into the shadows and walk along the wall, and though I have to move away from the quarantine cells and stick to the edges so I won't be seen, I eventually make my way closer.

There's only a few on guard tonight, as always, but two of them are on the upper level of the walls that look out over the edge to the outside, only one is circling the ground. Now all I have to do is figure out where that guard is.

The scent of smoke fills my nose and a small flicker of red only a few yards away catches my attention. I nearly cough before I realize what it is. A cigarette. I haven't smelled one in over two years. I clap a hand over my mouth and crouch down where I am, using a stack of empty crates to help conceal me.

Foot steps crunch on the dirt and gravel mixture of the walkway that runs along the edge of the hive.

I hold my breath and wait. The footfalls are slow and lazy, half dragging. And for a second that makes me worry that whoever is nearing my position is actually a runner. My heart picks up pace and thumps so loud it drowns out the approach. I press myself further into the tight space between the crates and wall.

Whoever it is comes into view and stops only a yard away. He lifts his head and the light from the moon shines on his face. *Fred.* I narrow my eyes at him. He *would* be the guard on duty.

He half turns toward me and I hold my breath tight. For a second, I think he sees me, and it's the longest moment of my life. If he does spot me, I have no doubt he'll be more than happy to assert his authority that Ross has bestowed on him.

He flicks his cigarette to the ground mere inches from my own foot and grinds out the small ember with his boot. Fred breathes in loudly then groans obnoxiously as he stretches his arms in the air. My lungs begin to ache from holding my breath and I wonder if he's ever going to leave.

A too long moment later and he finally turns back to his original path, rifle in hand, and moves away.

It's several seconds before I allow myself to breathe again, and I end up nearly gasping as I try to pull in the air my lungs demand. I wait a few more minutes after that before I move. My legs have nearly cramped from the uncomfortable crouching position.

I've wasted enough time, so I take the chance that Freddy over there is not paying attention to anything behind him. It's not as hard of a task as it could have been making my way to the quarantine, thanks to Garcia sneaking me this way to see Jace when he was down in the cells.

When I reach the door to the quarantine cells, I let myself relax, but only for a second. I wonder who's on guard in there. I move slowly, scanning the area, and grab the door and pull it open just wide enough for me to slip through. Inside, I guide the heavy door closed to keep it from slamming.

I wipe my forehead with the back of my hand, barely able to believe that I've even made it this far without being spotted. I certainly don't have the sway that Garcia holds. I doubt I could talk myself out of a situation if I get caught.

Seconds later, I regret even going there with my thoughts as I hear footsteps enter the room and stop.

Crap. Slowly, I turn and face the guard I know to be at my back.

"The fuck are you doin' in here?" he demands. I have no idea who he is, so I stutter, trying to find words, an excuse, anything that could make what I'm doing not seem so bad. His blue eyes narrow and he snatches my arm. "Fine, you want to be in the cells? Then let me help you."

What is it with the guards at this place using force first? He drags me down the hall and I finally manage to sputter, "W-wait, no."

I tug on my arm, but he doesn't loosen his grip or listen to me. We go through two sets of heavy doors and walk down a long hall. His strides are so large I have to nearly run to keep up.

He pushes open the last door and shoves me in. I stumble and barely catch myself before falling to the floor.

"What—" another man's voice says.

"I caught her sneaking in here. I figure if she wants to be here so bad, a night in a cell will keep her from pulling this kind of shit again. Ross can deal with her tomorrow."

I straighten and push my hair out of my face and see Phillip's shocked face staring at me.

"Ah, what the hell, Ray?" Then he actually rolls his eyes. "Why are you sneaking in here? Jace is in the med bay."

"Would you believe I mixed this up with the med bay?" I ask. Phillip rolls his eyes, knowing it wasn't a mix-up.

"You know her?" the guy who dragged me down here asks with a snort.

"Yeah, I train her." He turns to me again. "Going to see Jace after visiting hours is one thing, but you can't go sneaking around like this unless you want to get both of you kicked out of this compound for good." Phillip admonishes gently.

To lie, or tell the truth… I weigh my options, but ultimately decide on truth. He knows me well enough that he can probably smell a lie coming a mile away. I take a deep breath, then blow it out. "I wanted to talk to the doctor."

"We can't let you do that. Who the hell do you think you are?"

Phillip rubs a hand over his face and holds up a hand to the guard at my back. "Give me a minute, Corey." He looks like a massive headache is forming, and I'm sure it is, but I stand my ground. "Why exactly do you want to talk to him?"

I quickly toss a glance over my shoulder before answering. "It's something he said before he was taken down here," I start, noting the confusion that crosses Phillip's face. "He said something about needing to do something that couldn't wait."

Phillip walks up to me and pulls me a little farther from Corey to give us a little more privacy. "That's not for you to decide, Ray. We have protocols for a reason."

"I know… I know. I'm really sorry, I just have this…" I twirl my wrist in a circle. "I can't explain it. I just have this feeling that I need to know, *now.*"

"You should go," he starts, but I cut him off.

"Please? Just give me a few minutes with him—I'm already here."

He considers for a moment before his shoulders droop in defeat. "Fine, you can have ten minutes, then you need to leave." I smile, but he shoves a finger in my face. "Only on one condition: you don't pull any more dumb stunts like this again."

I nod.

"Are you kidding me?" Corey snaps from near the doorway.

"I'll take care of her tomorrow, but she's already here, it can't do any harm to give her a few minutes," he explains as he leads me down another hall to the quarantine section.

These are cells on this level have glass partitions with a rounded six-inch section of few holes in the glass near the door.

Phillip knocks on the glass. "Wake up, doc, you have a visitor." The man startles and sits up, looking at me confused. "I'll give you some privacy," Phillip says and walks away.

The doctor doesn't move at first, but then I see curiosity getting the best of him and he stands and walks over to me.

"Who are you?"

"Uh, hi, I'm Raylinn, but my friends call me Ray." I cringe inwardly, and a little on the outside. *Yikes that was a little too casual.*

"Why are you here?" He looks over my shoulder and narrows his eyes on the two men behind me. "I doubt you have clearance to be here right now."

"I heard what you said, about not being able to wait... it sounded important," I stumble on my words a bit. "I just thought someone needed to hear you out."

He takes me in from head to toe before chuckling to himself. "Well, in that case, Ray, I'm Doctor Simmons. It's nice to meet you. And yes, I do have some urgent information."

For a second, I wonder why he hasn't tried telling the two guards in here. But I suppose I can't really blame him. He's being treated like a prisoner. Who would feel open to chatting with their captors?

My heart thuds against my ribs.

"I would offer you something to drink..." He sweeps an arm, indicating his cell. "...but alas, my current arrangements prevent me from being very hospitable."

I step up to the glass and press my palms flat against it and lean my mouth closer to the holes. "Yeah, it sucks staying here. At least you get a bed."

"Ah, so you're familiar with the kindness." When I nod, he continues, "Well, enough of these pleasantries, I will tell you what you came here to learn." I lean closer. "At the Rushmore compound, we have been working hard on trying to find a cure. We have not succeeded yet, though we have managed to get close, thanks to the bonded couples who have volunteered to let us study what it is about them that seems to make them immune."

"What?" I ask, my jaw dropping in disbelief.

A sad smile crosses his face and I catch the quick glance he throws toward his arm. "We didn't manage to create a cure. But we were hoping to at least be able to suppress it enough that those effected could regain the majority of their former selves." His eyes glaze over as his words fade.

"What happened?" Though I can guess the answer.

"There was an outbreak at Rushmore before we could figure it out."

Holy crap. This was huge. "Can you all finish it here? I mean, I know you came alone, but if we went to go get the others—"

His shaking head stops me in my tracks. "They were all killed, turned when one of our test subjects got loose. I am the only one who made it out. I was lucky to find a fueled up truck or I never would have made it here."

A sense of hopelessness envelops me. "And there's nothing

left? Do you at least have a sample, anything? Maybe we could start from there? There's a doctor here and—"

He shakes his head again. "I'm afraid a cure is impossible now that we know what we are working with. The one man who could have got us there was shredded in the initial attack."

"So it's hopeless then…" I drop my hands from the partition. I don't get it. He'd said there was no time to waste, but all he's told me is that they were close to helping and now there's no hope.

"No, it's just nearly hopeless at this point. All of humanity is depending on this compound now." I furrow my brows in confusion. "We might not have found a cure, but we have a vaccine… you should know it hasn't been tested, but I believe it will prevent someone who was scratched or bitten from turning. There is also the possibility that it will weaken the infected so we can easily overpower them."

I press my hands against the glass again, only this time it's to steady myself. If his theory is true… we could reclaim this world. We can rid ourselves from these runners and start building this world again.

"Unfortunately, I think the infected are much smarter than we believed. At first we thought they were driven by pure blood lust, but one of our scientists was turned and the runners in the compound seemed to congregate near the labs, trying to destroy everything they could. It seems likely that they have some way of communicating that we don't know about." He steps closer and presses his hands opposite of my own. "It is up to this compound to make sure every last infected in the area is eradicated so they can't communicate that news to the others. And you must get the vaccines from the lab. I managed to change the code before I left so the infected can't get in without the pass code."

"You have to tell Ross first thing in the morning," I say.

He shakes his head. "It will be too late by then." Again, his eyes flick to his arm, lingering this time.

"Oh no… but, if what you say is true, then we need you," I whisper. He's been scratched. If it were a bite, the blood would have seeped through his sleeve. He isn't going to make it the full three days. In fact, he'll be lucky to see tomorrow night.

"Memorize this code, Raylinn."

I nod numbly. Doctor Simmons spends the next few minutes drilling the nine digit number into my head and makes me repeat it several times in a row. Then he goes over where he keeps his notes. With the vaccines and the notes, he believes we can replicate the results. Once he's satisfied I have everything down pat, we lapse into silence for a moment.

"How did you manage to escape?" I ask.

"Raylinn," Phillip's voice calls. "You need to go soon. Say goodbye."

I quickly turn back to the doctor. There are so many things I want to say. And knowing his time is almost up, I want to stay with him, I want to offer him comfort, companionship, so he doesn't have to be alone. After all, I wouldn't want to be alone if

I knew I was about to die.

"The air vents." He chuckles lightly. "I thought I was going to die in there. You can get anywhere in the compound through those vents—remember that."

Something tells me that he expects me personally to go to the Rushmore compound to do this. It's not like I have a choice, but I have to try. "I will."

"Raylinn, your time is up. You have to go now." Phillip's hand lands on my shoulder.

I want to argue and make him let me stay until the doctor changes so he's not alone in his final minutes as the man he is before he turns into a runner.

But I don't. I don't say a word. It's not my secret to tell, and I won't shorten his life. If they knew he was scratched or bitten for sure, they wouldn't hesitate to put a bullet in him this very moment. He will tell them when, or if, he wants them to know.

"Thank you," I say quickly. "I'll do my best."

"Tell me the code, one more time," he orders.

"What code? What—" Phillip says at my side.

I ignore him and repeat the numbers without hesitation. Doctor Simmons smiles and nods. "Good girl."

Then I let Phillip lead me away. I look behind me at the doctor until we walk through the door and down the first hall.

"What was that all about?" Phillip asks.

I just shake my head, unable to tell him anything right now. There's too much to process.

Once we reach the door to the outside, he holds up a hand and tells me to wait while he checks to see if the coast is clear. When he returns, he tells me to wait five minutes before leaving and to stick to the wall, heading east to get back to the underground bunker door. When I look at him confused, he points to the right.

"I have to get back, but be careful."

"Thank you," I say sheepishly, knowing he's none too pleased with me right now.

"Ray," he says, and I lift my eyes to meet his gaze. "We will talk about this tomorrow. I won't say anything to Ross, and I'll make sure Corey doesn't say anything either, but you're damn lucky I was here tonight or you and Jace would have been out of here… or worse, just you. Ross doesn't want to let any of the Vor'onins leave, their tech knowledge and defensive abilities are too valuable."

I suck in a breath, grasping the meaning. I had risked far more tonight than I'd realized. But I believe it was worth it.

Chapter Twenty-Two

The Good Doctor

I was down in the cells a lot longer than I realized, and a lot longer than the ten minutes Phillip said he would give me. Visiting Jace after hours is probably not the best idea. The moon has moved a fair distance across the sky.

I yawn by the time I reach the door to the underground area. The red lighting makes the hall look like it's bathed in blood. It's creepy. Each night at ten, the white florescent lighting turns off to make way for the red, signaling night, and stays on constantly until six the following morning.

Once I get into the stairwell that leads to the living quarters, the full weight of exhaustion settles on my shoulders. I only spot one guard who's getting ready to start his shift for the day. I mumble something about not being able to sleep and taking a walk and he moves me along.

I collapse onto the bed still fully clothed and stare up at the ceiling. I don't think I could be any more tired at this moment, but my mind refuses to settle. I can't stop thinking about Doctor Simmons and wondering how he's doing, how far along he is, what he's feeling. Wishing I could hold his hand, as impractical as that is.

Rolling over to my side, I stare at the clock on the wall and watch the seconds and minutes pass slowly until it's time to wake.

Even though I didn't sleep, resting seemed to have replenished a minimal amount of energy. I get to my feet and change my clothes before leaving and heading to the morning dining hall.

There's a small line leading up to the surface, and I trudge up the stairs between small groups of people as they talk. I avoid making eye contact with anyone, just in case they feel like engaging me. I just want to get some food in my belly and then go see Jace before I have to start my chores for the day—which I'm pretty sure will include a strongly worded lecture by Phillip. The one small thing I can be grateful for is that it won't be coming from Ross.

I'm halfway to the surface when I hear a scream, then a gunshot followed by another and another. Everyone around me seems to duck and cry out, but I just push my way to the surface, fearing the worst.

Please not Jace, please not Jace, please not Jace! I chant silently as I force my way through the others around me.

I burst out into the morning light and can't see anyone near the med bay, but there's a small group of people by the doors leading down into the quarantine cells. Phillip is among them.

The small group of guards parts and I can see the body of the doctor, lying face down in the dirt.

I clamp my hand tight against my face to keep a cry that rips its way up my throat, or to keep from vomiting. I run to Phillip without thinking.

He sees me and shoves his gun toward one of the others, catching me up by the waist before I can get too close. "No, Ray, you need to stay back."

Tears slip down my face at the horrible death Doctor Simmons suffered. "How did he get up here? What the hell happened?" I demand.

"Ross commanded us to bring the doctor to him. There was going to be a meeting," he explains. Though we both know he doesn't owe me an answer, he's telling me so I don't push away and run to the fallen man. "He… he turned as we got outside. We didn't know he was bitten."

"Scratched," I correct softly before catching myself.

His fingers dig into me and he spins me around to face him, pure anger flashing in his eyes. "What the fuck did you just say?" He thrusts one hand toward the cells. "You *knew* and you didn't fucking say anything? You could have gotten us killed by not telling me," Phillip whisper shouts at me.

He's right. I hadn't been thinking about anyone but the doctor last night. It was stupid. "I'm so sorry, I didn't... I thought he would have told you. I didn't know you were going to bring him out before the three days."

"I'm going to take care of this disaster, and then I'm going to come find you and we're going to have a serious chat about everything."

I nod, knowing I deserve whatever punishment he cooks up. I'll be glad to take whatever it happens to be. Because at least I won't be exiled. I'm an idiot. I put everyone at risk because I was only thinking about one person instead of the well being of the whole. But making that kind of decision for someone... I'm not sure I can make those kinds of decisions. It's the trolley problem, a question where there is no perfect answer. Either way, you are doing harm to someone.

"Just do yourself a favor and don't go far." With that, he turns away and strides back to the other guards.

A small crowd has formed in the time I spoke to Phillip. They keep a safe distance, not daring to get as close as I am. A few guards are working on trying to move them back even further and ordering people to go about their day. But their words are, for the most part, ignored.

Suddenly, food is the last thing on my mind, so I decide to go visit Jace now instead. I push back the tent flap and a terrifying thought sparks in my mind. What if Doctor Simmons had gotten past his guards and made it to the med bay? Jace wouldn't have been safe with a measly unlocked door protecting him.

Doctor Vasquez looks up from his small desk off to the side, surprised to see me. "You're here early," he says as he stands. "But something tells me that I don't think Jace will mind."

He motions for me to follow him to the far side of the tent and past a makeshift wall made from a hospital changing screen-like-thing. He doesn't ask about the commotion outside. He was probably one of the first to know. There was nothing anyone could do for someone who turned. Nothing but offer a quick death.

Jace lies on his back, his hands are clasped together over his stomach and his eyes are closed. He looks as though he fell asleep waiting for true love's kiss to wake him.

I walk quietly to his side and gently place a hand on his upper arm. Jace's eyes flutter open and he blinks several times, then a smile forms across his lips.

"Morning," I say. He must be tired because his eyes hold the gloss of sleep. He's always woken up with bright, alert eyes, even when he had little sleep. I wonder for a second if he'd been drugged to make him sleep. It would explain why the gun shots hadn't woken him.

"I missed you," he says.

I laugh. "I missed you too."

He looks toward the front of the tent as if he can see the doctor through the screen. "He says I can get out of this bed today. My cuts weren't as deep as he initially thought and they are nearly healed."

I throw my arms around him, so glad that he'll be with me again. Lately, it feels as if the world has been conspiring to keep us apart. Without him, I feel as though part of me is missing.

Jace returns my embrace, one hand stroking my head. "Hey, what's wrong, Raylinn?"

I pull away just enough to look him in the eye, and I don't realize I'm crying until he brushes his thumb under an eye, wiping away a tear. I swallow hard and lick my lips, not sure where to start. "So much has happened…"

He sees the overwhelm in my expression and squeezes one of my hands in his. "It's okay, just take a breath, then start from the beginning."

I pull in one breath and let it out slowly, then another and another until my emotions are tempered and I can think clearly. Then I tell him everything that happened since the last time I saw him. From the doctor arriving, to my sneaking out, to the conversation I had with him—even the code I was given—to what happened first thing this morning.

Jace's warm amber gaze darkens as I finish. He's quiet for a long moment as he takes in all the information I just spilled.

"We have to tell Ross," he says grimly. He's right, but the thought of approaching the man is more than a little unpleasant. "Hey, don't worry. I will be with you."

I blow out a relieved breath. "Thank you."

"Sorry to interrupt, but I just want to check the cuts one

more time. If they are closed completely, then, Jace, you'll be free to go."

We both perk up at the doctor's words. I slide off the edge of the bed and move to leave. "I'll see you later," I say to Jace, hating to leave him but knowing that this time, it won't be for long.

"You can stay, it won't be but a minute before I know," Doctor Vasquez offers.

"It's okay," I say. "I have to get something to eat then get to training." I look at Jace then say, "I'll see you at dinner."

Of course I wanted to stay, but if Jace can get out of here now then I need to get my lecture from Phillip done and over with. I only make it part way toward the dining hall before a hand grabs my arm. Our pace immediately picks up.

"Phillip, slow down," I snap.

He jerks his head in my direction and glares, but he slows a bit so that I can keep up. He looks ahead once more without a word and stays silent until we get to the training room. It's empty, as everyone is either at breakfast or starting their jobs for the morning. A few lucky people even get to head to bed.

"I'm sorry," the words blurt from my lips before he has a chance to say anything.

His eyes dart around. "Don't move."

Phillip closes the doors then locks us in. I take a single step back at the feeling of being trapped with someone so pissed at me. Phillip strides back toward me, and it's all I can do to keep my feet planted in place.

He lifts his hands, his mouth open, and he looks like he wants to scream at me while strangling me. Which, after the danger I put him and everyone else in last night, I kind of deserve. Okay, more than deserve, but I can only get murdered for being an idiot once.

"I don't even know where to fucking start with you!" he yells.

I can't help but flinch at the sudden noise in the quiet room. His breath comes quickly now, and I can see every emotion as it crosses his face.

"I know! I messed up. I should have told you about the scratch."

"It's not just that, Raylinn." He groans in frustration, but it comes out as half a growl. "Do you have any idea how much trouble you could have been in? Do you know that Ross would be more than happy to toss you out on your ass while keeping Jace here?" He runs his fingers through his hair and tugs. "Damn it, and you not only put yourself in danger but all of us. What do you think would have happened if he'd scratched or bitten someone? We could have had a fucking epidemic. All of us could have ended up dead. What the fuck were you thinking?"

I can't help the tears that well up in my eyes. Phillip has become a better friend in these past months than I'd realized, and knowing I'd let him down this bad hurts much worse than I ever would have imagined. "I'm sorry," I say again.

"Stop fucking saying that… and stop crying," he snaps. "I'm at a loss here, Ray. I don't even have the words to expressed how angry I am with you right now." Phillip starts pacing in what I can only assume is an attempt to keep from strangling me. "I should get you reassigned to someone else. I can't fucking do this anymore."

"No!" I lurch forward and grab him by the arm, stopping him. "Please believe me, I never meant to put you in danger like that. I swear, if I'd known you were going to take him in the morning, I would have told you about the scratch. I just … I just didn't want to shorten his life any more than it would have been."

He softens a little bit, but his anger is still the strongest emotion. His posture is still rigged and holding back his energy. But his eyes hold a lot of hurt in them. "You should have trusted me, Ray. I wouldn't have let anyone shoot him until he turned, or asked. I'm not some heartless bastard. I thought you would have figured that out by now. But I sure as hell wouldn't have taken him from the cells."

"I know… I'm sorry, I wasn't thinking."

"Why the hell did you even go to the cells last night?" he asks again.

"I told you, he said there wasn't time and there was something important." I take a deep breath before I say the next words. "And I don't regret going."

Those last words get his attention and, for the first time since he locked us in here, Phillip can see past his anger. "What did he tell you?"

"A lot." I pull everything I have to me and stand with my shoulders back. Putting everyone's lives in danger better have a good reason, and I don't want to leave anything out. So I explain everything, down to the code.

When I finish, Phillip stares at me, his anger all but forgotten for the moment. "We have to tell Ross and the others." A thoughtful expression crosses his face. "Have you told Jace?"

I nod. "Yes."

"Good, the more of us that tell him, the better." He eyes me, as if he's planning something I won't like very much. "You'll have to tell Ross, there's a meeting tomorrow afternoon, I'll have one of the others take you—"

"Whoa, whoa, whoa," I say, holding up my hands. "There is *no* way Ross will believe a single word out of my mouth."

"He'll have no choice if there are enough of us who can corroborate your story. I know Jace and I will, and I'm pretty sure I can get Corey to as well."

"What about me getting kicked out? You said if he found out—"

"Don't worry about that. I'll make sure he can't, not without losing everything he takes pride in." I frown, not understanding what kind of threat he's making. I open my mouth to ask, but he cuts me off. "And don't think just because you told me all of this you're off the hook." The flash of anger returns. "Run."

I blink, not understanding.

"Run, Raylinn. And don't stop until I tell you to." He's quiet when he speaks, but his tone sends a spike of fear down my spine. I don't waste another second before I start running laps around the large room. "Faster!" he snaps.

I push myself as hard as I can go. I'm really feeling the lack of food ten laps in. My muscles don't have much energy left, but I don't dare let up. I'm panting hard and even though I'm starving now, I'm glad I missed breakfast because it would have been all over the floor by now.

Sweat pours down the side of my face and neck with each step. I don't remember him unlocking the doors, but an hour into my run, others begin to filter in. They give me strange looks as they pass but I just push myself harder.

The toe of my shoe catches on the ground and I stumble. My legs are so tired I can't catch myself and I tumble to the ground, gasping for air. Spots dance before my eyes, then Phillip appears, hovering above me.

"I didn't say you could stop," he says flatly.

"I can't…" I wheeze in response.

He reaches down and pulls me to my feet. I'm so weak, my legs half buckle from under me and I fall forward into him. For a second, I don't think he'll catch me but then he does.

"What—" he starts, then pushes my head back and looks into my face. *Really* looks. "When was the last time you had anything to eat or drink? Did you sleep at all last night?"

I'm still hopelessly trying to catch my breath and can't answer. I hear him swear under his breath.

He puts my arm around his shoulders and walks me out of the training room. I can barely focus on walking, let alone where we are going, until we stop in front of another door. My door. Phillip shoves it open and drags me to the bed, half throwing me on top of it. I manage to roll to my back to find him glaring down at me, fists balled at his sides.

"This is the kind of shit I was talking about." He huffs then helps arrange me full onto the bed so my legs aren't hanging off. "Get some sleep. I'll send Lilly in with some food later. Get some rest before tomorrow." Then he storms out and slams the door behind him.

I wake up to Jace shaking me gently by the shoulders and whispering my name. "Ray, what happened? Are you all right?"

I shift to sit up and suck in a breath through my teeth. Damn, every muscle in my body hurts.

"Uh, yeah," I mutter. I press a hand to my head to try and stop the incessant drum solo happening inside my brain. "Hard training day."

Jace hands me a glass of water, which I gulp down. It's room temperature, which doesn't feel as good as ice cold water would have, but it makes it easier to drink. When I finish, I set it down next to the plate of cold food sitting on the small nightstand. I must have been dead to the world to not have heard Lilly drop off the food.

"What time is it?" I ask, still way beyond tired.

"It's after dinner." I'm relieved knowing that, for the rest of the day, it's our personal time together. "No offense, Ray, but you stink."

I laugh then try to get to my feet and end up stumbling. Jace catches me and helps me to the shower. He hesitates leaving me alone, then even though I say I got it, he helps me undress and somehow we both manage to fit into the tiny shower. He helps me wash and I'm glad he ignored my earlier protest because I would have ended up falling asleep in here.

After we get out, he dries me off and even helps dress me in my nightclothes. I stumble my way toward the bed but, before I can lie down, he shoves the plate of food into my hands and makes me eat it all.

Chapter Twenty-Three

Threats

I wait outside the doors to the meeting room. This part of the underground had been conveniently left out of the tour. Over and over, I roll my shoulders and pace in a tight circle, waiting for Phillip or someone to come get me. I wasn't too surprised when he came to wake us up early so Jace could make the meeting.

We barely spoke last night, but I don't think I was in the right space to do much more than blink. Apparently Phillip had filled Jace in on everything that happened between us at practice, as well as his plan.

Just as I'm debating on going in there, the door opens, and a Vor'onin woman ushers me in, leading me down another long hallway. I know we near the meeting room when Ross's voice rings past the open doorway.

"What's going on, Phillip?" he demands. "This better not be

a waste of my time or I'll send you to kitchen duty for a year."

I knew kitchen duty was a punishment! I quickly push that thought away. That's not important right now. The Vor'onin woman knocks on the doorframe then guides me in.

As soon as Ross's eyes meet mine, his face turns an awful shade of reddish purple. He stands and slams his hands on the table. "What is *she* doing here?"

"She did what you should have done," Phillip says lowly, then before he can be interrupted, he adds, "Hear her out. She has information that can change the world."

Ross scoffs, as if me knowing anything useful is a far stretch, let alone me knowing something that could change the world.

"We should listen to what she has to say, then we will decide if it's worth heeding or if punishment should be enacted," says the woman at my back.

Though I know what I have to say is important and true, the pressure still feels suffocating. Ross sneers then motions for me to take a spot at the table. Several people I've seen around the hive sit at the table, along with Jace and Phillip. Seeing their friendly faces gives me courage.

I stay standing and take a moment to look everyone in the eye before starting. "Late last night, Doctor Simmons informed me of a vaccine that is stored in the center of the Rushmore compound."

"Ha!" Ross bursts out. "Why would he tell you, of all people, something like that? Get back to work and quit making up stories and wasting everyone's time because you want attention."

I feel my anger toward him ignite. I keep my voice cool as I say, "He told *me* because *you* couldn't find time to talk to him before he turned. He told you that he had important information, but you thought you knew best. He told *me* because I was the only one to ask him what that was. He told *me* because I was the only one to listen to him. *That* is why he told me."

Ross sits back in his chair, arms crossed against his chest but not saying anything more, so I continue on.

"He said the vaccine will prevent anyone who's bitten or scratched from turning and could possibly weaken the runners so we could overtake them." I keep going until I tell them everything, except the code. Something tells me that for now, I need to keep at least one card close to my chest.

"There's no way we can send our people out to that death trap based on your word alone," Ross says when I finally finish.

"May I be excused for a minute?" Jace says. I can clearly see the anger in his face at the way Ross addresses me. I suppose he's never seen it before, as I have tried my best to avoid him, or he hasn't had the pleasure of being around. He stands leaning over the table, as if he almost can't control his feelings.

Ross seems taken aback by the sudden request. "Make it quick," he says, giving in.

Of course, he doesn't argue with him, always wanting to be on Jace's good side. Can't lose those Vor'onins. I know he's upset, but I wish he wouldn't leave.

Once Jace leaves and is no doubt out of earshot, Ross says, "As for you, Miss Marrow, we will discuss the terms of *you* leaving us within the next several hours."

I know he's insinuating that *when* I leave, I'll be going alone. As if that would ever happen. Unless he killed Jace or locked him up, there's no way he'd let me leave without him.

"I'm not lying."

To my relief, Phillip jumps in. "I was on duty last night, guarding the doctor. She's telling the truth, they spoke for a long time."

"Of course you would say that—you're her trainer," Ross waves him off with a hand. It's clear he's struggling to keep dismissing me.

"She told me everything," Jace says. I start, not realizing he'd already returned. "I believe her. She would never lie to me about something like this, and she's not the type to pull stunts like this for attention."

"Of course you would say as much, you're her mate," Ross spits the word *mate* as if it were an insult.

With this, the Vor'onin woman who led me inside nods her head. "If Jace'el believes her, than so do I. We do not lie, nor do we tend to fall for lies so easily."

Ross blusters only to be silenced by another voice. "She's telling the truth," he says reluctantly, and we all turn to stare at Corey. "I caught her sneaking into the cells. I was going to keep her until morning for you to deal with—" Phillip clears his throat. "Anyway, she talked to the doctor for a long time. She's telling the truth."

A long silence follows. There seems to be something about Corey's simple testimony that resonates with everyone in the room who had yet to voice an opinion or express what they thought of the situation.

"May I return to duty now?" Corey asks.

Ross waves a hand in his direction, not taking his eyes off me.

Once the meeting is back on, Ross motions for me to sit as he stands and addresses the room. "It seems Miss Marrow has managed to get several to collaborate her story. If what she says is true, then we must begin planning a rescue mission to the Rushmore compound to gather whatever is left of the vaccine. This could be a game changer. We will reconvene again after dinner tonight. You are all dismissed."

Everyone turns to leave, but I wait for Phillip and Jace to reach me before heading toward the door.

"Oh, and Miss Marrow?" I turn to him. "We will discuss your punishment in the morning."

With those words, I feel the blood drain from my face.

"No, she won't be punished." Phillip steps between us. "She did something *you* should have done and there are plenty of witnesses to that. Imagine what the people of this compound would think if you punished the one person who dared to find out such important information. Information that you should have taken the time to find out. Furthermore, you will allow her to be as much a part of this mission as she wants."

"No, I will not allow her that. She disobeyed orders and this is *not* a game. I will not allow her to risk this hive by allowing her to do whatever she wants."

"As far as I can tell, you're the only one turning this into a game. She might have snuck into the cells, but what she learned could give us the upper hand against the infected that we've been needing."

Jace slips his hand into mine and the three of us leave, walking down the hallway in silence. We don't even speak until we are all within mine and Jace's quarters.

I walk to the table and sit on the top. "I thought I was going to pass out at one point."

"You did great," Phillip says.

Jace wraps his arms around me and places a kiss on my head. "He's right, you were wonderful. You should be proud of yourself." I smile, but his fades. "I don't understand why you never told me how he was treating you. We've been here for months, Ray."

"I'm sorry," I say, ducking my head. "It wasn't really that big of a deal, and I didn't want you to worry."

"Next time, don't keep something like that from me."

I agree to be more open about things before steering the conversation back to our victory. "I can't believe you turned his threat into one against him."

Phillip shrugs. "He's predictable and I knew he'd threaten to kick you out on your own, but if enough people know you are responsible for getting this information then there's no way he could force you to leave like that. That's not how this place is supposed to run." He shakes his head and glowers at the floor boards. "This was always supposed to be a democracy with all of us deciding what's right for everyone here, not a dictatorship. He'll do as much as we let him get away with."

"Thank you, for helping to protect her," Jace says, still holding on to me.

"We have to look out for each other now that the world has gone to hell. The information she found could end up saving us all."

He backs up a few steps. "I need to get ready for dinner so I can eat and get some rest before duty tonight." He pauses at the door and looks over his shoulder to me. "Oh, keep that code to yourself for the time being. It could come in handy during tonight's meeting."

Chapter Twenty-Four

The Z Word

I adjust my backside for the tenth time in as many minutes, my chair creaking under the movements of my bouncing knee. If it wasn't so old, I might take exception to what it's implying. Jace places a hand on my knee below the table to offer a small amount of comfort to my frayed nerves as we wait for everyone to finish arriving.

There are a lot more people than in the earlier meeting. Most of them are people I've seen on guard duty over the last several months, others I've seen in the shooting range when Phillip trains me to improve my aim.

I never thought I would enjoy shooting targets, but it's a great stress reliever on bad days. My stomach twists into knots. Speaking to a dozen people this morning was one thing, this will be like having a full fledged audience.

I'm glad to see Garcia enter the room. It's been a few days since we've talked. I feel a stab of guilt for not sharing what I learned with her before. Mon'te, Des, and Jos'lin enter near the end... trailed by Brian. *Well crap on a cracker*, it seems my luck in avoiding him is now over.

As soon as everyone is here and settled, Ross enters. I half expect some of the people in the room to stand when he comes in, as if he were a judge as he takes his place at the head of the long oval table.

"Thank you all for coming to this last minute meeting. It has been brought to my attention by Miss Marrow," he manages to make my name sound like an insult, "that Doctor Simmons had some urgent information he shared with her before his untimely turning, and that there is a vaccine in the Rushmore compound. Well..." He lifts a hand in my direction. "I will let her explain the details of what the good doctor has told her."

Letting out a low breath, I use the table to push myself up to standing. I nervously wipe my hands down my hips before I catch myself and force my hands to remain still. Jace shifts in his seat, a silent reminder that he is here by my side.

I spend the next half an hour, once again going over every last detail the doctor told me—minus the code—only taking my seat once I've finished. Jace squeezes my thigh.

"Yes, thank you, Miss Marrow. You are excused," Ross says.

I frown. *That dirty son of a—*

"I'd like to stay and help with this mission," I say, trying to sound as pleasant as I can manage. He sees right through that façade just as I see through his seemingly pleasant dismissal as if I had asked to be excused.

I can't be sure, but I think I see his eye twitch before he gives me the worst fake smile in the history of ever, and says, "Of course."

Besides Jace, Phillip, and Garcia, no one else seems to catch on to the hostility between us.

"Our number one objective is to get the vaccines, but there is a store of weapons here." Ross points to some place on the map he'd spread out. "And there should be explosives here." He points to a different spot.

I stand on my toes trying to make myself a little taller to see. But the map is at a terrible angle for where I'm sitting.

"Teams Alpha and Delta, you will be in charge of finding the armory and gathering what weapons you can, Team Bravo, you will gather the explosives. Once everything is clear, Bravo will set some of the explosives to go up and take down the compound from the inside. We can't have whatever infected remain there to get loose. Teams Charlie, Foxtrot, and Tango, you will be in charge of getting those vaccines out of there. Do not break a single one of them." Ross shoves a stubby finger toward one man. "We don't know if we can replicate the formula, and right now, those vials will be worth more than diamonds if they can do what the doctor claimed they can. Each team will take one of these labs." Ross points to several different spots on the map.

The meeting soon becomes a huge strategy discussion, going into detail of where each team will be and when. I struggle to keep up with it all. I have no prior experience to this type of strategy, and it's moving a bit fast. Whatever I don't catch, Jace, Garcia, and Phillip will help me to understand. At the end of the day, I know I'm capable of doing what needs to be done. And I'm willing to risk my life, along with the four dozen others in this room, for the sake of leaving this world with a chance of saving it for future generations.

It's only about the time when they start dividing everyone into teams that the meeting actually starts to pick up. Before I know it, Jace and I are assigned different teams. I'm sentenced to be a driver, and to keep my butt behind the wheel the entire time. Normally I don't mind the idea of driving, but I *need* to be on the inside of Rushmore. I suppose if push comes to shove, I can make sure the people I know I can trust have the code.

Jace is on Alpha team. I hate the idea of him being in the middle of danger without me to have his back, especially when Brian ends up on his team. I might not be the best trained person around, but I'm the only one who will risk everything for him.

The meeting ends before I can figure out what I can say to protest my assignment and get placed on the inside. I don't exactly have any seniority or power here, not among people who have been here for far longer.

Though I'm less than thrilled at the job I'll be doing, I marvel at the idea of being in a working car after all this time. I hadn't even realized they had vehicles here. I've never seen any sign of them. Apparently they keep them well hidden and guarded so the fewer people who know about them, the less likely it is that scavengers will find out about them and storm the hive if they happen to capture one of the scouting parties.

Jace, Phillip, Garcia, and I make our way back to Garcia's room.

"What the hell, Raylinn? Why am I just now finding out about all of this?" she asks, though I sense more hurt in her words than anger. They aren't as sharp or cutting as usual.

"I'm sorry, it just all happened so fast." By the look on everyone's faces, I can tell I'm not the only one still processing the meeting as well as the past two days.

"Pfft, I guess." She runs her hand through her long black hair. "So, what did you do to get assigned driving duty? I've seen you shoot, you're a better marksmen than some of those idiots who are on the infiltrating teams."

I burst out laughing, as though what she said was a lot funnier than in reality. "What haven't I done?" I ask rhetorically when I can breathe enough to speak again.

"Yeah, she's pretty lucky she didn't get kicked out on her ass," Phillip adds helpfully.

"I never would have let that happen," Jace says defensively, glowering at me.

I think he's upset at me for not telling him about how Ross has been treating me. I don't really blame him. I'd feel the same if someone had treated him that way.

"We wouldn't have let it happen either," Garcia says sitting on the edge of her bed and leaning back on her arms.

"Hey, guys?" I say, feeling unsure of what I need to say next.

"What is it, Ray?" Jace's hand wraps around mine tighter.

"Since I'm not going inside the compound, I think you should all memorize the code." I can't help but feel disappointed that they will all be going inside and I won't.

"There's a code? A code to what?" Garcia asks.

I mentally slap my forehead, then quickly explain that part to her as well. A smile creeps over her face when I finish, and I'm not sure if I'll like the words that will come out of her mouth or if I should be terrified.

"Right, as if we'd let you get away with sitting in a truck twiddling your thumbs while the rest of us risk our necks for these vaccines."

Jace, Phillip, and I exchange looks then lean forward to listen to her plan. Apparently I am to drive Phillip's team there, and the two of us are supposed to stay in the car.

As terrified as I am at being in an underground military bunker with ravenous runners milling about, I'm also comforted knowing that my friends won't be risking their lives alone. I'll be by their sides, and we'll all have each other's backs.

Satisfied with our plan to make me part of the reconnaissance team, the three of us head out, leaving Garcia to her space. Jace and I part ways with Phillip as we stop at our quarters and we wave goodnight.

Butterflies fill my stomach with nerves and anticipation that I can't decide if it's a good or bad thing. I have a week to decide how I feel. Though, either way, I am determined to be a part of this and not shoved to the sidelines. They'll need all the hands on the inside that they can get.

As Jace and I settle into bed for the night, he kisses the top of my head and holds me, nearly crushing me to his chest. "I'm glad we found such good friends here."

"Me too," I murmur. My eyelids grow heavy. "Hey, Jace?"

"Mmm-hmm?" comes his reply, as he's falling into the embrace of sleep.

"I think I want to spend my day in the shooting range tomorrow—I want to brush up on my zombie killing skills." I feel the chuckle rumble in his chest more than I hear it, and I laugh with him.

I must be tired if I'm using the Z word.

It takes me a long moment to understand what woke me up. I sit up in the dark, the soft red glow of the hallway lights leaks through the crack along the bottom of the door. Jace is sitting up silently next to me, listening.

Thump, thump, thump.

It's a little hard for me to make out where the pounding is

coming from, but Jace throws the covers off him and is at the door in two long strides, throwing it open.

"Wake up!" *Thump, thump, thump.* "We're under attack by the infected!" a man shouts from down the hall.

My blood freezes in my veins. There wouldn't be any sirens. Those would only alert the runners to our underground position, which for now, is a small advantage.

Somehow, I manage to yank myself out of my stupor and grab the first clothing items I can find and throw them on. Jace is dressed before me, but he waits. He holds his hand out to me when I'm ready and I take it.

Then together we run down the hall toward the weapons room to grab anything we can to fight these monsters off.

CHAPTER TWENTY-FIVE

Planned Attack

The second we burst out onto the surface, I have a moment of helplessness. People are running about, shooting, using blunt objects, and fire to defend themselves. The runners are easy to spot, once they set their sites on someone, they zero in and charge like a wild animal would, though their movements are jerky. The air is orange and smoky from all the fires. So much of the compound is burning.

How the hell did this happen?

Jace and I run into the fray, we each have a blunt object of choice strapped to our backs. Mine is my trusty golf club and Jace has chosen a thick metal pipe—our "just in case" weapons. We start by seeking out the nearest person who seems to be overwhelmed by the number of runners they are fending off.

We stop and take aim with our hand guns, taking them down one by one. A runner reaches the man and stretches out it's long, gnarled fingers, ready to pull him in and make a meal out of him. Jace lifts his gun one more time and fires. The runner's head jerks to the side, then he crumples to the ground.

Then we are off again, looking for the next closest group of runners.

"How did they get in here?" Jace asks.

I'm wondering the same thing. It almost seems too organized, with the timing and the sheer number of them. But we don't have time to figure out the answers. We keep fighting our way through the seemingly never ending horde.

Something reddish catches my eye and I turn. What I see makes my heart break all over again. A few yards in front of me stands Scotty. Deep gashes mar his skin, and the look on his face is murderous.

"Jace," I whisper, afraid to take my eyes off the specter before me. "Jace…" I say again, a little louder when he doesn't answer. My throat constricts. I want to tell Scotty I'm sorry. I want to thank him for saving our lives.

I quickly look away, wondering why Jace hasn't answered, but I don't see him anywhere.

A loud bang makes my bad ear ring, and I stumble back a step as my equilibrium takes a hit. Something heavy falls at my feet and slides into me. I look down to see Scotty's still form, then up to Garcia where he had been only seconds earlier, her gun still raised.

Our eyes meet and I can see the pain in them, and I know she can see mine. It only lasts a second before she jerks her head for me to follow her. I can't bear to look down again as I move into a sprint right behind her.

"There!" she calls over the noise, pointing.

I nod and we run toward the dining hall. There are so many runners pounding on the doors and windows, trying to break them and get to those hiding within.

We each start on opposite ends of the building and aim at one runner then the next. I hit one in the shoulder and it turns and lets out a horrific, roaring scream, as if it was in the worst agony in the world. I hesitate for only a second before I put a bullet between its eyes.

"Where's Jace?" Garcia asks between shots.

"I-I don't know. He was by my side, then he was gone."

She puts a bullet in each of the final two attempting to smash their way into the building then faces me. Blood is smeared along her jaw on the left side and partially down her neck, but it's not hers. "Let's go find him… and Phillip."

I am more than willing to go along with that plan. While the number one objective right now is to rid ourselves of the runners, finding those two is a close second.

We manage to empty one and a half clips each before we

make it to the far side of the compound, where we spot Jace fighting next to Doctor Vasquez. We run toward them, putting down several more runners as we go.

"Ray," Jace says, deep relief in his tone. "I didn't know…"

"It's fine," I say. "Let's finish these monsters off."

He nods and follows behind Garcia and me, and to my surprise, the doctor comes with us. We move in a tight group looking everywhere for Phillip. We don't see him and I know Garcia is starting to worry. She's chewing the hell out of her lip, and her brows are pinched tight.

I'm worried we started looking for him too late and that a runner got to him first. I shake my head, banishing the thought. No, I have to believe he's still alive and unhurt.

"I'm out of ammo," Jace says.

I dart a quick glance toward him and do a mental count of the ammo I still have. Two clips left.

"Take one of mine," I say, handing one to him. He doesn't take it.

"I'm out too," Garcia says.

"Stay with Ray. Doctor Vasquez and I are going to get more."

Sweat beads at my temples but not from exertion. "No, we can't split up," I start to protest. We just found them.

"You and Garcia need to stay out here and help the others."

"Then take my extra clip." I hand it toward him again, but he's shaking his head.

"Give it to Garcia. You two will need all you can get. We'll be fast."

Then the two of them take off before I can say another word. I hand the clip I have to her and we stand back to back, turning in a slow circle, pausing to take aim at the closest runners.

"Let's make every shot count," she says. Garcia points toward the cells. "Let's head that way. We still need to find Phill."

We make our way toward the cells. The air is thick with smoke now, making it more difficult to tell runner from human in the late night sky. The growls of monsters and cries of pain and anger echo through the air and mix to become one horrible sound that comes from all sides at once.

Clouds of grayish orange light spill from the stock pile of wood crates I hid behind days ago. The glow is weak, but there's enough that I can see someone moving closer. I can't tell if it's human or an infected. I raise my gun and take aim, waiting on it to come close enough so I can tell. The movements are jerky which could mean a runner, or it could mean a survivor with a twisted ankle.

The last thing I want to do is make a mistake, so I wait. A rivulet of sweat trickles down my spine. The figure moves closer and closer. My palms grow damp, and I fear this gun will slip out of my grip.

Finally, I make out a face through the smoke. Fred? I cringe, not trusting him even if he managed to escape the runners without so much as a scratch. But the second he opens his mouth, an inhuman groan of agony issues from between his lips. Blood gushes from his shoulder by his neck. He was bitten and he's already showing signs of being infected.

Still, I hesitate.

I'm shoved to the side and a gun fires. Fred's head jerks back and a spray of dark blood speckles the smog behind him. Then he drops to the ground and doesn't get back up.

"What are you doing?" Phillip demands. I open my mouth to answer, but he just says, "Never mind, we have to take cover." Then he proceeds to drag me and a relieved looking Garcia toward the door that leads down to the cells.

I look around, trusting him to lead me as I look for Jace. But I don't see him anywhere. He should have been back by now. My stomach twists into knots as my mind jumps to every horrible conclusion possible.

The metal door slams shut, and all the noise from outside is blocked out. The silence rings in my ears.

Garcia and Phillip take deep, relieved breaths, but mine start coming in short, quickened bursts. *Jace will never find me in here.* He'll think something bad happened to me… he won't stop looking. I have to go back out there and look for him.

In my panic, I grip the door handle and yank, only to have Phillip throw his body against it and slam it closed.

"Get out of my way."

"Ray, what are you doing? You're going to get killed—you are out of ammo."

Something about Phillip's words make me drop my hands from the door and look at him. "What?"

"You were shooting at that runner, but you were out of bullets," he says calmly but on guard, as if he expects that I'll flip out at any second and run outside.

"I was?" I blink and look over to Garcia, who has a completely worried expression, devoid of any of her usual attitude. I'd thought I had hesitated.

"It's fine, we have extra weapons here." Phillip moves to the black metal cabinet behind one of those old school metal desks and throws it open to reveal four rifles and what looks like two tackle boxes. He grabs one box and drops it on the table with a heavy thud. When he opens it, there's a crap ton—and yes, that is totally a valid measurement—of ammo.

"Ummm," I say, eyeing the guns and the bullets. We only practiced with one of these twice, opting to practice with a hand gun the rest of the time. "Do you have anything smaller?"

He looks at me as he hands Garcia a rifle. She immediately starts gathering ammo and loading her weapon.

"I'm sorry, we should have trained you more on the rifle, but we'll have to make due." He crosses the distance between us. "Don't worry, you just keep shooting, we'll help you load."

With that, I take the proffered weapon, amazed at how much

everything has changed in only two year's time. But now isn't the time to reminisce. We need to rid ourselves of these infected so I can find Jace.

We place the buckets of ammo just inside the door, then making sure we are all ready, Phillip throws open the door. We all huddle in the doorframe so, if need be, we can jump back and close the door and bolt it. We each aim in a different direction, Phillip standing, Garcia kneeling, and me on my belly so the ground can help keep my aim steady. We shoot any runner we see, and none can get close to us. It's a lot harder than the gun I'm used to, but the more I shoot, the more accurate I become.

Eventually, the agonizing cries fade and the screams of pain from those fighting to protect this place quiet, and the smoke clears.

Silently, Garcia and I follow Phillip out of our hiding spot and venture out into the open, checking on the fallen as we go. Most are either dead or alive and hiding. There are a few who have been scratched or bitten but have not yet turned. We get the uninjured to help escort them to the cells, none of us able to deal the killing blow.

The whole time, most of my attention is on searching the faces and making sure none of the injured or dead are Jace.

Then we cross one man who we had thought dead, but as we pass, he moans. Phillip has his gun aimed at him in the blink of an eye. "Bitten or scratched?" he demands.

The man takes a moment to look at us all then says, "Bitten."

"We need to take him to the cells," Phillip starts.

"Nooo," the man moans. "Don't let me become one of them. Let me die a man."

Garcia and I exchange looks.

"We can't—" she says.

"Please, we all know what's going to happen. You have to do it now."

My heart aches. I understand his request, because it would be what I would want. Maybe it makes me a coward, but I don't think I can pull the trigger.

The man reaches out a pleading hand and I can see the circles under his eyes deepen unnaturally fast. The change will happen soon.

Phillip looks green as he says, "You two, go over there."

He doesn't point or indicate any direction but both Garcia and I understand his meaning. We do as he says, then as soon as we are a good distance away, the sound of the shot goes off in the silence. Garcia and I jump in unison as we clutch each others hand and huddle together.

Several minutes later, Phillip rejoins us, his eyes red and face blotchy. None of us speak. We continue moving, and I'm thankful most of the bodies we come across were runners. Somehow, we all push through the horror of what happened, knowing we'll have to process it later and continuing to make sure there isn't a single infected still lurking about.

After what feels like forever but must have been only about an hour, I hear a voice that makes my heart soar.

"Ray!" Jace's voice calls out to me, and I've never been happier.

I shove my gun into Garcia's hands and run to him. He catches me and lifts me up so I can wrap myself around him and hold on tight.

"I was so worried when you never came back," I murmur into the space between his shoulder and his neck.

"I know, I'm so sorry. There was an attack on the entrance to the underground." I jerk back to look him in the face at his words and nearly end up toppling us over. "It's okay, the entrance bottle necked them and we were able to get to them one by one. I meant to come back to you sooner." he finishes his story, then starts peppering me with questions. "Where did you go? What happened?"

I hold up a hand. "We ran out of ammo but we found Phillip. He took us to the entrance to the cells, they had more ammo there."

I hug him tightly and kiss his face a few more times before he sets me down and we rejoin our friends. I hold his hand and squeeze tight, beyond glad that the small group that had become like family all made it through the terrible night.

Dawn slowly creeps closer, setting the sky to a deep purple

and lining the clouds with red and gold. A few stray gunshots ring out then all is silent as we collectively hold our breaths.

The smoke from the dying fires finally clears completely. Bodies are everywhere across this small compound. It had felt so big last night, now it seems small and confining, reminding me of why Jace and I avoided walls this entire time. We had seen our fair share of runners as we spent each day trying to survive, but we had never seen anything like this, not since it first started.

Something Doctor Simmons said to me when I snuck down to see him comes back. The pieces snap into place.

This wasn't just a horde coming for their prey. This was an attack. *This was planned.*

And I know exactly how they did it.

Chapter Twenty-Six

Running Off

Everyone, except the children, spend the rest of the morning cleaning up. Many get sick from the gore. I don't blame them. It's all I can do to keep myself from hurling my guts up. The runner bodies are weirdly soft, as though they were in the process of decomposing for far more than a few hours. It takes longer than it should to purge the hive of the bodies. There are two people per body and a third to guard in case a runner infected one of us and they "wake up" as we carry them outside of the compound.

The trucks with their limited gas supply are used. We load them up and they drive them off to a far enough distance several miles away. I'm told they will stack them all and burn them, so there is zero chance at any coming back.

As the last of the bodies are moved out, I swipe my arm across my forehead, wiping a layer of dirt and sweat away.

It's nearing breakfast time, but I have a feeling we'll all be skipping at least this meal. I can't imagine eating after what happened. Some of the guards are issuing orders to others as a select group begin repairs on the walls and start to fortify the weak spots where the runners broke through, so nothing like this can ever happen again.

Sometime in the late afternoon, Ross walks out from the underground layer and stops one of the guards, they speak with their heads pulled together. Then the guard nods to him and they part ways. Each of them find another guard, and so on, then the guards spread out and one by one collect those of us who have been in meetings over the past few days.

We all exchange a look as, finally, one of the guards approaches us to say there will be a meeting in one hour and everyone who is involved in the mission next week is expected to be there.

Jace and I walk into the meeting held in the same room as usual. There are already several dozen in the room when we enter, but still several more groups of people enter after we manage to find seats next to Garcia and Phillip. Everyone in the room is silent. We didn't lose a lot of our own last night, but there were enough losses that everyone is feeling the pain of knowing they'll never see several of the members of this close knit community again.

Ross stands at the head of the table, two guards on either side, giving the look that he is the commander and they are his generals. It's a deviation in how this place is run and it worries me. It's a community with rules set up by the few who established this place, but in this moment, it feels as though everything is about to change.

I glance over at Jace and he meets my gaze, I can see that he's thinking the same thing. We can't stay in this place if we don't have a voice. We will go back to living in the woods, traveling from town to town until we find a place that feels like home. A place where we can protect ourselves, where no one will find us, and we can grow everything we need on the land we claim. Hopefully it doesn't come to that, I've come to care for this small makeshift family I've found and would hate to lose them. Having a backup plan is essential.

We turn to listen to what Ross has to say. He rambles on about how he's proud of us all for fighting, that our constant training has paid off. Looking around the room, a long pep talk isn't what anyone here needs or wants. As time ticks on, I wonder why this meeting was mandatory, but then he says something that makes my attention snap to him.

"… As of this moment, we are still unsure of how the infected managed to break through our defenses."

Garcia's eyes meet mine and I know I have to say something. I jump to my feet before I can think too hard on it. Raising my hand, I say, "I know."

He stops and drags his eyes to take me in. He's too stunned at my audacity to dare speak up and interrupt him in the middle of his speech for him to respond.

Yeeeaaah, I probably should have waited until the end… but damn it, everyone needs to understand this. Despite mentioning the doctor's theory when I explained it the first two times, no one seems to have paid attention to that detail, having chosen to focus on the vaccines and weapons instead.

Okay, so maybe a tiny part of me is feeling a little smug about pissing him off. It would probably be easier to respect the man if he didn't hate me so much upon first sight.

I clear my throat. "I know how they got in." A low murmur kicks up surrounding me. "They are smarter than we all thought, they aren't just brainless and driven purely by hunger. They knew the weaknesses and how—"

"Young lady, will you please sit down. There will be time enough for questions later," Ross cuts me off.

I immediately plop down in my seat.

A few others speak up in disagreement. "Let her speak. We want to know," pipes up a voice from behind me, and an "I want to know what she has to say," comes from somewhere to my left.

Ross smiles at the crowd, but it doesn't reach his slightly narrowed eyes. "Oh course," he says, turning to me. "Miss Marrow, please tell us what you think you know."

I hesitate, but Garcia nudges me lightly and encourages me to stand again. "Doctor Simmons said he believed they had a way of communicating among themselves."

Ross chuckles as if I had just said something adorable, which burns away any lingering uncertainty I have left. "There's no way to prove that," he says condescendingly.

I grit my teeth. "Scotty was among them. When we were on our way here, we had thought they—" I pause because I don't want to say *ripped him to shreds,* even though that's exactly what everyone had thought. "—killed him. But they didn't, they turned him and somehow used him and his knowledge of this place to penetrate the weak spots. I believe the doctor was right—they are able to communicate. And at the very least, we should approach them as if they are intelligent."

Murmuring erupts throughout the room as Ross looks around taking everyone in and doing a good job at keeping his composure, except for the flaring of his nostrils. I can't make out most of the talking but catch a few words here and there. *Scotty. Each other. Impossible.*

"Very well. Thank you, Miss Marrow, we will go ahead with that information as if it were true. But we will also expect a good deal of mindless attacking. We cannot let our guard down around them."

I can barely keep my jaw from dropping.

"You did well," Jace whispers in my ear once I take my seat.

I give him a tight smile. Butting heads with Ross could cause me nothing but trouble, but standing up for myself, making sure everyone has the facts they need, will only help in the long run.

I have Jace by my side to back me up, and I know Ross wants every Vor'onin he can get his hands on, so he won't do anything too horrible if he wants to keep him around.

He'll just make my life a pain, and I can live with that.

Ross goes on to say that the mission we have set for six nights from now will be moved up to tonight.

Garcia grips my hand and squeezes it in both of hers. I barely manage to keep from jumping. She's been so still and quiet in the meeting, I almost forgot she was there. She doesn't look at me but her jaw is clenched tight, and there are tears brimming in her eyes. I pat her hand with my free one, and she answers with the slightest twitch of her lips turning up into a ghost of a smile.

I sit in a daze through the rest of the meeting, trying to absorb everything. The meeting drones on for hours, as we go over everything again and again. Until the changes in the original plans have been solidified and memorized by everyone.

Then in a way that feels almost too abrupt, we are all dismissed. Everyone files out quietly and heads to the dining hall or their quarters. The halls are eerily quiet and I'm glad to be inside our little one room home with the door shut firmly behind us.

"I can't believe he didn't tell me to get out," I say in awe as I plop down on the bed.

Jace moves about the room. "The others in the room believed you, so dismissing you would only make things harder on him. It helps that you shared that information in the original meeting."

He stops getting ready for the impending mission and crosses the room to me and takes my face in his hands. "You standing up there was important. Never second guess that. Only you spoke to the doctor before he turned, so only you were able to make that known. It will save lives. I think deep down, even Ross knows that."

"Thank you." I lean my face into his palm and close my eyes, enjoying the simple touch.

"Come on," Jace says after a moment. "We should get ready, then get some rest before tonight."

I tap my fingers on the steering wheel as I drive down a long dark stretch of highway. Jace, being on a completely different team, was in one of the first vehicles. Four men sit in the back of this one, all clutching a rifle with two more guns—one on each hip—and a variety of pointy weapons strapped to arms and legs.

"Hey, it's going to be okay," Phillip says, placing a hand on my shoulder. "We have a plan. We'll get through this and all of us will make it home."

I drag my gaze from the never ending darkness ahead and frown at him. "We are basically running head first into a hornets nest. We'll be trapped underground with who knows how many runners. What if something happens to Jace? Or Garcia, or you?"

A rock settles in the pit of my stomach as my nerves grow.

Somehow I had stupidly pushed aside how dangerous this all was. But if I'd stayed behind, as Ross would have preferred, I wouldn't be able to live with myself. I loathe the idea of letting everyone I care about go inside that compound while I sit safely underground at the hive.

He gives me an understanding smile. "I get it, Ray, I'm worried about the same thing—we all are. But we have a plan— all four of us have memorized the code just as everyone else has. The important thing is getting that vaccine and those notes so we can start fixing this world."

I pull in a deep breath then let it out slowly, trying to calm my racing nerves.

"How long is this drive?" I ask, looking at the clock for perhaps the hundredth time since we left the Tower.

"It's roughly a little over two hours, but…" He holds up a hand to stop me from speaking. "We are moving slower, trying to keep quiet… come on, Ray. You know this. It will take between three and a half to four hours to get there. You've been staring at that damn clock every thirty seconds. It's going to be a long night, try not to make it worse on yourself."

I'm too tightly wound up on the inside, but I can tell my anxiety is starting to effect him, so for his sake I sit back and relax my posture, trying to appear at ease, though my brain continues to worry over every detail of the plan.

Eventually the monument comes into view. I follow the truck in front of me into a large parking lot, and when I find a spot, I cut the engine.

Phillip looks at me and says, "Stay here. I'll come back for you in a few minutes."

I listen, going over the steps to our plan in my head over and over as I squint into the dark at the looming monument ahead. I'm about to start questioning everything when the men who'd been in the back jog past me in a stealthy military fashion, then Phillip opens the door and jumps back in.

"We can't get closer?" I ask.

"Sorry, it's easier this way." He turns on a small screen that has been attached to the dash.

It displays a grainy black and white feed that separates the small screen into four quadrants. The top left is Jace, and he's already made it to the vents. I bite my lip, hating that he's in there without me. The second is Garcia's group, they are even further into the compound, while the third and fourth are groups I'm not familiar with.

We watch silently together, waiting for the final vehicle to arrive and the men to go inside. Then it will be our turn. Only two more left and we can move in.

My heart plummets when the bottom right feed fizzes out. Phillip and I look at each other, eyes wide.

Something is not right.

"Ray," he says slowly, holding his hands up as if I'm a wild animal about to pounce.

Then the bottom left feed goes out and I know we have

to go now.

I turn and throw open the door and Phillip grabs my hand to stop me, but I've already launched myself out of the cab and his grip falls away.

I run through the avenue of flags and take a sharp left once I get to the visitor center entrances and head left, toward the trail that will take me to the base of the monument.

Chapter Twenty-Seven

The Shattering

I have to get to Jace before whatever is happening reaches him too. If I lose him… I shake off the thought. I can't go there right now or I won't make it to him. I have to believe that I can still get to him before it's too late.

Phillip catches up to me as I hit the narrow, paved path. "Ray," he pants. "We should wait, we don't know what's happened." I don't slow down as I say, "That's exactly why we have to go in now."

He curses under his breath and grabs my shoulder, forcing me to a stop. I'm about to shove him away when he thrusts a holstered gun into my hand. "Then take this, and let's go."

He takes the lead and when we reach the spot where it veers to the east and runs along the base of the monument, we head off path to a solid large stone and the crevice behind it where a thick door is propped open by a rock. Together, Phillip and I pry it open enough so we can fit through. It's on some kind of mechanism that no longer works to open and close it without the use of brute strength.

Inside, the walls, ceiling, and floor are covered in thick metal. It is exactly what I always imagined a secret government bunker to look like. We can hear shouts and groaning from further inside. The tunnel heads straight for what seems like a long time then forks in two directions. Dim, flickering emergency lights above light the way.

I start to move forward in search of a vent, but Phillip's arm shoots out in front of me.

"There," he says pointing to an air vent in the wall. "Come on, I'll lift you up. We'll be safer in there."

He kneels down and cups his hands, creating a foothold. I place a boot in his hands and press my front against the smooth metal wall, reaching up for the ledge. He boosts me up and I quickly scramble inside. Immediately, the walls seem to close in on me but I force myself to crawl forward.

Phillip pulls himself up and in after me. I balk at the darkness before me now that his body blocks the dim light shining inside.

"It's a tight fit," he grumbles more to himself.

"Is this the vent we planned?" My question barely makes sense but he seems to understand me.

"Yes."

There's a click and a faint glow, followed by a rattling as he tosses a glow stick up to me attached to a string so I can loop it around my neck. There's another click and a soft glow emanates from behind me. I try to visualize the map as I navigate my way toward the lab. I count the turns we pass until I get to the first right we're supposed to take.

"Ray," Phillip's voice startles me. "I'm sorry… I need to go left here."

"What? Why?" I panic at the thought of being left alone. He's supposed to go with me. That was the plan.

"I have to make sure Garcia's team is okay."

The look in his eyes tells me this is something he has to do. I know that look. It's one I've seen on Jace's face, and one I have worn in the past. I can feel it in my very soul. He loves her, even if he's never said it, even if he doesn't realize it yet. I understand him with every fiber of my being.

"Okay. We'll meet up at the lab later?"

"No, you and Jace get the notes and as much of the vaccine as possible and get out. We'll meet at the truck. The keys are in the ignition, so if you have to go, then go. Don't wait for me."

"We can't—"

"Don't argue with me for once, Ray," he snaps. "Just do what you're told for once in your life." He starts to move past me at the intersection.

"Be safe," I whisper after him.

Phillip pauses but doesn't look back. "You too, Ray... I'll see you on the other side."

With that, we part and I continue to move toward the lab. I don't know what happened to Jace, and as much as I want to go to find him now, I know I have to get the vaccines and notes first.

I hate being alone in the dark. I feel like a child stuck in a nightmare turned reality where all the monsters have come to life and are hunting me. Which I suppose isn't too far from the truth. The path my thoughts have taken make me move faster out of pure instinct. I have to concentrate on slowing to avoid making the metal creak and groan.

Turning down what should be the final stretch, I see a grated vent ahead of me. I inch forward until I'm forced to stop. I stick my fingers through the grate and try to move or dislodge it.

It doesn't budge.

I press my face up against the dusty metal and peer down. It leads to a hallway, and on the other side is a door with a lit up glowing keypad. There's a large panorama window to the left of the door and a window in the upper half of the door. I can't see through the glass to what lays beyond it as it's pitch black on the other side, but I know it's the lab.

I thought this vent would take me directly to it, but it must have a separate ventilation system.

Twisting in the too tight space, I finally manage to turn so my feet face the vent exit. I brace my arms against the sides and kick with both feet until the metal bends and warps under the force. I hear a groaning but I can't tell if it's echoing through the vents from another hallway or if it's *in* the vent with me.

I kick harder and one corner pops free. Focusing my strength on the other lower corner, I kick and kick until it too comes free. I flip to my belly and back toward it, pushing my legs through the opening. The covering scrapes over the backs of my legs as I shimmy myself through. It presses down on my back, leaving scratches but somehow I manage to make it out until I'm dangling by my fingertips.

I look down to the floor still several feet below me and instantly regret it. Taking a deep breath and bracing myself for the impact, I let go. I try to keep my knees bent but I still manage to roll backward and land on my butt, but the momentum keeps me falling until I'm flat on my back.

Rolling to my side, I push up to standing and brush off the pain.

A groan bordering on an animalistic roar echoes from down the hall.

"Shit," I whisper and lunge for the keypad.

With shaky fingers, I enter the code, hitting the wrong final number. The glow flashes from green to red and beeps at me. My breathing increases. I try again and once more hit the wrong combination.

"Slow it down, Ray," I say to myself then take two

calming breaths.

On the third try, it finally beeps once and flashes green. The mechanism for the door disengages the lock and it pops open. I quickly slide through and shut it. I press my back to the door and slide down.

Gripping my bag, I slide it around to my chest, clutching it tightly. There's no way I'm getting out of here through the vents again. Not by myself. I'll come to that problem after I find the vials of vaccine first.

I give myself one minute to pull my nerves together then I stand and run to the door in the back of the lab leading to the room of refrigerated units. They are labeled but I don't know what the codes mean. Doctor Simmons never mentioned batches. I rub my temples trying to focus instead of panicking.

Okay, the doctor said he had files in the back room, those might have the notes I need. I back out of the cold lab and into the main room, looking around until I find a door that leads to the only office space I can see. I try the knob, but just my luck, it's locked.

I find a fire extinguisher strapped to one of the tables in the room and grab it, taking it to the door and smashing it against the doorknob. Each time it connects with the metal, the vibration rattles my bones. After several hits, the knob finally moves and hangs loose. I kick the door open and groan at the mess within.

This looks like the office of a mad scientist or a very

scatterbrained man. Papers are scattered across the desk and several drawers from two file cabinets in the corner are left partially open.

Crossing the room, I start at the desk, skimming the papers as I straighten them in the best semblance of order that I can figure out. Some pages are stained by what I can only guess is spilled coffee. I doubt those are the notes I need, but I flip through them anyway. Nothing on the top seems to be what I'm looking for so I move down to the bottom drawer and pull it out. Stacks of papers are shoved in there. Again, I can't imagine he would treat something so important as the vaccine with such carelessness. Nevertheless, I pull all the papers out and sort through them.

This is starting to feel hopeless. I'm spending way too much time searching.

I move to the other drawer and find much of the same. As I'm pulling out the mess of papers, my fingers brush against something more solid. I snatch it up and find it's an old leather notebook with sticky notes poking out from between the pages and a leather tie wrapped around it.

I quickly flip through the pages, hardly able to believe my eyes. These are the notes I'm looking for. There's a combination of scientific scribbles, formulas I don't understand, and thoughts written and dated much like a diary. At the back, I find a passage talking about how this is the closest they've come to a cure. He named it *Phoenix's Retribution*. I roll my eyes at the cheesy name but I suppose it's something that held meaning for him. Next to the name is what appears to be a batch number: PRZ-42. I memorize that code then shove the notebook into my bag before returning to the cold room.

I scan the batches of vials and am halfway through when an explosion shakes the room all around me. Debris falls from above as part of the vent falls down and knocks over the three cold units.

I dive under a metal table, trying to avoid getting crushed, and cover my head as glass shatters from everywhere.

When the dust clears, I lift my head. Every unit has fallen.

No, no, no, no, *no*! I rush to the fallen units and finally locate the batch of the vaccine I was looking for. More than half are shattered. The red liquid within spilling over everything. My fingers are cut as I sort through the mess looking for any that might have survived.

I only manage to find a little over a dozen unbroken vials. I search the room to find something to put them in that will protect what little remains and spot a hand cloth that I quickly shred into slices. I wrap them individually then all together. It will have to do for now. But my hands are bleeding so I slice off my sleeves and wrap them the best I can.

Now to get out of this hellhole and find Jace.

I make it to the main room only to find the glass window to also be shattered. Moaning comes from just outside and I can see shadows cast along the far wall, backlit by the orange glow of fire as smoke billows around the ceiling.

It looks like getting out through the vents isn't going to be possible after all, even if I could reach and lift myself up.

I draw my gun for the first time and take the safety off as I quietly make my way between two tables that had been blasted together from the explosion. I manage to fit in the tight space of shadows my cover provides and cover my mouth with my hand to stifle the sound of my breathing.

The moans grow closer until I see several feet shuffle before me.

I could reach out and grab one of them if I wanted to. Instead, I watch as they move to the cold room en masse.

Then the shattering begins.

Chapter Twenty-Eight

Unsatiated

I suck in a breath and make a dash for the door while they are in the other room destroying what they believe to be the cure. Now, what I hold is the key. It's all that is left. I have to find a way to make sure that no matter what, these vials and notes make it out and into someone's hands who can do something with it.

Out in the corridor, several bodies are scattered on the floor. I look left and right, trying to remember the maps from the plans, trying to remember the route Jace and his group have taken. Left will take me toward the entrance, but Jace is somewhere to the right, keeping inside.

I look at my watch—we still have time. There's an hour before the explosions are set to go off if everything is going to plan. I feel sick at the decision before me, but in the end, there's only one choice I can take.

I head to the left and run. I leap over the bodies and sprint through the lingering dust and smoke in the air. I stop as soon as I turn the corner. A horde of runners stands about halfway down the hall. One swerves and spots me, and then they all turn.

They barrel through the hall in a tidal wave of limbs, shoving each other out of the way, trampling one another, all in an attempt to get to me. I lift my gun and aim. I fire and one falls, but is quickly replaced by another.

The gun fires, again, and again, and again.

Three more runners fall. I shoot, taking one down with every bullet until only one runner remains. I press the trigger and it clicks, letting me know I'm out of ammo.

I turn and run as fast as I can back the way I came. The runner is on my heels as I fumble to see if I have another clip in my bag's side pocket. I was so stupid to rush into this mountain without checking my bag first. My fingers catch on something cold and metal. I pull it out and thank Phillip for being far more prepared than I was.

I drop the old used clip and pop the new one in. The noise of unsatiated hunger and violence follows close behind. I turn and aim, firing at the runner as it leaps toward me. Its head snaps back from the bullet but its body still flies forward and crashes into me. I land hard on my back, sprawling on the ground with its heavy body on top of me.

I lay on the ground in pain as I attempt to regain my breath.

The dead runner on top of me is heavy and oozing goo from the bullet wound.

Struggling to push him off, I push with my arms and roll out from under him. I need to get out of this area and fast before more runners come, called by the sound of my gun. I check my bag quickly to make sure none of the vials have broken. They all look intact.

I take off down the hall and head in the direction the armory should be.

Navigating the halls littered with bodies, I try not to look at them as I pass but am unable to help myself from scanning their faces to make sure none of them are Jace. A few I recognize, most I don't. I keep my gun out and pointed up, ready for another surge of runners.

The armory is picked over and empty by the time I reach it. I search for more clips anyway. Somehow I luck out and find two empty and a few small boxes of ammo. I load the clips then tuck them into my bag, stuffing an extra rag I found between the vials and spares.

"Ray?" a voice makes me freeze in place. My mind spins as I realize who it came from.

"Jace?" I call out a little too loud. I spin around, expecting him to be right there, but I don't see him.

"Here," he says from behind a wall that sticks out several feet. I run to him but what I see crushes my heart. Jace is on the floor, his back up against the wall, legs spread out before him and his hand pressed tight to his arm, his other against his abdomen.

I fall to my knees at his side. "What happened?" I try to pry his hands away but he won't let me. "Jace, let me look at it. I need to see how bad it is."

"You need to leave, Ray," he says, but he sounds defeated.

"I will, with *you*, once we get you fixed up."

"Stop, Ray. I've been scratched." His words are harsh, but I know it's not directed at me.

I'm still not sure what to do with myself, with that news. The bodies of his teammates were outside this room, all dead. But they had left him. I know the runners wanted him to change, to become one of them.

He winces and I pull the hand on his abdomen away, it's a clean cut.

"What happened?"

He grimaces. "One of the guys tried to kill me after I was scratched."

I don't know if he says anymore because my vision fills with red and my blood roars in my ears. One guess as to who the guy who stabbed him was. "I will kill him," I snarl.

"I'll never make it, Ray. Please go. I love you."

"Shut up, you idiot. I'm not leaving here without you."

"You need to leave," he says again. I move from my crouching position and sit next to him. "I can't leave here without you... I need you."

"No, you need to find the vaccine and get out. Save this world, Ray."

My head snaps up at his mention of the vaccine. I reach into my bag and fish out one vial.

"What is that?"

"It's what is going to keep you with me," I say. I pop the top off to find there's a small needle then I work the rubber part of the bottom off exposing a plunger. A built in syringe. Handy. I thought the rubber was around the top and bottom to protect them, but they managed to serve another purpose as well. "Move your hand."

"No, don't waste it."

"Jace, you know I love you but I am *this* close to knocking you out so I can give this to you. You are not a waste. And don't you dare tell me to leave you here again, when we both damn well know that you would never leave me here if our situations were reversed."

We have a silent battle of wills, then I get tired of it, of wasting time, and I push his hand away. The thin sheen of sweat that has built up on his forehead is telling me we don't have much time before the change starts.

This time, he doesn't fight me. I plunge it into his arm right over the scratch, probably a little rougher than necessary, but I don't want to take the chance that he'll try to martyr himself. I watch the red liquid disappear into his arm.

"Where are the others?" he asks.

"I'm not sure." I sit against the wall, leaning on his good side. "When we were waiting, the feeds started to cut out, so we ran in here. Phillip went in search of Garcia, I came after you and the vaccine."

"Did you find the notes?"

I nod against him.

"Good."

"Do you think you can walk?" I ask, sitting up. "We need to get out now. There's twenty minutes before they blow this place."

He nods, and with some difficulty, I help him to his feet. Jace drapes an arm over my shoulder until he finds his balance. I have everything that matters in this world and I'm getting them the hell out of here.

Chapter Twenty-Nine

Goop and Gore

We were lucky Jace still had his handgun, because I don't think he could shoot the rifle right now. I made sure we both had as many full clips as possible before we left the armory.

The halls have quieted some and I worry that everyone who survived this mission has already left without us. But we will deal with that as soon as we get out of this maze.

"Do you remember how to get from here to the exit?" I ask. Glancing down both ends of the corridor, I feel turned around. I can't remember which direction I came from and there's at least five hallways sprouting from this one.

Jace nods his head in one direction, picking up the silent way of communicating that we used for so long. I follow his lead and we move slowly and quietly down a maze of halls. I am glad he remembers the way because I never would have figured it out, since I came in through the vents.

The reek of dead bodies permeates the air and it's all I can do to avoid vomiting. Most of the rooms we pass are either locked or open and trashed, a few are on fire, billowing smoke that leaks slowly into the hall, but even those are beginning to die out.

After several turns down identical hallways, Jace stops and turns to me. Bringing his mouth down to my ear he says, "We are almost there. Stay here, I'll make sure the hall is clear."

He presses his back against the wall, flattening himself and peeks around the corner for a second before returning. Jace grabs me by the arm and pulls me into an open room that's been trashed. Desks turned over, papers thrown about, everything not nailed down is toppled. He drags me behind a knocked over bookcase where we crouch.

What is it? I mouth.

Runners.

How many?

He doesn't answer, only hangs his head. I tap him on the shoulder, insisting he tells me.

Jace shrugs. *Too many.*

We sit and look at each other, then at the bag slung over my shoulder. How could we get so close only to die yards from the exit, and the cure with us. There's no way for us to get word out. No way to radio for help. No way to escape except through a horde of runners. Going back the other way would take too long.

I'm falling into a pit of despair and feeling the anger rise up when Jace waves his hands and points to the bag, then mimes giving myself a shot. I frown at him, not understanding why he'd want me to waste a perfectly good sample when we already have so few and we are doomed to die here.

He shakes his head then leans in close. "Give yourself a shot, and trust me."

I do as he says, hoping that whatever idea he has will work, because, at this point, we are screwed anyway. If we die, the hope these vials contain dies with us.

Once I do, he motions for me to follow. We turn back the way we had come, toward the armory until we reach a pile of three fallen runners that seemed to be further along in the rotting process than most.

Trust me, he mouths, which makes me want to question whatever his plan is.

He bends down and motions for me to hand him my knife, which I reluctantly do. Then I watch in horror as he cuts the runner open and reaches in, scooping out some of the innards and smearing them on his clothes and exposed skin, keeping it well away from the stab wound.

I hold up my hands and back away into the wall behind me, shaking my head. He gives me an impatient look but I'm barely able to keep my stomach from revolting as it is.

This is the only chance we have.

I don't want to agree, and I'm adamant that we can find another way. A glance at my watch tells me otherwise. Thirteen minutes.

Another boom shakes the entire underground. Dust plumes from behind us, as if to say that through the horde is the only way out.

I swear and surrender to his plan. I let him smear the goo all over me, glopping some extra around my neck, presumably to disguise any pheromones I'm emitting. Then for good measure, he runs his gore-covered hands over my face and hair. I'm about to be sick, so I back away.

If this doesn't do the trick, then no amount of corpse innards will.

He points to the bag, and when I bring it forward, he covers the outside with two fistfuls of the stuff. Then slowly, he leads me down the hallway just before we turn into the section where the horde awaits us.

Jace takes my face in his hands, pressing his forehead against mine. "I love you, Ray. I was born to be with you and I'll stay by your side until the bitter end. I don't plan on letting us die now… but I want you to know before we walk into that horde, that you are my heart, my soul, my everything."

I'm taken aback by his declaration. I've always known we were meant for each other, that I belonged with him since the moment we met… but we never said the words like this. We just knew it. Hearing them out loud like this is more powerful than I could imagine.

If we make it out alive, then I'll make it a point to say the words out loud from now on.

"I love you too, Jace'el," I say his full name, a habit I'd dropped for a shortened version long ago. But it seems to make him happy. "Not even the stars could keep us apart."

He squeezes my hand once before dropping it to the side. Quietly, we slip into the side room from earlier and hide behind the door. Then Jace picks up a plant in a ceramic pot and hurls it down the hallway.

Just as predicted, the runners rush by our room toward the sound. As the last one passes, we exit, doing our best to run in the somewhat awkward and clumsy way they have.

Once we enter the main foyer, I recognize the hall as being the one Phillip and I entered through. I'd somehow managed to go in the full circle of this compound. We almost reach the exit when the runners rush us. I keep my head down to hide that I don't have the same deathly pale eyes they do. Somehow, I keep from screaming, trying to wander as Jace does.

The runners encircle us, sniffing and grunting. They aren't sure about us but the smell of death on us makes them believe we are one of them. My heart skips a painful beat as I realize one of the runners is Brian. He'd stabbed Jace in the hopes of using him as bait to get away, and he ended up as one of them anyway. I hold my breath and squeeze my eyes shut, hoping against hope that he doesn't recognize us.

After a too long moment, he moves on and faces the small opening of the door. After each has had a chance to inspect us, they resume mindless milling about.

The runners tighten the space between them at the entrance, blocking the door. Gradually, Jace and I work our way closer and closer to the propped door.

But Jace stops in the middle and slowly reaches into a pocket and pulls out something that looks like a grenade. My eyes go wide and I almost shout at him not to before I remember where we're at.

The look on his face asks me to trust him, so I give him the barest nod then continue to push my way closer to the door. They can feel the fresh air coming through the small crack, but they don't seem to quite know the origin.

With a flick of his wrist, he pulls the pin then flicks the thing back down the hall. Immediately, all eyes turn toward it, sniffing. One runs after the noise, then another and another, until they've all passed us. Jace runs to me and slams his body against the door while pushing me out.

We stumble and fall to the hard ground. He shoves the rock propping it open, it doesn't move. I jump to my feet and pull on the door and he shoves it again, moving it out of the way. I let go and the door slams shut, just as arms pass through the opening.

I turn my head, not wanting to watch the dismemberment.

We run down the slope toward the parking lot.

I take in huge gulps of air, never happier to be outside than I am in this moment. It feels almost eerie to pass the avenue of flags now. In the dim light, I notice many of them are tattered into strips from a long time of no one to care for them. It almost feels symbolic.

We make it to the parking lot and find all guns of the remaining people on our teams aimed at us. Most of the vehicles have already left, only three remain.

I can only imagine how we look to them. Like runners. I'm a little shocked that they haven't gunned us down and taken off yet.

We raise our hands in the air as we wait for them to give us a command. The only thing we can do now is act human because we sure as hell don't look it.

One man slowly approaches as many more surround him and narrow in on us. They all stop a fair distance away.

"Are you scratched or bitten?" the front man asks.

"No," Jace and I say in unison.

"Do you feel ill?"

"No," we say again.

There's a long pause as the man questioning us moves back to speak in hushed tones to another. When he faces us again, he asks, "What are your names?"

I can feel a twitch develop under my right eye. He's clearly making this all up as he goes along. Whoever was supposed to be in charge at this point must not have made it back out. That realization bothers me.

"I am Jace'el and this is Raylinn Marrow," Jace says.

"You're telling the truth about not being infected?"

I take half a step forward, cutting off anything else Jace was about to say and making sure all guns are on me. "Of course we're not lying. We wouldn't endanger everyone like that. We know how the virus spreads. But I need you to listen to me now. There is a horde of runners trying to get out from the inside, so we need to get going before they figure it out."

"You look like one of them," the man pipes up, ignoring what I just said.

I grit my teeth and say, "We had to disguise ourselves." I take another half step forward.

"Stop advancing," he shouts.

"Look, you can see we aren't infected, we are talking to you—"

"I'll decide."

I'm about to say something that will most likely get me shot, but Garcia's voice calls out from behind them. "Stick them in the back and let's go, we can interrogate them when we're on the road."

"But they might be—"

She groans loudly and stomps over to where the guy is standing and pushes between them and up to me. "Raylinn, have you been bitten or scratched?"

"No," I say clearly.

Garcia grabs me by the wrist and turns to him. "See? Not infected, just really disgusting." Then under her breath she whispers, "Did you find it?"

"Yes."

"If you know what's good for everyone, you'll get your butts in the vehicles and we'll leave this place before it blows."

My heart hammers at those last words.

Still, the guy hesitates a long moment before having every armed man in his semicircle escort Jace and I to the back of one of the trucks. There's a small metal cage with substantial bars. It sucks, but I'll take it.

They slam the door closed and make sure it's locked tight.

Garcia lifts her shirt and pulls it off, leaving her in a tank. "Here, change into this, you'll need to make yourself somewhat presentable for when we get back."

She starts to turn away but stops to give me a sly smile over her shoulder. "I'm proud of you."

"Thanks," then before I can forget, I ask, "Phillip?"

Garcia nods. "He's alive… for now. He was scratched trying to save me. He only has a few days before they'll shoot him."

Then she eyes me, though she doesn't mention the vaccine.

"Wait," I say as I hold out my bag for her to take.

She shakes her head and says, "Keep it, you'll need it."

I understand her unspoken words. I defied the plan, and my friends might have helped, but I'd never tell. Ross will kick me out with or without Jace. I'll need the vaccine and the notes so we can replicate it as insurance.

The driver of our truck sticks his head out and calls, "Move out!" as he circles one finger in the air.

Desmond comes running into the lot from the avenue of flags and jumps into the open door of the vehicle in front of us and yells "Go, go, go!"

At once, all the vehicles peel out and drive as if they all floor it. I'm thrown to the side and only manage to avoid smashing my face on the metal trunk bed thanks to Jace catching me and holding me to him.

We are several miles out when an explosion rocks the ground, followed by another and another, in a chain of more than I expected. I watch as Mt. Rushmore becomes smaller and smaller as we put distance between it and us, then it falls from view.

The world feels stuck in slow motion as a cloud of dust rises and spreads out in all directions. It takes a few minutes before it reaches us. But by the time it hits, washing over us like a wave, it has lost most of its power.

Jace and I are coated in a layer of dirt, being pelted by small pebbles that sting but otherwise don't hurt. We cough when the dust clears and the vehicles all slow to a safer speed.

The Rushmore compound is no more—a once great monument to a world that no longer exists, gone forever.

Jace and I settle back, trying to get as comfortable as we can in the chilled morning. He wraps his arms around me and pulls me into his side.

The drive back is long and cold. We watch the sun rise behind us as the beams break through the billowing smoke that still drifts up into the sky. I clutch my bag to my lap, holding onto it like it means the world.

And it does.

It means a future. A chance. It means... everything if humans and Vor'onins alike are to survive.

CHAPTER THIRTY

One Bag to Save Them All

We reach the Tower around mid morning.

"How's your arm?" I ask Jace under my breath as we approach the gates.

"Healed. That vaccine has some of the healing serum from our ships."

"You mean those scary big syringes?" I ask.

He nods.

"Good," I say, relieved.

We grow quiet as our vehicle brings up the end of the line going inside the gate. One truck is let through at a time, making the process take forever. But I see why once it's our turn.

First those on the inside cab are told to exit one at a time and are closely examined for signs of bites or scratches before being sent to the cells or let go. Jace and I are the last to be looked at.

I'm glad we spent the ride back getting as much of the gore off us as possible and wrapping Jace's stab wound. Thankfully, he wore a black shirt so the blood isn't visible through the cloth. We look like two people blasted by a dust storm and nothing more.

He is let go but waits for me a few yards back so he's not in their way or perceived as a threat.

"What is that?" the guard asks, pointing to my bag.

"It's important," I say.

"Give it here," he says, holding out his hand.

I steel my spine and pretend to have more courage than I do. I don't know if he was told to confiscate anything or if he's just curious, but I know I will not be letting this bag out of my hands without being in a meeting. My gaze flicks to Jace standing back and looking at me, waiting patiently. I have too much to lose.

"No," I state firmly.

The guard checking me for bites and scratches only raises a questioning brow.

"It's too important. Call a meeting with Ross and all those who went on this mission, and whoever else is in charge. Then I'll explain."

He doesn't seem to have any real authority so he shrugs and says, "He won't appreciate you trying to call a meeting, but I'll tell him you're looking for him. Anyway, you check out and you're free to go now."

I don't waste another second, I run to Jace's side. He picks me up in a tight hug and I throw my arms around his neck. He kisses me then. The relief at finally being back apparent, knowing that we have answers, knowing that we still have each other, and for once, feeling as if our life is more than trying to survive one day at a time.

"We have to find Garcia," I say in hushed tones as we walk toward the underground entrance.

We walk as fast as we can without drawing attention to ourselves, but as soon as our feet hit the landing of the underground area, we come face to face with Ross. Jace tries to stand protectively in front of me as he senses the all too clear irritation on Ross's face.

"I was informed that you went rogue on the mission, I knew it was a terrible decision to let you go. And now you want to call a meeting?"

"You will not—"

I squeeze Jace's hand to remind him that he can't fight my battles for me when it comes to Ross.

"You're having a debriefing meeting anyway, aren't you?" I demand, and he nods. "Then make sure we are there." Then I walk around him and continue on my way, knowing Jace will be only a few steps behind.

Once I'm around the corner, I sprint for Garcia's room and

knock on the door. She opens it, her eyes rimmed in red. She stands there almost as if she is in a trance, then throws her arms around me and I hug her back.

She only pulls away once Jace joins us.

"Can you visit Phillip?" I ask in a hushed whisper as we all move inside.

"I-I think so, I know the guys on guard duty now. I can make them let me in."

"Good," I say then reach into my bag and pull out a single wrapped vial. "I need you to go in there now and give him this."

She stares at the red liquid syringe in my hand. "But won't we need that to replicate?" she asks. But the hunger of hope glistens in her eyes.

"We have enough, and he's family. We can save him with this… we have to."

She nods and takes it from me, gripping it firmly in her hand.

We leave her quarters soon after that. Garcia is to make her way down into the cells. I don't see or hear from her again until evening, and Jace and I are to clean up before I escort him to the med bay. As much as I wanted to take him first thing, it would have raised red flags. So we let things settle down.

I'm half tempted to give the doctor the vaccine right then and there… but I need it for the meeting.

The doctor gives Jace a few stitches and the wound is already doing much better, thanks to the vaccine's Vor'onin medicine in it.

Garcia walks into that meeting, her head held high, and I know she was successful. *One last mission.*

I'm glad to see both Desmond and Mon'te there. Of course I had caught a glimpse of Desmond as we were leaving Rushmore, but I hadn't seen or heard of Mon'te's fate until this moment.

The meeting is long and I am on the edge of my seat the entire time, waiting for my turn. When it is, I stand on shaky legs. Still clutching my bag to me.

I take several deep breaths before I speak. "What I have here in this bag will change everything." I look around the room and make eye contact with everyone. I want their full attention. "Inside, I hold the only vials of the vaccine created by Doctor Simmons. And while there are only eleven, I also have his notes."

The room erupts in chatter, and questions. Many questions are thrown at me, but I can't make them out in the dim of whoops and hollers. The doctor here, Doctor Vasquez runs forward and grips me by the shoulders, pure elation on his face. He hugs me and it's finally then that I hand over the bag.

After answering all the questions to the best of my knowledge, I sit and listen with half an ear to the rest of the meeting, unable to concentrate.

We did it. Nothing went to plan but we made it back, and

Phillip will be fine, they'll see that in a few days when he doesn't turn.

Hope wells in my chest, knowing for once that this world isn't doomed to be slowly ripped apart.

A week later, there's a bonfire held in the center of the hive's open area for all those who died in the attack and in the rescue mission at Rushmore.

Jace, Garcia, Phillip, Desmond, Mon'te, and I stand together, all holding hands as people take turns talking. Garcia leans into Phillip and rests her head on his shoulder. He places his cheek against the top of her head.

They read off a list of names. Some I knew, others I didn't. But the one thing we all have in common is that we each lost someone. Scotty's name is read last, which brings a fresh wave of emotion to our group.

I silently add the names of my parents, Toby, Miranda, Shane, Josh, and even Brian—as horrible as he was. No one deserves that fate. Everyone I ever knew or encountered whose name I knew, and if I didn't know, then I think of who they were to us on our journey.

Alive or dead, I think of everyone.

After everything that brought us here, after everything that happened, this world now has a chance at a new beginning.

Epilogue

The End of it All

Two years later...

It took thousands of years for civilization to reach the height we knew it as. Then this world was plunged into darkness by what was once thought to be impossible—nothing more than fiction, and only weeks, if not days to fall.

But some of us have survived, and we lock ourselves away behind barriers and walls, always on guard, always watching and searching. This is how the world is, at least for now.

There's a long road ahead of us and it might even get worse before it gets better. But it *will* get better.

We have the vaccine, the key to stopping this infestation. Scientists and doctors are working hard on replicating it. Everyone gets one to keep the runner population from growing. It's not our endgame, though it is a start in the right direction.

Thanks to Doctor Simmons and those who worked with him to develop the vaccine, we will declare war on the runners and take back what is ours and leave the future generations the tools and the weapons needed to make it happen. Human and Vor'onin alike, we will heal this world.

One day at a time.

Jace having had experience under Doctor Lar'ruk is assisting Doctor Vasquez with replicating the vaccine and rescue missions are putting in renewed efforts to find the materials needed.

Every day we continue to search for more survivors and focus on opening up ways to communicate with other compounds, getting them our notes and helping them develop their own batches of the vaccine. We aren't out of the woods yet, there is still danger out there waiting for us every step of the way.

But one thing's for sure... We will never stop fighting to right this world and rid it of every last runner.

Reclaiming this world might not happen in our lifetime, it might not even happen in the next, or the one after that, but one day, future generations will be free to walk the earth without worry of runners and build it to be better than it was before.

For now, the world is a dark place, and it will remain so for a long time yet to come, but dawn will break, and with it, it will bring the sun.

There is hope for the future. I place a hand over my belly and smile, knowing that the small life just starting to grow inside me will have a chance now. It took me a month to realize I was late, and the doctor confirmed it this morning. I will tell Jace tonight, then together we'll tell the rest of our makeshift family.

A knock on the door brings me out of my thoughts. I sit up just as Garcia and Phillip walk in. He's holding their little girl in his arms, completely smitten with her.

"Are you ready to go?" Garcia asks.

I stand and walk over to Phillip. "Shouldn't you be there already?"

He shrugs with one shoulder, not taking his eyes off the baby that has become his reason for living. After our return from the Rushmore compound, when things settled down, Phillip confessed how he felt about Garcia. Jace and I were in complete support of them. Garcia was reluctant at first, still feeling the loyalty of her lost love. But once she and Jace had a long talk about how he'd want her to be happy, it didn't take long for her to fall for him. I think she already had feelings for him but needed time to realize it wouldn't be a betrayal to Tris'an.

"Hand her over and get out of here," Garcia says.

Reluctantly, he places their daughter into her arms. Little Miranda. She looks like her mother, but with her father's eyes.

"All right, we need to get going or you'll be late for your own wedding," Garcia says. She eyes me up and down. "Really, Ray? You couldn't have found something better than cargo pants and a white tank to wear?"

"It's the post apocalypse, what do you expect?" I stand next to her and drop my head on her shoulder. "Thanks for giving me away today."

She wraps an arm around my shoulders and says, "That's what family is for."

We leave and walk through the hallways and up the stairs to the outside. I blink into the light and, when my eyes clear, I see Jace waiting under a makeshift arch and smiling at me.

My heart warms, filling with so much love that I feel I might burst.

Outside the walls, the world is still a dangerous place, but day-by-day, we are working to make it a better place than it ever was, and in the end, that is all any of us can do.

ACKNOWLEDGMENTS

This series was one I'd had on my mind for a long time before I set pen to paper, (fingers to keyboard?) I was sitting next to my husband on the couch and working on another project, feeling stuck when the documentary he was watching sparked the idea. I believe it was about what would happen to the earth if humans just suddenly vanished, if I remember correctly.

The idea of a global peace started to swirl in my mind, then a fact from school popped up to join it. (Something along the lines of 'For all of recorded history there have only been 300 years combined where there was not a war somewhere in the world.')

And idea for world peace and how it could be achieved bloomed, combined with my love of the Twilight Zone and from that, Sound of Silence was born. My only regret was that I failed to mention jackalopes.

I used a few real towns in this book, but took a bit of creative license with them to avoid adding unnecessary fluffy details on getting from one place to another but I still wanted to give a nod to a few small towns and their unique features.

I never intended to write the second book when I wrote the first, though I knew exactly what would happen after. But I couldn't shake the story and finally I decided fighting it was useless and I forced a space in my schedule for it.

Thank you Kelly Hashway for all your feedback and support. You've been amazing!

To Michelle and Konstanz, thank you for your unwavering support and love.

And of course, always thank you to the Atomic Indies: Lexi, Tiki, Trish, April, and Jon. I don't know what I'd do without you hippies.

ABOUT THE AUTHOR

Ali Winters is the USA TODAY Bestselling author of several series filled with romance, magic, and adventure.

Her first love will always be fantasy, but she fully admits to being obsessed with coffee and T-Rex, and has a weakness for love interests that walk the line between gray and villainy.

Ali was born and raised in the PNW but now currently resides in the wastelands that time forgot, with impossibly cold winters, and summers that are too short. She spends her days with her husband and alpha of her two dog pack. (They have assimilated her as one of their own and since she's the only one with opposable thumbs, have made her their leader.)

When she's not consumed with creating magical worlds for readers to get lost in, she can be found walking, reading, designing graphics, and creating art in various mediums.

Visit Ali on the web at www.aliwinters.com
Facebook.com/authoraliwinters
instagram.com/authoraliwinters

To subscribe to Ali's monthly newsletter for new releases, exclusive sneak peeks, and visit
www.aliwinters.com/newsletter